COTTONWOOD CREEK

by Ashley Walsh

Cottonwood Creek

HPID: AJB-384946-1060822-02

Hooked Publishing, LTD
P.O. Box 200804
Austin, TX 78720-0804
www.hookedpublishing.com

Dedication:

For my grandparents, Al and June.

Not a day passes that I don't miss and love you both. I never forget, never will. With each new day, I carry on, bursting with pride and gratitude for all you were and will always be. Thank you for the love, the "constant" sense of home, and the gift of Bueny.

I'm blessed by an angel in heaven. I call her Nana. It means everything to me that I finished *Cottonwood Creek* on what would have been her birthday. There were so many signs from Nana as this story evolved, they were everywhere. When I'd get stuck, I'd ask for help, and there she'd be. Like always.

Special Thanks

To my cousins, my sisters, and especially my dad.

There's no order to my appreciation, but I must first thank Todd. He always let me tag along, taught me how to fish, what spinners to use and had the patience to unsnag my line. Many, many times. To the rest the "bucko" clan—so many memories, so much love! Finally, to my dad. Because of his sacrifices, love, and loyalty to his parents, his girls, and Buena Vista, the legacy lives on.

P.S., Debbie A and Whitney S…you know! Thank you!

Author's Note:

Cottonwood Creek is a story of my lifelong love affair with a small town nestled in the heart of the Rocky Mountains. It is not a sequel to *Breakthrough*. However, after many restless nights and the convincing from a few influential gurus, I reluctantly decided to break my own heart and go for it. Writing it was an emotional challenge, but gradually, I waded into the river and let the words flow around me. By doing so, I allowed my characters to speak for themselves, which meant accepting that one key component (a favorite) from *Breakthrough* needed to join the journey. I intended to sprinkle her here and there, yet somehow, she had something else in mind, and so the story—as it was destined to do— went its own way.

PART ONE

Summer

CHAPTER ONE

Journal Entry 324 / Letters to Jordan

I got out of bed to get a glass of water and to look for you, but of course, I couldn't because you died eleven months ago.

Your death has not been kind. You don't mean to hurt me yet continue to rip me to shreds. Losing you has shown me that grief is really just another form of love, a desperate kind I need to share but can't. You're gone.

It's been almost a year since a man took eleven lives, including yours. Three hundred and thirty-one days later and here I am. Still sitting by the lake where you're resting peacefully beneath a silver oak. And still with so many questions. The most prevalent is why I never got to say goodbye.

All I want to do is pretend it's not true. Instead, I continue to relive those first few days, recognizing now that I pushed through your funeral. That first week, I almost got away with it. I refused to face it, wouldn't talk about it, and did everything I could to not think about it. And then it came crashing through, blinding me with pain.

I never know when the door is going to swing open and pull me through. With every passing day, I'm struck breathless by memories before they shift, and the agony becomes too much. It's gut-wrenching. Just the other day I heard our song and broke down in the middle of the grocery store. It happens all the time. I can't even walk at sunset without smelling you, feeling you beside me, holding my hand. I still feel you here. Everywhere.

The cruelest tears are the silent ones. They're different from what comes each night when the rest of the world sleeps. They come with a burning sensation inside my throat when my eyes blur from feeling helpless. I catch myself holding my breath and gripping my stomach to keep from screaming. Those are the darkest moments when I fight what's left of my faith. Afterward, I force myself outdoors to search for a star, convincing myself whichever shines the brightest is you.

By the way, it's been a while, but it happened again this afternoon. Your brother. There are times I'm confident I can hear his heart breaking all over again. How can I comfort him when I don't even know how to do that for myself? Then

4

Ava rounds the corner, and our eyes instantly light up, and for a short while her joy gently replaces our sorrow.

Our daughter is quick to remind me how love looks and feels. Ava's the spitting image of you, has your sense of humor, your wit, and shares the same zest for life and learning. She's wise beyond her years, the essence of you in every way. With what little time you had together, you taught her to be brave when the world is terrifying and often difficult. If I had to guess, it's why she keeps your picture with a pressed lily from your service on the kitchen table. She insists you be with us.

Ava is the reason I have to gather whatever strength I have left to carry on. I'm still here. I've survived. Even though I feel lost, I can't help but hope the broken pieces of me are in heaven with you. I like to imagine that someday we'll meet again, you'll glue me back together, and I'll be whole once more. Until then...

Please don't be mad, and I'm begging you not to stop me or interfere. I need to leave. I cannot move on here, so I'm taking our little girl and moving away. For now, I need to be in a place where there aren't constant reminders, and no one is trying to fix me.

It's time. I have to try to find a way to rebuild myself around losing you.

In this life and all others, forever yours,
Samantha Xx

#

"Did I sleepwalk when we were kids?"

"You have to ask? Either that or you snuck into my room and slept on the floor more times than I can count."

"Not true," Dean Sterling argued, ignoring the amusement flashing through his cousin's eyes. "I saw something by the footbridge," he offered, not mentioning how misty and early it had been, the time of morning when the trees still protect everything from being touched by the sun. "Seems strange now, so I'm wondering if it happened at all."

"You do strange well." Jenna smiled and shook her head. "What do you think you saw?"

"A dark-haired woman with a golden dog." Dean shrugged. "She was by the creek, coming from the forest. The kind of woman you don't think exists except you're watching her, she's real, and she's standing on your mountain, inside your world. Or, she will be soon enough."

"And you say I have an active imagination."

"No, I say you exaggerate. There's a difference."

"Right," Jenna responded, holding her mug to her chest, keeping the aroma close and her hands warm. "Let me guess, in this dawning fantasy of yours this woman was a collection of all your favorite parts of many women combined into one."

"Now that you mention it."

6

Jenna Sterling was younger than Dean by three years and more of a little sister than a cousin. It was a relief for him to see her unwind as the year had been rough. She was different, he noticed, watching her lean against a log bean on the expansive deck with her ankles crossed. There were times it was hard to separate this woman in her early thirties from the little girl who rarely left his side growing up. The days of her unruly ponytails were long gone, replaced with soft wisps of pale honey hair that swept her shoulders when she turned, catching his gaze.

"I'm fine," she said, expecting his questions.

"Are you?" His brows raised, lined with something between worry and wonder.

"Absolutely." For several seconds they held their ground, staring at one another.

"Jen, just because the truth is out there, doesn't mean it's finished with us."

Dean had learned to read Jenna well over the years, learned to read her emotions by looking into her eyes. As always, the intensity of the green irises with specs of liquid gold, heavy with unshed tears betrayed her.

"It's more than…" the words stayed thick in her throat like something she needed to swallow but couldn't. "Never mind. Let's not ruin a beautiful morning talking about it. Besides, it's finally May. We've got three weeks to get ready for summer. It might just be our biggest yet."

Agreeing, Dean balanced a laptop on his knees as he slowly rocked on one of four blue, patio chairs. He'd been browsing their website, skimming through reservations and updates before Jenna arrived, disrupting his morning routine.

"Rising dramatically from the Arkansas River Valley, Mount Princeton sits just southwest of Buena Vista," Dean read aloud. The verbiage was new, recently added by Jenna. "Princeton, flanked by fellow Collegiate Peaks, is among a group of fourteeners in the Sawatch Range. Mount Yale, Columbia, Harvard, and Oxford are included in the assembly with elevations above fourteen thousand feet.

"We look forward to seeing you in the heart of the San Isabel National Forest between Princeton and Cottonwood Pass at the base of Sheep Mountain South (a straight shot seven miles west of town) for your next adventure with Cottonwood Expeditions."

"It needs work," Jenna admitted. "That last bit is lengthy. I could always replace all that with Sheep Mountain, a mere 12k in elevation, is a humble one among the plethora of towering peaks in the range. Or simply that it sits between Princeton and Yale and acts as a landmark to the town."

"Wordy, but I like it. Leave it." Dean closed the laptop. "It's time to gather the troops. Can you arrange it for this afternoon? And, Jen—"

"Stanna Truitt is shitbrained!"

"Hey, Colbs." Jenna stifled a laugh, setting her mug on the rail and reaching for her niece, technically her second cousin, as Colby stomped onto the patio from the kitchen.

"Seriously, Colby? It's like rinse and repeat with you. I mean it. Stop cussing!"

"But, Daddy, she is!" Colby confirmed, with her hands on her hips. "What kind of person hates rocks? Stanna Truitt, that's who! She hates me, too, as if I care!"

"I doubt that."

"It's true. Stanna told Macy, who told Joseph, that I gave Danny Weber one of my lava rocks from the Capulin Volcano Monument in New Mexico!" Colby's eyes bulged in disbelief. "And if you can believe that, you know what else she told them, Daddy?" Colby asked, shaking her arms which were spread wide above her head. "She's saying when I gave it to him, I said, "I *lava* you, Danny Weber." It's a big, fat lie!"

"Let's hope so. Got your backpack?" Dean stood, looked over Colby's head and winked at Jenna. "Hard to believe school's almost out and you're going to be a second-grader."

"Am I doing sports this summer?"

"Softball?" Dean asked, hopeful.

"I'm not good at throwing or catching."

"What are you good at?"

"I'm really good at not throwing or catching. I like to swim."

"Okay, unless you're grounded. It's a deal."

"I'm grounded?"

"Cussing." Dean reminded. "Again."

"I can take her to school," Jenna offered, jumping in. "Besides, I need to swing by and spend some time with Nana Sterling. Let her try out one of her new coffee experiments on me."

At the thought of their grandmother's experimentations, Dean cringed. "You might as well drive down with us then. I've got a few things to pick up. I'll drop you off, say hello, and run before she has time to fill a mug for me."

"Chicken."

"Says the woman who's about to be poisoned."

9

He'd made a mistake. Observing them too closely this time, leaning against a widely ridged moss boulder, wiping clean the stainless-steel blade of the ten-inch hunting knife he called Justice. He tapped the cherry wood handle against his chapped lips, and then sheathed it, watching Dean Sterling drive his family toward town.

#

It's my first fishing license ever, and I'm so proud I almost tripped stepping out of the makeshift store which was once a hotspot for vacationers. It's something else now, and only temporarily, but the previous name is still sprawled across the outside of the building in large, block letters. I've learned of its history, a popular gift and tackle shop for over six decades, from a seasonal yet chatty clerk running the register.

Apparently, I'm not the only fresh face in town. A couple from Nebraska is renting the space, and by the end of summer when the short-term lease ends, they'll either buy in or bow out. I'm predicting their departure, as I overheard chatter in the backroom of snowbirding in Arizona for the winter. There was more gossip that followed of a local merchandise company with the interest of moving in, but I was too excited with my purchases to continue eavesdropping.

From what I gathered, whoever settles in for the duration will be sharing the building with a telecom company. Essentially, I've acquired a fishing license and a pole in the same location also used for a permanent link to fiber drop broader internet throughout the valley. Technology I didn't quite expect in the one-stoplight-town.

As I'm leaving, another customer enters the store promptly behind me, clanking the bells together. I'm quickly discovering the bells hanging on the doors around town are to welcome, not warn. I smile, sidestepping a knee-high whiskey barrel overflowing with pink, yellow, and red flowers. Nasturtiums, I think. Shifting my purchases from one arm to the other, I glance up to see a man by my Toyota 4-Runner, petting my dog.

"Hello," I say, approaching. I feel slightly betrayed that my golden retriever, Bodie, continues licking this man's hand. "Checking out my dog or my ride?" I'd left the liftgate up, trusting Bodie to stay put and guard our belongings. I reach over Bodie, setting down the bag of fishing gear and a new pole.

The man turns and locks his eyes on mine, although I'm wearing aviator sunglasses. I lift my sunglasses to rest on the top of my head where they spend a good amount of time. I should be cautious, I realize this, but I'm curious. Before he manages to speak a word, we're in some kind of anomalous stare down. There's a split second of recognition, a spark of intrigue, and then it's gone because I tell myself it's ridiculous. Evidently, it doesn't matter. Before common sense kicks in, my mind is already made up to engage. Something I rarely do with strangers.

He's easy to look at, appears friendly, but then again so was Ted Bundy. Now seems like a good time to remember first impressions are usually wrong impressions, and I trust nothing, definitely not the quick grin spreading across his

11

handsome face. A face with distinct cheekbones and an angular jaw. *And those eyes*. Earthy brown with flecks of copper like light shining through a clear glass of whiskey.

"Both," he says, as his eyes move over me. "I've seen you before."

"Don't think so." It takes a second or two for that to sink in. He shakes his head, choosing to believe me. It's true. I've never met this man before. He extends his hand to shake mine, and instead of reciprocating, I retreat.

"I'm Dean," I hear, as I round the corner to the driver's side and open the door to the garnet red SUV. It's bizarre how openly people provide information in this friendly, little town. I can't help but wonder if I seem different here. If approachability is something I suddenly convey. Will I be expected to be as sociably welcoming as those around me have been? Well, except for the old man at the gas station. However, to be fair, that was in Johnson Village three miles south.

"Take care, Dean."

"What kind of fishing are you hoping to do with that?" he asks, delaying my departure.

"Any kind."

"With that?" He's eyeing the fishing pole. The judgment is evident in his tone.

"That's my plan."

He looks at my license plate. I sigh. *Here we go*. He begins laughing, driving the rest of my goodwill away. His laughter holds just enough arrogance to annoy me, so I climb out and face him. Twice, and both within the past hour, I've been laughed at over Texas plates. I remove my sunglasses for the second time and wait for an explanation. He's yet to

12

look at me. I'm confident that once he does, he'll fold, and then I'm out of here. Except I'm wrong. When he looks up, we're right back where we started. Staring.

"There's only one other person I've ever met with eyes as green as yours, and she's my cousin," he says, and blinks. It's unsettling to look into this stranger's eyes, and again, recognize a spark of something, regardless of whatever that something may be. "Let's start over. I'm Dean." He waits. "You are?"

"Ryan." I refuse to tell him my full name which is Natalie Ryan McCray. I have never gone by Natalie, and never will. Not because I don't like it, but because it's my aunt's middle name, and that's a whole other story.

"Ryan," he echoes, mostly to himself. "I'm usually a little better at this. For what it's worth, I wasn't laughing at you. Not directly, anyhow."

"You weren't the first." He cocks his head, studying me. "I stopped for gas," I offer, waving my hand southbound. "I was at the pump and about to clean my windshield when an older man approached me. I won't lie, he was pretty adorable. We got to talking, and before I knew it, he was insisting on cleaning my windshield. But in the end, he laughed at me."

"Saw your plates?" Dean asks, as his face falls into a look of sympathy, the combination of a frown and sigh are a little too much.

"He did. And after he did, he asked me if I knew the difference between a Texan and a pig?" I see the corner of Dean's mouth twitch as he waits to hear the punchline. He's trying not to laugh again. "There's just some things a pig won't do."

13

"Sounds like you met Flip."

"Flip?"

"Believe it or not, Flip's famous. A world-renowned trekker back in the day. Published even. He's helped carve countless trails throughout the Rockies. Flip's his trail name."

"You people have trail names?"

He smiles. "Flip was fortunate to pack with the right kinds of hikers who gave it to him. When you're out there," he nods toward the mountains, "for long periods, people get to know things about you. Flip changes his mind a lot."

"What do they call you?"

"Lots of things." He's grinning again. "C'mon, don't take it personally, we like Texans well enough. I admit, sometimes we get our backs up over the condition tourists leave our state. Not everyone is respectful while visiting. For the most part, we like everyone, especially the ones who add movement to our economy." He finishes by reaching for my pole and walks back to the store.

"Stay," I tell Bodie, and am hot on Dean's heels.

He enters the store, and this time it feels like the bells on the door are mocking me. He walks no more than ten feet before turning left and stepping down into a side room equipped with an abundance of fishing paraphernalia. I missed this room earlier, and instead picked out a packaged set displayed by the counter where I filled out paperwork for the fishing license.

"Trevor?" Dean sets the pole on the counter, confronting the boy who helped me with the application. "You let her buy this?"

"Am I missing something?" I ask.

14

Dean narrow's his eyes, his amused expression drawing me in. "Are you sure we've never met?"

"I'd remember, and I need to go. Can I have my pole back?" I turn to the boy Dean called Trevor, and ask, "Is there something wrong with what I bought?"

"Normally, no, but if you're going fishing with Dean, you'll need something better. What you have here is for beginners. And, uh, mostly for children."

"Fishing with Dean?" *Not happening!* "Can I exchange this for something more appropriate and be taken seriously?"

"No. I mean yes. I didn't mean to imply you weren't serious."

"What do I need?" I ask Dean.

"For river fishing, you'll want a spinning reel, not a casting one. If that's your intention?" Of half a dozen, he points at a blue one inside the case. "Lightweight, smooth handling, but solid."

"Sold. I think I've got it from here."

"We're not done." Dean leads me to a hearty display of hooks and other garb. "Panther Martins," he says, grabbing a handful of spinners with yellow bodies, red dots and silver jackets. "I prefer size six, but you should start with a four. I've used these since I was a kid, and I'm loyal." I roll my eyes. Oddly, it feels normal, like meeting Dean is just the next step of my life story.

Outside, I attempt another goodbye, although Dean has something different in mind and reaches for Bodie's leash. My eager retriever jumps down, betraying me all over again. Dean points to a park banked along Cottonwood Creek. It runs through town, behind the legendary tackle shop, beneath the bridge, and back again to flow beside the park. "I'll show you how to use the reel."

I shade my eyes, forgetting the aviators on the top of my head, and spin in a half circle, pointing across the road. "Why not the lake over there?" I ask, registering the small body of water with another park adjacent to where we're standing.

"I don't go there."

"Why not?" I ask, as something new replaces the sparkle in his eyes. Something dark and cryptic. "What's with you and that park? I like the lake."

"Lakes are no good."

"Where'd you hear that?" I scoff.

"I didn't hear it. That one I had to learn." He increases his pace. "Besides, it's no more than a pond. Columbine Park is better." I stop walking. He turns, looking over his shoulder once he realizes I'm no longer walking in stride beside him. "It was a long time ago," he says, and I wait for more. He stops, and then turns to walk back in my direction. "When I was a kid, there was a little girl. She lived behind us. She was my cousin Jenna's age when she disappeared. I was the last person to see her, and I saw her there, by the lake." Dean's eyes lift briefly towards the small lake then away.

In the back pocket of my jeans, my phone vibrates. It's work, and I'm reminded of why I'm here. I ignore the call but not my obligation. "I need to hit the road, but Bodie thanks you, and so do I."

"I'd like to see you."

"You are seeing me."

"I meant again. I'd like to see you again, Ryan."

16

"Maybe you will," I say, putting my sunglasses back on. I inch away, trying to further communicate that I'm attempting to escape. For now, at least. "I like this place."

With the windows down, I drive away with the mountains in view and cool air against my skin. In the rear-view mirror, I can see Dean standing where I left him, watching me go.

CHAPTER TWO

"Mommy, where are we?"

"Trinidad, baby. It's our last stop before we're there. Do you need to potty?"

"Kinda. How much longer 'til we get there?"

"Three hours, maybe a little more."

On Raton Pass, thirteen miles north of the Colorado state line, Samantha merged onto the off-ramp. They needed fuel, Ava was hungry, and Sam could use the break to stretch her legs. For hours she had anticipated the exit, a stop she didn't want to make, in a place she didn't want to see. A place where Jordan had proposed on a whim for no other reason other than spontaneity was what Jordan did so well.

Sam waited outside the bathroom stall for Ava to finish, reminiscing of the last time they'd passed through Trinidad. She swallowed, tasting reality. This wasn't a vacation. This was starting over.

When Ava sprang from the stall, wound with energy from the long drive, Sam smiled halfheartedly. "Come on, kiddo, we've got a pretty cool place to get to."

Clasping her small hand around her mother's, Ava looked up to Sam through bright, blue eyes. "Mommy, do you think the mountains have special powers?"

"I hope so. What kind of powers do you want them to have?"

"The kind that takes our sad away."

#

There was nothing unusual with Drew's whistle setting the tone for a meeting. He enjoyed aggravating his brothers and flirting with Garrett's lifelong crush had come to be expected. When the boys were younger, Drew and Reece Young's mother met and married Garrett Dillon's father to form their tight-knit family. Later that same year, Jenna Sterling had given Garrett his first kiss—a kiss that only knew one direction—and for Garrett, there was no turning back.

"You're predictable, ornery, and good for my ego," Jenna said, patting Drew on the shoulder as she passed him.

"These meetings feel more like family gatherings."

"We're not related." Dean crumbled a sheet of paper full of notes and threw it at Drew. "I can fire your ass anytime I feel the urge. And get your boots off my desk."

"Close enough. My brother's the godfather to Colby and wants to marry your sister. Plus, there's that time you and

Garret built us that fort in the woods, and we all made a pact to be blood brothers."

"She's my cousin, not my sister. Are you really holding on to something we did when I was ten?"

"Just saying, blood isn't always thicker than water."

"Still, not related. Hey, not to knock the concept of a family barbeque, but are you about ready to talk work?"

"Ready, bossman. Green light on all things motorized. Dirt bikes, quads, jeeps are all in good shape. Registration and maintenance are good on all but the Kodiak. That engine's shot. I've asked Jenna for the add-ons to insurance and considered taking on another guy from Tahoe but sticking with what I've got. Back to toys? I want to talk about adding a couple of side-by-sides. Got my eye on an RZR or a Viking. Other than that, my department is ready to roll."

"What about the snowmobiles?"

"Got the last of the sleds moved over to storage early last week. Minimal repairs on two."

"Good." Dean turned his head to Reece, Drew's older brother by a year and a half. "How's it going on your end?"

"Besides crazy?" Reece, laughed, kicking the leg of Drew's chair, knocking it down to all fours. "As of yesterday, I've got just under thirty river guides lined up. The stragglers should roll into town by the end of next week after finals."

"The perks of employing college kids from all over the world," Jenna chimed in. "I motion to pass out a bar of soap and shampoo with paychecks."

"I second that. I'm missing certificates on a few, that a problem?" Reece asked Jenna.

"All rafting outfitters licensed by the state of Colorado require guides to be certified in First Aid and CPR."

"I'll take care of it. Still planning to separate rafting check-ins from rentals?"

"Yes," Dean and Jenna answered in unison.

"Good, that will help make the busy days less complicated. The only other things I've got on the list are buses." Reece pointed at Drew. "Seeing that they have motors, I'm hoping that jackass can look them over and make sure they're ready by next week for training."

"Already done," Drew beamed, using his finger to make a checkmark in the air. "Now back to the side-by-sides?"

"You got thirty-grand to pitch in?" Dean asked, then waited.

"You giving me a raise?"

"Funny guy. Okay, moving on. The woman from Texas taking over the stables starts Monday. She's got a lot of experience with horses and just about every other animal imaginable, so utilize that. With her extensive background in the veterinary world, I'm sure we can all learn plenty. We'll need to familiarize her with the trails and quick. Things are different up here, so we need to get her acclimated. Word on the street is she also plans to run some rescue operation for animals throughout the valley. Let's not get in the way of that."

"She single?" Drew asked.

"Drew Young, please hear me," Jenna annunciated carefully, using a stern tone. "Give her space. Plenty of it. Also, heads-up, guys, she'll be here later this afternoon, along with her daughter. They'll stay in the first cabin off the creek. Next to them, I've got the photographer booked for the summer. The three smaller cabins across the road are reserved every weekend through August. Lots of activity, so keep things tidy and run a tight ship."

"That leaves TC and me with anglers and packers." Dean's eyes traveled the room, landing on the former marine with a jagged scar along his lower cheek and a five o'clock shadow to try and hide it. "TC, you're here because most of the time I'm not. Consider this a promotion. You get to be me, so when people come bitching, I'm pointing them to you. Aside from Dumb and Dumber over there, you've been here the longest, and I trust you to keep an eye on all areas. If last summer was any indication of how many times I'll be called out, you'll be busy filling in here when I can't. You good?"

"Appreciate it, Dean, I've got you." TC turned. "Jenna, thank you."

"I feel good about the season, let's do this one well. We'll have dinner at the house tomorrow to kick things off. We'll even let Drew pretend it's a family reunion."

"Bring your money for poker after dinner," Drew added, getting to his feet.

As the gang slowly shuffled out of Dean's office no more than a hundred yards from the main house, TC hung back, lingering longer than usual. He scanned the pictures of various magazine articles, newspaper clippings, and certifications on the wall before sitting. Framed beside the monitor, he examined the image of Dean in the middle of a group of smiling faces, all wearing the same red jackets with CCSAR-N patches. Finally, TC centered his attention on Dean who waited patiently across the broad, weathered desk made of driftwood.

In addition to Cottonwood Expeditions, Dean trained and coordinated for the Chaffee County Search and Rescue North Unit—a cohesive and highly skilled group trained to respond to difficult circumstances. Dean's widely recognized expertise had earned him a spot with the special operation team, a team that executed high-angle, swift water, and avalanche rescues.

"The committee is locked, so no budget adjustments yet" Dean began, "but if you want it, I can get you the lift ticket." He watched TC's blank expression shift. The opportunity to participate in special helicopter training from Flight for Life was something TC had hoped for. "You'll be trained and flown into the backcountry to respond quickly to severely injured parties. You do understand the lifted SAR members are responsible for hiking their way out?"

"Wouldn't want to do it otherwise. The promotion…and now this," TC paused. "I appreciate it, Dean. Everything you do for all of us."

#

Denver is exceptional if you enjoy a metropolitan pace, which I do on occasion. There was a time when all I wanted was to escape to a big city. A place with a million different faces I didn't know, and none knew me. A city where constant motion wouldn't allow me time to wallow in self-pity. Not anymore. Instead, I'm looking forward to this quaint little town where I'm on location for the next two to three months. I'm eager to get acquainted with the locals and

23

adapt to a moderately relaxed lifestyle. Alas, the quiet. I have daydreamed of the forest's tranquility for months.

While gathering bags from the 4-Runner, I turn to set a large duffle down and am met by a little girl standing with her hands on her hips. For a fleeting second, I'm startled. The girl has appeared from nowhere, confirming I need to pay closer attention and be hyper-aware of my surroundings. I'm far from the city now, and although I'm definitely dramatizing the situation, she could have just as easily been a bear.

"Hi there," I say, allowing her time to form an opinion as she looks me slowly up then down.

"I'm six."

"Really? I was thinking eight, at least," I counter, attempting to win her over on the first try. "I'm Ryan."

"I know. My aunt told me. You take pictures?"

"I do."

"'Cuz if you want, I could help sometimes. Nana Sterling says I got a good eye."

"Good to know. I'll keep it in mind."

I hear the crunch of footsteps over gravel and turn. After talking on the phone several times, I put a face to the voice of Jenna Sterling. She's All-American and cute in a Rachel McAdams—a deep dimple in her right cheek—sort of way. "I see you've met Colby. She's pretty much our meet and greet." Jenna ruffles the top of Colby's head then rests her hand on her niece's shoulder.

"We were just negotiating her offer to be my assistant."

"She works fast. Need a hand?"

"I've got what I need for now. I'll come back for the rest later." I feel a nudge against my thigh. "This is Bodie. He's generous with his affection," I say, as Bodie licks Colby and receives a giggle in return. "Bodie and I came through early yesterday to get a glimpse before I had to be in Denver for an appointment. That drive didn't disappoint."

I think back to the route lined with pine trees. I felt the climb up and up again, right into the sky along the black asphalt slab slicing through the mountains. I even honked, receiving a look from Bodie, as we traveled through the Eisenhower Tunnel which carries the interstate under the Continental Divide in the Rocky Mountains. Stats excite me, and so does knowing it's the highest tunnel in the world and the longest mountain tunnel in the country. *Take that Smokies!* Not that I have anything against the Great Smoky Mountains.

"*You're* the golden dog?" Jenna asks Bodie like he understands and with more excitement than it warrants, and then her eyes jump to me. "And you're the dark-haired woman!"

"I'm sorry?"

Jenna's laughing. There's an inside joke here I know nothing about, but my smile spreads because Jenna's jubilation is contagious. "My cousin…" Jenna shakes her head. "I teased him for his overactive imagination, except you are real. He *did* see you!"

Fortunately, I'm spared an awkward response as another mid-sized SUV, a deep gray Range Rover, pulls in and parks beside us. The woman driving has long, blonde hair. If I didn't know better, I'd think she's talking to herself, but then I see a small person vault from the back seat to the front. I notice the plates and exhale, eternally grateful. I'm no longer the only Texan on the mountain.

The woman emerges from the vehicle, reluctantly at first, then forces a smile. The little person, however, is a bundle of pent up energy and springs from the car. She embraces Bodie without acknowledging the rest of us. Animal lovers, I gather, before noticing Jenna's amusement fade as she softens with an empathetic expression.

The blonde, there's something about her, something desolate yet kind. I feel a vibe, one I don't often pick up on, if ever. It's premature, but I choose to trust my most basic instincts, hoping they're right, and we'll be friends. "Ryan McCray." I extend my hand. "Looks like we're going to be neighbors."

"Well, this makes it easy. I can show you all around at the same time. That," Jenna points to a large log home, "is the main house."

"Me and my Daddy live there," Colby adds, earning a glance from the other girl who looks to be Colby's age, or close.

"Right. You'll meet him sooner or later. I live in an apartment above the office, just there." Jenna gestures toward a smaller log structure no more than three hundred feet from the house. "Half a mile down the way, our friend Garrett has a place. You'll bump into him a lot too. There are five smaller cabins—"

"Named after animals," Colby jumps in. She's quick to enlighten us after interrupting her aunt as if there's a contest between them.

"Right," Jenna says. "Two on this side of the road, and three across the way."

"What kind of animals?" The newest little girl asks. She's a beautiful child with long, wavy locks and striking blue eyes.

"This is Ava," the woman introduces her daughter, while I stand back and watch the interactions. "She's a quick study," the woman adds. It feels like a friendly warning of many questions to come.

"We're standing on what was once Ute Indian territory." Jenna says, and I instantly like her. She reads and responds to people quickly and well with little effort. "We try to keep that in mind, so the names of your cabins are *Kava* and *Pari*."

"*Kava's* a horse and *Pari* means elk," Colby shares, staking her claim in the conversation.

The younger girls eye one another, silently deciding if they want to bother with a friendship. The jury's still out because Ava shies away and grabs hold of her mom's hand. They exchange a look. The shyness doesn't come across to be the norm. If I had to guess, I'm betting that once we're all settled in and comfortable, these little people are a promise for things to get interesting.

"Your cabins," Jenna points, "are by the creek. Both have one bedroom and a loft with a sofa sleeper. We swapped the sleeper in The *Kava* for a twin, so that Ava will be more comfortable. They have fireplaces, cable, WiFi, and small kitchens equipped with cooking essentials. The patios on those face the creek and have wood stacked by the back doors. The other cabins are across the way on the hill. They have a view. You have the water," Jenna winks, "as well as a view."

"Do they have Indian names, too?" Ava asks, intrigued.

27

"Bear. Fish. Beaver," Colby answers, matter-of-factly.

"*Kviag'ant, Pag'ii, and Pavintc*," Jenna clarifies, smiling warmly at Ava. "Do you like books, Ava? There's a lot of them in the main house about the Ute Indians that lived in these mountains and throughout the Rockies. You're welcome to borrow any of them."

"Or do you like rocks?" Colby asks Ava, changing gears. "'Cuz I do. C'mon, I'll show you my collection." They dart off, and the jury is no longer out.

"That didn't take long." Jenna laughs. "I should probably tell you both now before you get besieged in town, or God forbid Garrett hears. He'll tease you endlessly for it. The quickest way to be singled out by locals is to mispronounce our town's name. No one is trying to butcher the Spanish language with the wrong pronunciation, but it was chosen by the town back in 1879, and it is *our* town. Much debating goes on over it. I can't begin to tell you how often we hear Boynah Vista or Bwayna Vista. No, those are just *so* wrong. It's BV, Bueny or Buena Vista, like Bew-na Vis-ta."

"Got it," I say, unable to contain my smile. Jenna's feisty and I like it. "Beww naa Viss Taa!" Jenna claps, and if I'm not mistaken, from the corner of my eye, I see the blonde crack a smile.

"I'm sure you've guessed already the creek is Cottonwood Creek. We're sitting on one of three runoff tributaries. North, middle, and south. Ours is south. The stables are up that way, just around the bend. Motor rentals too. The rest of the facilities are in town on the Arkansas River. Other than that, welcome to the mountain!"

"Thank you," the blonde says. She glances at the serenity spread exquisitely around us. She turns to face me, resuming

28

our initial introduction. "I'm Samantha. It's nice to meet you. To meet all of you," she finishes, smiling genuinely for the first time.

#

Denver, Colorado

The excitement made him smile. It was thrilling to watch the intensity of the thunderstorm from the fifty-third floor of the Republic Plaza. There was little he enjoyed more than negotiating while the gods cursed him from above for a transaction he was about to make. The power was his now, to control and take. Not even the persuasive wisdom of his late wife could diminish the pleasure he would get from stripping Dean Sterling of his heritage to build an empire for himself.

Jonathan Prescott turned away from the storm to search his son's features for the slightest reluctance. When he saw none, Jonathan arched a brow, prepared to hear the rest from Henry. "He's the one, tried and true. He's liable, equipped, and already in place, unlike the former vagabond with no family or ties to speak, whom I might add has gone missing. This guy, he blends. He's masterfully common and unsuspecting. Don't worry, Dad, when this is all over, he'll vanish. He won't exist."

"You found him easily enough."

"Technically, he found me," Henry paused, noting the tremors of the storm disturbing the structure of his father's

29

high-rise office, escalating vainly in the center of downtown Denver. That was true, the individual in question had begun earning Henry Prescott's trust by performing illegal operations to ensure Prescott's power and prestige years ago. Although, it had taken longer than expected to gain the privilege of meeting the patriarch of the family—Senator Jonathan Prescott. "He's fearless and compliant," Henry added for good measure.

"He's expensive."

"He's the best, knows the area."

"Expertise?"

"Terrorism Counteraction for four years. Demolition and Control Blasting Specialist for another nine. All phases of blasting. Demolition, underwater, highway, railroad, logging and quarries."

"He's aware our interests are strictly reactive explosives?"

"Ammonium Nitrate. Nausea, headaches and often unconsciousness. Blood has difficulty carrying oxygen when exposed. Death is a possibility. He understands."

"Bring him in. And Henry, discretion guarantees liberties we can't afford to lose. He's never to show his face here again." Jonathan Prescott turned, enthused by the malevolent storm just beyond the glass.

CHAPTER THREE

Ambushed on sight, Dean caught Colby mid-air. She jumped from one log poking out of the water to another before lunging into his arms as he crossed the creek. Dean tightened his hold, hugging her close. With her head resting on his shoulder, he paused long enough to embrace their surroundings. *Enchanting*, he thought of the forest as the sun was setting. It was his favorite time of day when the trees allowed minimal light to seep through, highlighting the golden riverbed. A color that always made him think of butterscotch.

"Reece called Drew a mother-effer! But, Daddy, they didn't know I was listening, so don't be mad. I'm not the one who said it, so don't go trying to ground me again. I was with Ava, and we were sorta hiding in the workshop. I know I'm not 'sposed to be in there without you, but I was showing Ava around."

"Colbs, there's so much wrong with everything you just said, I don't even know where to begin. Let's start with Ava. Who's she?"

"She's the kid that's gonna live here this summer with her mom. The picture lady came too, and she's super-duper pretty, Daddy, with brown hair like me. They all got here at the same time, so Aunt Jenna and me showed 'em stuff."

"Sounds like I dodged a busy afternoon."

"Got a minute?" Reece asked, coming through the trees.

Dean bent, letting his gear slide off his shoulder, handing it to Colby, "Run that to the house and wash up. I won't be long."

"Alright, Daddy. Let's go, Rutger!"

"Rutger?" Dean asked Reece.

"Her dog." Reece shrugged. "She introduced him to me earlier. Your daughter has a lot of imaginary pets."

"She gets it from Jenna, not me. Healthy imaginations are hereditary in the females around here. What's up?"

"The photographer, she's here. Jenna's got her all sorted. It's just that…" Reece toed at the river grass with the tip of his hiking boot. "She took off up the mountain not long after with her dog and camera. Says she parked near Cottonwood Lake and went in before the campground and Miners Lodge. Not much of a trail there. Claims it was rocky and steep, so she stuck close to the center of the gulch before stumbling onto a few discarded items and a freshly banked fire. I assumed she meant Porphyry Gulch and checked it out."

"How bad?"

"Hard to tell what they were at first. Mostly charred topographic maps and oddly a notepad of horror stories."

"Horror stories?"

32

"The gory kind, yeah. Most of it was blackened, but there were parts of one. Pretty graphic. Something about burying girls alive only to come back a bit later to rescue them."

"Let Garrett know, otherwise keep it between us. I'd rather Jenna not find out. I'll talk to the photographer."

#

The most valuable reward I get from the work I do is fatigue. Things are going exceptionally well when exhaustion eliminates the possibility of dreams waking me up in the middle of the night. My muscles are tight and sore from the hike, which is another result of a great afternoon. It's unfortunate I crossed paths with a careless hiker's campsite and their tales of who knows what. The gruesome story that I found still has my stomach in knots.

I have every intention of showering until the hot water runs cold. My jeans are off, and my shirt is halfway over my head when the excessive knocking begins. I jump, not because I'm prey to old fears, but because it's forceful enough to rattle my little cabin. Walking quickly from one room to another toward the door, tugging my jeans on, I catch a glimpse of the sinking sun between the gap of the curtains. I almost forget about the pounding on the door to search for my camera until another round of banging begins.

Swinging the door open, I come face-to-face with the same man who hijacked my fishing pole the day before. Dean's eyes widen in surprise. I'm not at all what he expects either. He takes two steps backward as I take one forward, jabbing a finger into his chest.

"Are you following me?" I ask.

"Are you serious?" He steps back once more. "What are you doing here?"

I turn to read the cabin's nameplate hanging just above the porchlight. Sure enough, it says *Pari*. I'm in the right place, and he has some explaining to do. It matters none that his eyes are prettier than I remember, and how did I miss the tall, solid frame. Or did I? Never mind, the examination ends when my dog escapes our quarters and soaks Dean's hand with kisses. There seems to be no end to this betrayal.

"Hey, boy." Dean kneels, giving Bodie a good rubdown. "How about we start over? We're good at that."

"How did you find me? And why?"

"It's probably easier to try this in reverse. If it applied here, and I had to say why, it's because I haven't stopped thinking about you since you sped off from me in a hurry. As for how…it's more accurate to say you found me. I live here."

"Here? As in *here*? Is this place yours? Are you the cousin? Wait, you're the *daddy*?"

"Yes." Dean extends his hand to shake mine as casually as he had done before. "Dean Sterling, this is my place, and Colby is my daughter. We live there," he nods to the main house. "Just the two of us." Eventually, he lowers his hand, realizing once again I'm not budging.

"This day continues to surprise me."

"It was you, wasn't it? Yesterday? You and your dog by the bridge at sunrise? That's an image I'll never forget."

34

"Are you always so…" I trail off, thinking of the right term, still avoiding his first admission that he'd been thinking about me. "Straightforward?"

"I have no idea. Maybe." Dean smiled. "It could be that I just like girls from Texas."

"In that case, you'll like my neighbors."

"How do you know I wasn't talking about your dog?"

"Because Bodie's a boy? *Holy*…did you see that?" I ask, excitedly.

Dean ducks, covering his head with his hands, stretching the blue fabric of his shirt tightly across his back. Evidently, I've triggered a deeply rooted paranoia. "Is it a bat?" he asks. "It is, isn't it? *Shit!*" He shrieks. I can't help it. I bend over at the waist laughing. He peeks between slowly spreading fingers, grasping the predicament he's put himself in, though he continues to stoop. "It was only a hummingbird, wasn't it?" he asks, cringing while dropping his hands. "Some people are afraid of spiders or snakes. For me, it's bats." I watch as he shudders. "I can't stand those bastards."

"For now, your secret's safe with me. If it helps, the hummingbird was exceptional! I've never seen one with such a vibrant violet throat and emerald head before. Or *that* tiny."

"Calliope Hummingbirds," Dean offers, trying to save face, standing tall and mighty now. "They're the smallest birds in North America and prefer higher elevations. The average male weighs less than an ounce. Don't you take pictures all over the world? Aren't you used to this sort of thing?"

"I usually have to risk breaking my neck to get the shot."

"Speaking of…would you consider taking someone along when you go out? There's a lot of unknowns in these parts, a lot of things can happen unexpectantly. I'd feel better if you pair up."

"Do you suggest this to all hiking enthusiasts who roll through town?" He doesn't respond. Instead, we're back to the staring routine we perfected the day before. "Is this about what I found this afternoon?"

"Nevertheless, I'm asking as a favor. That's what this is about."

"Should I expect you to bang my door down often, asking me to be careful?" I notice the truck behind him. It's blue. I'm beginning to recognize the pattern here. This guy loves blue.

"Do you have everything you need? You like the cabin?" Dean asks, dodging my question.

"I do." I begin to back up, snapping for my dog to get back inside. "Good night, Dean Sterling."

"Where are you from, Ryan?" he asks, masterfully delaying my exits.

"We've been over this," I remind him.

"Where in Texas?"

Hell is the first thing that comes to mind. I sigh and give in. "I grew up in a place called Silver Valley. It's part of Coleman County which starts at the almost non-existent town of Bangs."

"Near Austin?"

"Closer to Abilene."

Dean nods, not that he can place it on a map, but he listens attentively anyway. I can feel the cool doorknob in my hands as I lean back on the door that I've closed to keep Bodie inside.

"Are your parents still there?"

"I lived with my aunt and uncle." Riveted, Dean stands in place. It's clear he's neither leaving nor letting me off too easily. "I know nothing about my dad, and my mother was sent away when I was young. Her mind isn't well."

It's more than I typically offer, and something I need to consider later when I have time to reflect on the direction this conversation has gone. I push thoughts of Mama from my mind as an image of Silver Valley flashes through. The memory of the uncompromising flatland with only one scarcely filled body of water in the vicinity of where we lived is unpleasant. Rough Creek. Rough was exactly what my life in Silver Valley had been.

"I like it here," I say to change the course of things. This earns the most endearing smile from an insanely good-looking man. But then again, I'm feeling nostalgic. "You grew up here?"

"Born and raised. Jenna and I stayed with our grandmother, Nana Sterling, in town. She's got a bookstore, Present Tense. We lived above it."

"And this place? Your business is literally on a mountain."

"In that way, I'm lucky." Dean laughs. "Okay, on my twenty-first birthday a representative from the Tribal Land Division came by when I was on break from school. I was gifted lawful possession of thirty-two thousand acres. I'm the oldest living male on my mother's side and fortunate enough to be the great, great grandson of Isaac Nakanchee. Isaac was part of the Mouache, one of seven bands of Ute

Indians that concentrated into a loose confederation. The land, though massively abundant to us, was all that was left for them."

"That somewhat explains your looks."

"If you say so. I should add my dad's Irish."

"He's around, your dad?"

"No, he lives in Denver. He was in law school when he met my mother on Copper Mountain. She was living in Leadville at the time and worked at the ski resort. When my dad found out about me, he took me, and then planted me with Nana Sterling. The rest is history."

"*Hmm*. What about your grandmother? How did she end up here?"

"Nana Sterling? She's always lived in Buena Vista, although she was born in Salida. You really want my family snapshot?"

"Shockingly, I do. You have to admit, it's fascinating."

"I'll test you on it later," he jokes. "Alright. From what I understand, one triple great grandfather claimed the summit region in honor of his father for fighting in the Arkansas River attack of the Comanches, Cuampes, and Kiowa. The battle ended with the death of Mouache chief, Delgadito. That's all my mother's lineage. I've never met her. As for Ray's side of the family…Ray is my dad, by the way. Another grandfather, a prospector by the name of Christopher Kenneth Sterling, was one of the forefathers of the valley below. He joined the Utes, Spanish conquistadors, American explorers, and mountain men to clear their way into the upper Arkansas River Valley."

"I'll never pass that test," I admit. He grins, and my stomach flips. *Ridiculous!* "And Jenna?"

"We have lousy parents, which is confusing. My grandmother is the kindest, most generous, easy-loving woman you'll ever meet. I'm being kind by stating it skipped a generation. Jenna's mother, Joyce, had Jenna very young. She pretty much did the same as my dad did with me by dumping her on Nana Sterling. Joyce is also in Denver. Or was. She passed unexpectantly last month."

"I'm sorry. Losing people, even the ones we don't like or understand is hard."

"Jenna's struggling. Unresolved issues," Dean explains. "Until recently, she's spent too much of her life believing her mother ended up doing well for herself by leaving Jenna behind. I don't see it that way. Departing the universe as a senator's wife cost Joyce a lot more than Jenna realizes."

#

Dean said goodnight once Colby hollered from their place to mine, her demands for dinner echoing throughout the narrow canyon. Behind the closed door, I run a hand over the high center of my chest. *What was that?* Maybe it's just me, but I don't feel like I'm the easiest person to get to know. Dean, on the other hand, opened up without any reluctance, revealing personal facets of his life, even ugly ones. I, of all people, understand how difficult the truth of our families can be.

After a shower, I attempt to sleep, but it wasn't long before I jump awake. In the dark, repetition isn't something I appreciate. Years later, the punishment following the abuse

39

continues to disrupt my dreams. The memories that come during the night are as much a part of me as the scars I escaped with.

The dreams remain the same: There's a screen door hanging by a hinge, slapping shut behind Uncle Jim, limping away on his damaged leg. He leaves, but not before shoving my aunt aside to reach for beer from an almost empty fridge, never bothering to zip the fly of his filthy jeans. The trailer shifts from the weight of my aunt moving toward me, hot oil dripping from the spatula in her hand. When she's finished, my bare legs are welted and blistered.

With the nightmare aside, and just after midnight, I decide to go for it. From the window above the kitchen sink, I can see my neighbor sitting on a wooden rocking chair. She's wrapped in a blanket, rocking slowly forward then back. The moon, as if daring me to go outside, brightens the short distance from my deck to Samantha's. I can hear the gurgle of the creek but can't see it. My pace is quick. I'm not ready to be mauled by a bear and need to figure out what my new fixation with bears is all about.

"Fellow insomniac?" I ask, coming up the few steps to her deck. She isn't startled by my appearance and instead wipes beneath her right eye. *Uh, oh!* I've caught her crying.

"Hard to sleep with a night as gorgeous as this," Samantha says, looking up. "The stars look like millions of fireflies from here."

"Stunning," I add, sitting in a rocker beside hers, separated by a small round table with an unopened book resting on top. "It's like they're winking at us."

"They are. At least, I like to think so."

"Not to pry, but are you okay?"

"Not really." I admire her honesty. I ask nothing more as several seconds tick by. Some moments are better without words. "What brings you to the mountains?" she finally asks.

"I'm a freelance photographer for several publications online and in print. A friend of mine is the founding partner for Shay & Blackwell out of Denver who owns the majority of those publications. I've been on a project with her for the past eight months that we hope to wrap up over the summer. "You? I heard Jenna say something about horses?"

"Twenty-seven of them. I'm here to take over that part of the business and keep them healthy, which includes making sure the guides don't overuse, mistreat, or neglect them. Initially, I was attracted by the genuine interest they seem to have for the well-being of their animals, considering the recreational use. Beyond that, and once we're into mud season, I hope to dive into a partnership with local animal shelters on an idea I have for wildlife rescue."

"Starting over?" I ask, unable to believe the invasive words that just flew out of my mouth.

"Whatever it takes to—" Samantha stops, catching herself before she speaks her emotions out loud, to a stranger no less. She looks me in the eye and something unexplainable clicks between us. A connection. An understanding. It takes a broken person to recognize another broken person. "A little over a year ago a student with a gun walked through campus and into an auditorium full of professors. He opened-fire, instantly killing the love of my life."

CHAPTER FOUR

"We're playing poker tonight. You should join us," Jenna suggested, bending to peer through the passenger side window.

"Thanks, but I've got Ava, and I'm awful at cards."

"The pizza's free, and trust me, we all cheat, especially Drew."

"Can I let you know later? Oh, and hey, thanks for keeping an eye on Ava for me. It was kind of Colby to ask her over."

"It's good for Colby to have someone around her age for a change."

"You do realize they're building a fort outdoors with every sheet and blanket from the house, right?"

"Dean's blankets, Dean's laundry." Jenna laughs. "Headed to town?"

"Thought I might as well get an early jump on enrolling Ava for school next fall." Samantha looked down at the keys in her hand. "That's actually a lie."

"You don't have to explain yourself, and certainly not to me. We all need breaks here and there. With all these buffoons around, I'm the timeout queen."

"I appreciate that, but we're going to be working together, so I need to start on the right foot. I'm usually honest to a fault and should tell you that I've been here before. Quite a few times when I was married. The first time we happened upon Buena Vista was when we were headed toward Independence Pass to get to Aspen but stayed here instead. We fell in love with it. I think it might be a good idea to walk through town a bit to get my feet back under me before I do so with Ava."

"Sam, stop by my grandmother's bookstore. You won't be sorry."

Samantha waved, deciding where to go first. Less than a quarter mile from the turn toward town, she skidded to a stop, nearly running over a man crossing the road. Wearing a dark green hoodie, a backpacker crossed the dirt road without a second glance in her direction then disappeared into the trees.

Ten minutes later, she parked by the bakery with a date plate of 1879 above the door then cruised the shops. It was nice, noticing the water bowls for dogs in the entryways of most storefronts. Strolling by the coffee shop on the corner of Main Street and Colorado Avenue, she ran into a woman. Smiling, she helped the woman who looked to be in her fifties untangle herself from the leashes of two cocker spaniels. After unraveling the last cluster around the woman's calves, Sam rose to meet curious eyes.

"Dawn?"

"No, sorry, I'm Samantha, new in town. Cute dogs, what are their names?"

"This stinker is Jasper, and this here is my sweetheart Olive. They make good company, my precious babies."

"I don't doubt it. Do you happen to know where I can find the bookstore Present Tense?"

"Oh, yes, you're close." The woman raised her arm and pointed a shaky finger down the walkway a half block away. "Before the bank, you can't miss it. Lots of flower pots out front."

"Thank you. What was your name?"

"That depends," the woman answered, chuckling. "I'm Juliann but folks I'm friendly with call me Jules."

"Well, Jules, it was nice to meet you. I hope to see you and your pups again sometime."

Stepping inside the bookshop, that familiar voice inside her head began whispering, "Pay attention, you've been here before." It couldn't be. It was the first time she'd ever stepped foot inside Present Tense Books & Blankets. The first time she smelled the spicy aroma, and the first time she heard those particular instrumental hums coming from a player behind the counter.

"Good morning," a little woman said, appearing from one of the many rooms shelved with books and knickknacks. Without another word, she reached for Sam's hand, tugging her along. They crossed one room to the next with burning incense, soft lighting, and a sleeping cat in the center of a round, colorfully braided rug.

44

She wore an unbuttoned, denim shirt with the sleeves rolled to her elbows. Under it, she had on a lime green t-shirt with the words "heavily meditated" in hot pink letters across the front. She was accessorized in feather drop earrings and an assortment of beaded bracelets. Her silver hair was pulled back into a ponytail revealing a lovely face with endless lines etched into her skin telling a story of a well-lived life. If Sam had to guess, the deep creases along her cheeks were from smiles she gave freely and often.

"You're my first customer of the day. That earns you a fresh cup of my coffee." She patted the top of Samantha's hand then flipped it over to skim her palm. "Interesting," is all she said, then resumed tugging Samantha through the shop. They stopped in a brightly lit room of many lamps and zero books. There was a small sink with a counter holding several coffee makers of varying types and brands, and a white, round table with four chairs. The screened door was propped open by a brightly painted rock the size of a grapefruit to allow the breeze through.

"You're Nana Sterling."

"Don't let that frighten you," she responded, with a wink. "Sit, dear, and let me test my latest concoction on you. I enjoy experimenting, even if my grandchildren gripe about it."

"I'm working with them. Jenna mentioned your shop. I hoped to pick up a book or two. Any suggestions?"

"Plenty, are you looking to escape or in search of information? Here. Try this." Nana Sterling set a mug steaming with the thick scent of peppermint on the placemat in front of Sam. "I'm calling this particular blend Merriment, even if it's summer."

"Thanks, and I'm not sure. Maybe both."

"I'm going with escape," Nana Sterling decided for her. She sat across from Samantha and reached for Sam's hands to hold loosely in her own. "You don't need more books, child. You need a heavy dose of disorder and commotion."

"You think?" Sam smiled, enjoying the eccentric woman's quick projections.

"I do, yes. You mustn't put your life on hold. I can attest it certainly doesn't wait for you."

"So, no books? How do you stay in business?"

"Oh, I do well enough. And you, my dear, have landed in our neck of the woods for a reason. Here, you aim to push through whatever it is that ails you, am I right? It's a good place to start, and you'll get there if you're gentle with yourself and realistic with a pace that will work for you. A good first step is knowing you're not alone. We all fight to hold on. It's only natural we fight letting go."

"Did Jenna speak to you? Of my situation?"

"No, your sadness speaks for itself. It takes courage to move on. But as I said before, you're here, so you're already working that out. When something's true, well, it's just that, true. Perhaps the next step is learning to believe in yourself again."

"I have a little girl," Sam announced, unsure as to why.

"She's a lucky girl."

"That's nice of you to say, considering I'm a stranger and this all feels so coincidental."

"I don't believe in coincidences. Surely you don't either. It's no secret others trust my intuition and ability to communicate. For me, it's been paramount in my recovery." Nana Sterling stood, removed a magnet from the fridge and set it on the table in front of Sam. This has always worked for me. You keep it."

Sam studied the magnet then read the words printed on it aloud: *"Well, look who I ran into," crowed Coincidence. "Please," flirted Fate, "this was meant to be."*

"Your heart is broken, that's apparent. If it can break, it's been loved. For your daughter's sake, and yours, use that love to rebuild." Nana Sterling smiled brightly.

"For me, the ground doesn't exactly feel solid right now, but there is one thing I've learned I can always count on," Sam said. "Behind every great smile, there's a good story. I want to come back soon and hear yours."

"*Ah*, yes, there it is. You're the best friend."

"Best friend?"

"Best friend," Nana Sterling repeated. "Think about it. All your relationships, you're the one, the invisible force holding everyone together time and time again. That says a lot about you."

"But what does it really mean? What good has it done?"

"Only time will tell. You have an opportunity here. Take it and remember that there are no coincidences, only fates. Use the time to be selfish, and to be your own best friend."

"To heal," Sam murmured, understanding. "Can I tell you something?"

"You can say anything here and are welcome to come by anytime to do so."

"I love your t-shirt, but this coffee is terrible."

#

47

"Cupid is stupid," I hear from Colby. Then, "Just like Stanna Truitt!"

"It's not even close to Valentine's Day," Ava adds, egging Colby on. "Girls like her think Cupid is cute. So dumb. Only smart people like us know it's scary to get an arrow shot through your heart by a flying baby."

"Exactly. That's why Stanna's a dumbshit!"

"Colby Sterling! Again? Really? You are so lucky your dad isn't here," Jenna scolds.

"Drew always says it, and no one yells at him for it."

"And no one is yelling at you either."

"My mom cussed *a lot*, and people said she was a genius," Ava adds.

"See!"

I watch Jenna soften, trapped between what's appropriate and their adolescent logic. "There's a difference. You're not a grown-up, and until you are, you have to follow the rules. Rules are to help, not hurt." *Poor Jenna*. She's getting nowhere with that reasoning. From where I'm standing, I witness both girls rolling their eyes in unison.

I'd come in just in time and without notice. I hitched my hip to the corner of the island taking up a chunk of the massive kitchen while Jenna rinses a glass in the sink. "What's the problem with Stanna Truitt?" I interject, hoping to spare Jenna.

"Ryan!" Colby screeches, lighting up. Ava, with dirt smeared across her cheek, walks to me and wraps her arms around my thigh, hugging me. I have no idea what I've done to warrant such adoration, but I like it.

48

"Oh, no, watch out! I know this tactic," Jenna warns. "They want something from you."

"Daddy says Aunt Jenna exonerates."

"Exaggerates. And, your dad would know." Jenna tosses the dishtowel over the edge of the sink, and then leans against the counter, crossing her arms over her chest.

"What's exaggerate?" Ava asks.

"It's what Stanna Truitt does!" Colby hops off the stool, preparing to educate us, using her body to expresses herself. "I got friends," she begins, convincingly. "Daddy says Stanna's either jealous or trying to be my friend 'cuz sometimes people are bullies when they want something bad enough. 'Cept, Stanna's always blabbing her big mouth about me." Colby spreads her arms wide. "So, what's Stanna go and do?" Colby pauses for effect, shaking her arms back and forth above her head. "She goes drawing pictures! All over the sidewalk at school!"

"Of what?" Ava asks. "Cupid?"

"Yep, shooting darts at stick people. They weren't even good stick people. Above the girl stick in purple letters—" Colby is using her finger to draw in the air— "it said, Colby Sterling! The boy stick had red, fat letters with hearts that said, Danny Stupid Weber!"

"Did it really say, Danny *Stupid* Weber?" I ask, trying to keep a straight face.

"Colbs, you need to stop calling people stupid. Find a different word."

"I tried that," Colby deadpans.

"Stanna probably isn't stupid either," Ava says, and we all turn to listen. "Maybe she's just got bad luck when it comes to thinking."

49

"Ryan, we got to talk later," Colby whispers. I nod, and the little people wisely run off before Jenna has a chance to zero in on her niece's cussing habit. We're alone now, and I have the opening I was hoping for. I need to talk to her without little ears tuning in, and more importantly without Dean chiming in to make matters worse.

"Colby mentioned the guy up the way is your boyfriend. What's he do?" I ask, working up my nerve.

"Garrett? He owns Dillon Lumber, and he's not my boyfriend." *Right*, I think. "He's usually around more, but they've been cutting over the pass near Tincup."

"Tincup? Didn't it get its name from a prospector who carried his gold dust in a tin cup? I'd love to tag along with him sometime, if he wouldn't mind?" Jenna chuckled at the enthusiasm in my voice. I tend to get excited when researching locations I plan to photograph.

"Do you exhibit? Use film or digital? Portraiture?"

"Wow." It's my turn to laugh. "You know about photography."

"Truthfully, I have no idea what I said. I literally used every phrase I know besides selfie. As for Garrett, he loves company. But I'm warning you. He will talk your ear off and tick off more tidbits of local info than you'll ever remember."

"Perfect. I look forward to it. And digital mostly. Eventually, my goal is to find the right place to settle and exhibit." I bite my lower lip. *Now or never.* "Jenna, is there something going on around here I should know? I'm only asking because I prefer not getting caught up in the middle of something dangerous that I know nothing about."

"The campfire incident," Jenna huffs, sighing. "I'm sorry you had to see that. They tried keeping it from me, but Drew has a big mouth."

"It's not that. I mean, that *was* grisly, but there's more. Even more than Dean suggesting I take measures to be safe when I'm working. It wasn't until after his warning that I did a little searching online. Reece tried to make light of it and blamed hunters. Jenna, it's not hunting season. Still, I understand that people don't always follow laws. It's going to happen, and I'm sure you get a lot of that sort of thing."

"We do. Trespassing is a common occurrence. Almost always unintentional and harmless."

"Right. That's what I thought. Until…" I pause, Jenna's eyes are telling. She's worried. "Late last night, I was with Samantha on her patio, talking. I saw something. I chose to keep it to myself and pretended to be oblivious. Samantha's got enough on her plate, and I didn't want to scare her or make an issue out of something that may be nothing."

"What did you see?"

"How wide is the creek? Twenty-five feet?"

"Roughly."

"It was dark. Occasionally I was able to make the outlines of trees if their tips lined against the night sky just right. Across the creek, in the trees, but not too deep, maybe forty feet from where we were, a man was watching us."

"Oh, my god! How do you know?"

"I have an eye for light. I usually keep my phone on silent. It's set on vibrate with a quick flash when there's a notification. I received a message, and my phone flashed. There was a slight reflection against something across the water. I'm assuming metal, belt high."

"How can you know for sure?"

"I have a habit of spinning my phone between my fingers, which I was doing while talking to Sam. Without being obvious, I was able to snap a few pictures. It was a longshot, but later when I looked at them, they were all too blurry except one. When I enlarged it, and with the help of several filters, I saw it. It's blurry but look. You can barely make it out, but he's there." I hand Jenna my phone. "Before I work myself up too much, I was hoping you would have a simple explanation. You know, like someone you know out for a midnight stroll?"

"I don't know who that could be and agree with Dean. You need to be careful."

I swallow. "Do you know why?"

"We're having some trouble, but so far nothing more than being scouted and pushed around. Dean has possession of something my stepfather wants."

"This land?"

"The mountain," Jenna confirms.

I'm relieved to find out she has an explanation, though not simple. I can deal with minor scare tactics as long as I'm not part of it anymore moving forward. There's no need for me to call Darien Shay, my boss-slash-friend, to relocate.

"My mom died," Jenna announces, abruptly. I look at her, confused at first. Then it sinks in, her desire to keep talking. She's around too many men too much and too often, men who attempt to protect her by limiting what they share. "She was the only sound of reason when it came to my stepfather, Jonathan."

"How did she die?" I ask, attempting to give this a whirl. I like Jenna and don't want her to feel as if the conversation has already served its purpose. Perhaps Samantha and I being around will balance the absence of female camaraderie.

"She played cards several times a week. She was vacationing with some friends from her bridge group when she passed. Aneurysm. That was a month ago. A week later Dean received the first letter from the County Assessor. My stepfather doesn't like wasting time. The senator has the power to pull strings which are proving to make things difficult for us."

"Why would he do that?"

"Ever been to Cripple Creek? Nice mountain town with legalized gambling? Jonathan has his sights on the mountain for a casino and hotel. What better place to launder money while making millions more? I'll never let it happen. He'll have to kill me first."

CHAPTER FIVE

"Here's one," Dean said, brushing his fingers along the claw marks of a bear on the bark of an aspen tree. "Oddly enough, the aspen is the more interesting of the two between the bear and tree."

"*Pssh*, right!" Samantha used her hands as if she were balancing the two. "Bear." Left arm up high, right arm down. "Tree." Left arm down, right arm up midway."

"We could always bet on it, but I'd feel bad taking your money. It's true. Aspen, they're the largest living thing on earth, and here in Colorado. We're in one of the biggest groves now. These things are interconnected by roots which can spread up to two-hundred acres wide. Garrett claims that's over six thousand tons worth of aspen."

"All from a plant?" Samantha asked, horseback riding above the Colorado Trail along the northern edge of Sheep Mountain. It had been Dean's idea to go, to familiarize Sam with the trails before the tourists started pouring in.

"Amazing, right? When our guides drop tidbits like this on the trail, clients soak it up then leave good reviews."

"Got it. Reviews. Go on then," Sam smiled, tongue-in-cheek.

"Yeah, yeah, just humor me and listen." Dean raised his index finger. "Genetic samples from underground shoots show they're separate but still part of the same root system, so yep…one plant. Nothing else compares in mass or area. Now it's your turn. You get to coach whoever you hire with scraps of local insight. You can thank me later."

"I'll be sure to do that. So, this trail? It's approximately a two-hour ride?"

"Just under and the most popular of the three. The ride crosses a footbridge and the creek several times, through this aspen grove, and along the mountainside with views of Cottonwood Canyon, Princeton, and Yale."

"How high are we?"

"Feeling it in your lungs?" Dean asked, chuckling. "It'll take a few more days, and I hope you and Ava are both drinking plenty of water. Altitude sickness is no joke. The elevation at Cottonwood Lake is ninety-five hundred, so we're maybe five hundred feet above that."

"Do you use fly spray?" Sam asked. "I need to check your horse's chest and belly when we get back."

"Why?"

"The skin there is thin and a feast for flies. Your horse is tense, in a hurry to get back and get that saddle off. Ease up just a bit. Not your fault, I can see you're an experienced rider, but it doesn't mean the horse thinks so. He's confused about how to respond to your leg pressure. Nine times out of ten they haven't been trained right and respond to pressure as a cue to speed up. Retraining him to respond to pressure by bending his body will show him pressure can have multiple meanings. Once he understands, he'll cooperate. He's new?"

"You can tell all that?"

"I can, and he's remarkable. He just needs a little assurance and help to know what we expect from him."

"Colby named him Gem. She has a thing for rocks," Dean relayed, detecting the thunderheads rolling in from a distance.

"Your daughter gave me a thorough presentation of her collection, but only after emptying her pockets of them. It took her a minute to strategically place each one, but once she had her display just right, she was well versed. She asked me if I'd teach her how to become a professional horsewoman then proceeded to share her intentions to travel the world. She plans to study petrology, you know?"

"Welcome to the mountain, Samantha, where things always change and never get boring. Let's head back. We're about to get one helluva sto—"

A blinding ray of light flashed through the already low billowing clouds rolling in no more than a quarter of a mile away. Bursts of orange flames punching their way through the shallow ravine chased the deafening explosion with a cloud of thick white smoke rising in its wake. Debris showered down, gradually landing on what was left of Golden Eagle Point, the basecamp for backpacking.

#

"I thought I might find you here." I step through brush onto the bank near Dean, who much to my surprise isn't wearing blue. "This is it? The place where you first saw my dog?"

"I'm not sure. The dog I saw that morning had a beautiful woman with him," Dean answers, looking up with only a hint of a smile.

He's kneeling with his fingers slowly sweeping through the current of the creek by a decomposing bridge. He's practically a silhouette surrounded by magnificent cottonwood trees, a few of which are nearly a hundred feet tall. From them, white cotton threads writhe free of their seeds on the limbs from the gentle breeze, floating through the air like dreams.

Dean suddenly stands, looming over me. He's intense, and understandably so. The explosion has stunned everyone. He raises his hand still dripping with creek water and gently brushes his fingertips over the fresh scrape on my arm. I close my eyes. It feels good to be touched. Just as quickly, I open them and step back.

"Please don't be afraid here."

"I'm not," I say, but I am still shaken. I was working when the eruption took place and was lucky to escape the area with only a few scratches. "Someone is trying to get your attention. Give it to them, if only to buy yourself some time. You'll figure this out, Dean."

"Jenna told you?"

"Very little."

"You might be right. I have always dreaded the day I'll have to ask my dad for help."

"The attorney?"

"He socialized in the same circles with my aunt and her husband."

"You really believe the senator is responsible for this?" I ask, lifting my hand toward the ridge where a portion of it had been blown to kingdom come.

"I don't think he has any idea of what happened here today, but I think people he pays to remove obstacles standing in his way do. What happened today is only a nudge. He's already steamrolling me in more practical and legal ways."

"How so?"

"Property taxes. Matters dating back before I was even born. There's no limit to the measures a man will take to steal land that doesn't belong to him."

Dean bends, picking up a pinecone and tosses it back and forth from one hand to another. I kick loose dirt on his hiking boot to lighten the mood. Above us a western bluebird, hidden in the branches, swoops by then flies upstream just above the water. I hear them first, then notice ducks nearby, bathing behind a boulder in the center of the creek. There's also a fallen tree with orange and yellow cosmos sulfur flowers growing through dead limbs. I'm beginning to appreciate that inside the forest so much life comes from death.

"Yes, this is the place I first saw you, and you are the most beautiful woman I've ever seen."

"Dean—" I want to say more but can't. I force my eyes down, finding it difficult to break eye contact and look elsewhere but they pop right back up, keeping him.

"The sun is always here," he says. "Even through the trees, this is the one place I can always find it. Before I was old enough to understand or appreciate any of it, Nana Sterling told me the sun represents the spirits who watch over my people. I didn't get it then, but I do now." He smiles that signature smile of his, and I'm sunk. "It'll be dark soon. Let's head back."

"On the way, you can tell me about Tincup. I'm headed there in the morning."

"Take Reece with you. Talk him into taking you by Taylor Reservoir. It's close enough, twenty minutes max."

"I'll think about it. He's definitely the better looking of the two," I tease, nudging Dean's shoulder.

"In that case, take Drew."

#

"Give me some singles, bro."

"Keep dreaming and please stop drooling," Reece elbows Drew, who's sitting sandwiched between us, hiding his hand. Samantha and Garrett fold. Reece calls my bluff, and now I'm out too. It's between the brothers while Jenna and Dean are having dinner with their grandmother in town. "Hurry up, the Rockies game is on and tied up at five," Reece says, winning with four of a kind.

Samantha passes the sofa, running her hand gently over Ava's head, as Garrett steps outside. Ava's been going through books for over an hour and taking notes in a purple binder. I consider the efforts Samantha's making for Ava's sake and notice the vast amount of blue decor throughout Dean's house.

Simultaneously, Samantha and I join Garrett on the deck. The night is too beautiful not to. At some point during the card game, it had rained lightly, leaving a fresh and earthy smell behind. A sliver of a crescent moon, glowing white, peeks in and out of ribbons of moving clouds while the trees whisper from a gentle yet crisp breeze.

"Slight change in plans," Garrett tells me. "We're cutting near St. Elmo tomorrow, not Tincup, but you and Bodie are welcome to ride along. The scenery at St. Elmo is hard to beat, not to mention it's a ghost town."

"Sold!" I answer enthusiastically, producing a slight chuckle from Samantha.

"We'll hit up Tincup in a day or two. A loader tipped on a skidder path, delaying the project." Neither Sam nor I have a clue what this means, but we both nod pretending we do.

"Bodie," Sam softly calls my dog. Bodie goes to her and rests his head on her knee then peers up at her through chocolate brown eyes. The exchange is simple yet tender.

"Jenna has a stepbrother and sister," Garrett offers, on the verge of saying more. More of what feels like is going to be essential we know as long as we're both planning to stick around. "There's no love lost between the two families. I'm telling you this because Dean and Jenna won't, and it may shed some light on the activity around here as of late.

"Jenna, she's no more than a second thought to Prescott, especially now with her mother gone. Dean's a different story. Sarah Prescott, Jenna's stepsister, concealed her way through town off and on for months trying to grab Dean's attention. It all went down while Jenna was away, so Dean

60

was none the wiser. He'd never met Sarah Prescott before, who introduced herself as Sarah Peyton. Peyton is her middle name, so not exactly a lie. Fill in the blanks, and we have Colby."

I feel sick. These people have their claws in Dean more ways than I can keep up with. "She gave up her daughter?" Sam asks, pulling me from my thoughts. "Who does that?" Samantha is from a close family, from loving and supportive parents, so she is completely baffled by this. Not me, I've seen my share of parents pull a disappearing act.

"Some women aren't cut out for it," Garrett answers, seemingly guessing. "It was all too easy, if you ask me. Dean's never had to fight for her, Colby's just his. I can't help but think it's all part of some grand scheme, a bigger plan. The Prescotts don't strike me as people who walk away from what's theirs."

"Or what's not theirs," I add, butting in where I shouldn't.

"Things might get ugly."

"Uglier than they already are?" Sam asks, not expecting an answer.

"Does she ever see Colby? I ask Garrett.

"Third Saturday of every month."

"Do Dean and Jenna do this a lot? Have dinner with their grandmother?"

"Every week like clockwork, but tonight was different. Nana Sterling summoned them with little notice. It's been a month since Jenna's mom passed and thirty years to the day Nana Sterling buried her firstborn son. Railroad accident. A coal train derailed from sun kinks. The track expanded, warped, then split. Several carriers toppled over, crushing him. If that weren't enough, it was right around the same time a neighbor, Dawn Jenson, went missing."

"No wonder," Sam begins. "When I met Nana Sterling, she tapped into my feelings instantly. Understood the things I'm going through. It's because she knows how it feels." Gently, Samantha continues rubbing Bodie. "She was so...*wait*, did you say Dawn? I ran into a woman in town, a sweet lady but a little confused, who asked if I was Dawn."

"That's Juliann Jenson, better known by locals as Jules. She's the mother of the missing girl. Jules spends a lot of her time walking through town asking girls, young and old, if they're Dawn. If you've got blonde hair, she's going to ask. Don't let her fool you. Ms. Jenson's sharp as a tack, but when it comes to Dawn things get fuzzy for her. It was a terrible thing what happened."

"Awful story," Sam agrees. "Where does she live?"

"There's a small neighborhood behind Main Street. Jules lives in a little, yellow house that backs up to Nana Sterling's."

"Ava," Sam calls. We hear footsteps coming closer before seeing a small head with a mass of brown, wavy hair poking out the doorway. "Come here, baby." Ava climbs on her mother's lap, as Sam hugs her close. "Tired?"

"Can't we stay longer?"

"You're still looking through those books?" Sam asked. *So much like you*, Sam thought, silently. "How about tomorrow we run a few errands? We can swing by the library and get you a card, so you can get books as often as you like. Then we should drive to Salida and look at bikes. You're big enough, don't you think?" Sam asked, smiling at the animated expression across her daughter's face.

"One like Colby's so we can ride together? For real?"

"Whatever you want."

"But, mommy, aren't they like a brazillion dollars?"

We laugh. The little people have a knack for that. In my gut, I know what I'm seeing will change the course of how things are going to be for them. Ava's blue eyes fill, quickly spilling over with tears. I sense why, willing to bet it's been too long since Ava's heard that magical sound. She wraps her small arms around Samantha's neck. Eventually, Ava pulls back and locks her watery eyes on her mother's.

"Mommy, you laughed."

CHAPTER SIX

I've lost count of the days that have passed. It's cold, and I'm scared. Something wild and hungry is lurking outside of our tent. It's not the first time. The only thing keeping me from freaking out is I can tell by the shadow that it's small. I close my eyes, willing myself back to sleep. The minutes slowly tick by.

Restless, I lie awake for another hour and then two. My mind is relentless, bouncing from one subject to another. Darien—my boss—has to be on the verge of firing me. Only figurately, I hope. That's not to say I'm not testing the limits. I came to Colorado with an understanding that a lot of work needed to be done in a short amount of time. And here I am, off on a Good Samaritan sabbatical. Lucky for me, Darien and I are close, and I am definitely having to play that card. She's also brilliant, and I have no doubt she's going to turn this hiatus into a headline that will receive national attention.

Having my camera won't hurt. The images I'm capturing will go a long way with putting food on the table for months to come. Which reminds me, the exposure will be good for Dean and Jenna's business as well. That will undoubtedly make things easier for Samantha who is with me out here in the wilderness. Not that I believe her position is in jeopardy.

Drew Young comes to mind. I'm adding him to the long list of random thoughts throughout the night. We owe him. He has stepped up, taking over Samantha's responsibilities without rebuke or hesitation, and it doesn't end there. Reece and TC have also jumped in to help. I foresee a long night at the bar, on me, and soon. Jenna, too. She has singlehandedly taken Ava under her wing while we're gone. The support we're receiving is proof enough that it really does take a village.

I turn to my side and see Samantha sleeping. Or at least pretending to be. I never had any doubt about how she would react. From the moment I explained the situation and the tragic circumstances surrounding it, there was no turning back for either of us. It continues to be a risk we're both still willing to take. A risk despite consequences, and there have been consequences. We never had time to organize nor did we initially realize how inept we truly were for what was and is in store for us. Even now, our determination can't be suppressed. We're on a mission.

It's hard to believe that it all started when Bodie and I caught a ride with Garrett to St. Elmo. But, even that's not completely accurate. It actually began with a fatal Jeep accident. Only I didn't know that yet.

St. Elmo had been a handful of abandoned buildings and few people. The individuals I did encounter were more interested in the chipmunks than the ancient magnificence lining the dirt road. I snapped countless photographs, working a myriad of angles. I had a goal. I wanted to score a glimpse of the ghost Garrett claimed was a disgruntled postal worker in the lower left window of what was once the post office.

When I was near the concrete remains of the Pawnee Stamp Mill, I recognized another flyer. It was easily the hundredth one I'd seen nailed to trees and trail posts during the thirty-five-minute drive on a winding road hugging Chalk Creek. The flyers were an assortment of bright colors to attract attention, although I had not read any.

I moved on to the General Store that I'd read was once a bank and before that a saloon. It was the only structure open for business, renovated just enough for the flow of light tourism. I bought two chunks of fake gold for two dollars. One for Colby and the other for Ava.

I proceeded to get a few more shots of the bell tower, formerly town hall and jailhouse before focusing my lens on another flyer. I zoomed in enough to recognize the image at the top of a single sheet of paper was a dog. My stomach flipped, and I turned away with Bodie hot on my heels. My dog means everything to me, so the thought of another one missing out in the wild wasn't anything I cared to know more about.

I wanted to see the Murphy Mine, hoping to catch the aftermath of mining for gold, copper, iron and silver sulfide. Instead, I found five wonderfully photogenic boxcars. I looked for tracks, some significant proof of railroad, but saw nothing more than an outhouse.

I needed to pee but cringed at the thought. Even Bodie whimpered as if he read my mind. I was close to succumbing before spotting the outhouse was partially made of an old dynamite crate, and there was a sound coming from the inside. A sound like claws scoring metal. I quickly turned away and walked directly into a post. I stepped back, releasing my grasp from splintered wood, and pulled a flyer free in my retreat. I could no longer escape it. The missing dog was literally in my hands.

Deacon, a two-year-old Bernese Mountain Dog, was thrown from a vehicle as it slid off a cliff and tumbled six hundred feet down the ravine. The driver, a woman in her forties from Omaha, guiding her Jeep in a caravan near Iron Chest Road, was killed in the crash. Her daughter Caren, a Nebraska college student, had been airlifted to a hospital in Colorado Springs. Family and friends were desperate to reunite Caren with Deacon, last seen running away from the scene of the accident.

And here we are. Well, not exactly. We had several stops to make first. Samantha and I drove to Colorado Springs to meet Caren at Penrose Hospital. Samantha was reluctant to go, wanting to begin the search immediately. "Every minute counts," she told me repeatedly. I delayed because I thought we needed more information. If we hoped to have any success, or at least find out what had happened to Deacon, we needed to talk to Caren first. I couldn't say this to Sam, but the odds weren't good.

We hummed along to a song playing on Sirius Radio as we made our way through Manitou Springs when I asked, "Do you think Deacon is alive?"

"The minute I let myself think otherwise, he's as good as gone." Sam turned her head toward me. "This girl lost her mom. It doesn't have to be us, Ryan, but I hope it's someone. Someone needs to find her dog." Another minute passed before she added, "It's awful imagining how frightened he must be."

Caren was a bandaged bundle under a mountain of white sheets and blankets. She was battered and weary when we arrived. It didn't surprise me when Samantha promptly moved a chair beside the hospital bed and took Caren's hand as if they've been lifelong friends. Sam wasted no time with introductions and explained our intentions. I brought Caren a tissue from a box on the counter once her tears began to fall.

"For as long as I can remember," Caren started, "we've gone to Colorado every summer to camp. The day it happened, I looked over and saw we were way too close to the edge of the road. I started to say "whoa, stay closer," but I couldn't finish before we started sliding." Caren dabbed her eyes. "My mom...we were close. And Deacon...he's out there somewhere. I know what everyone is thinking, but I don't believe it. He's alive," she sobbed. "He needs help."

"How are you, Caren?" I asked, hoping to offer an emotional respite.

"Lucky," she answered, collecting herself. "Broken leg and ribs, stitches here and there, compressed vertebrae."

"We can't change what's happened," Sam said. "But we'll do everything we can to help find your dog."

Two hours later, we were back in Buena Vista. We grabbed lunch to go then pulled into a tight parking spot outside of a locally owned and operated specialty store for outdoor equipment and apparel. We received tremendous assistance, an abundance of helpful tips from two knowledgeable employees. We left with our arms full of gear, but not before they supplied us with phone numbers should we need help. My adoration for the people in town leapt to a whole new level.

I've camped before, but never in the conditions we were about to encounter, even if it's summer. I admit I was worried. We're both in shape, but not for this. *This* requires training, not to mention acclimation. We didn't have time to consider the obstacles or allow our thoughts to even go there. Our strategy was to get packed and get out of dodge before Dean returned to put a halt to our plans. Again, thank goodness for Jenna and her willingness to mediate that minor detail.

We entered the forest above St. Elmo at an elevation just above eleven thousand feet. We were totally prepared, or so we thought, to hike to timberline if necessary and possibly higher. We're equipped for weather, but I swallow now, thinking of what concerns me the most. *Bears.*

For some reason, a mountain lion or whatever else prowling outside of our tent this very moment isn't nearly as worrisome to me as a bear. Have I mentioned that I tied tiny bells to my shoelaces for noise? It was silly but comforting to think if a bear hears me, he won't come near me. After several annoying hours that first afternoon, Sam made me remove my bells.

It's odd now that I think about it, but being out here, completely off the radar, I've unearthed more solace and sovereignty than ever before. It's a hard admission to make considering the circumstances, but I'm confident it's the same for Samantha. There are times it feels we are the only two people left on earth. We are *that* alone. For Sam, it's been more than a hunt. I have spent days observing her. It's as if she's gradually healing in the arms of Mother Nature. Earlier, while watching the sunset, I heard her say, "No one paints more beautifully than God," blowing my soul wide open.

Thus far, we've spent our days getting lost, aiding blisters, wrapping turned ankles and ignoring sore muscles. We're both losing weight we don't have to lose. Sam has a deep gash along the right side of her neck, and I'm pretty sure poison ivy. But luckily, no bears.

In addition to the occasional roadside check-ins with Jenna for Ava and Samantha to connect, Dean has tracked us multiple times, replenishing our supplies. To his credit, he never attempts to talk us down. He's encouraging when our spirits are deflated, and our endeavor feels hopeless. He lingers longer with each visit, and if I'm honest, I'm always sad to see him go. Something I have to face sooner than later.

I begin to fall asleep just as the sun decides to grace us with its presence and warmth. Unfortunately, Sam is ready to roll and nudges me awake. It takes two stainless steel cups of tar-like coffee to get me on my feet. Several hours into our morning, and we're not only heartsick but exhausted from trekking varying terrain for ten to thirteen hours a day.

My fingers are raw, my toes are numb, and my skin is burned and chapped. We've climbed, crawled, and even swam in water we should have avoided a time or two. I can add bathing in diverse bodies of insanely cold water throughout the Rocky Mountains to my resume. It doesn't necessarily mean we are clean.

We've been on the receiving end of icy nights, pelting rain, and a skunk attack. We've seen beautiful animals, big and small. We've slept cramped together in a small tent on the rocky and wet ground, and heard noises I care never to hear again, napping with our flashlights on. We're desperate and beginning to lose hope. Deacon has vanished. A miserable thought but one I have to let sit my stomach while it continues to ache.

On the trail following an old railroad grade from the ghost town of Hancock toward the partially collapsed Alpine Tunnel, I stop. At one time, it was the highest railroad tunnel in the world and the first to be built through the Continental Divide, but I cannot explore or search anymore. The view is spectacular, and I realize we've only been on the move for three hours, but I'm done. My body aches in unimaginable places.

I let my pack fall and unlace my boot, noticing I really need to shave. I'm sitting on a log less than a foot away from the lake, presumably one of the Hancock Lakes. Sam says nothing. We share in this despair. We've failed. I feel the weight of the world but realize it's only her arm draping across my shoulders as she rests her head against mine. I feel her stiffen and chalk it up to the anguish we're both feeling.

"Ryan?"

"Hmm?" I sigh, distracted and lost in thought.

"Please don't freak out," Sam whispers. Her arm tightens around my shoulders with her hand clamping down on my collarbone. "Don't scream, and whatever you do...please do not run." Slowly, I open my eyes and turn my head to the left.

Oh. My. God!

I faint. That, or I lost all recollection of several long seconds. The sharp odor surrounding us is strong, and my eyes bulge. "*Shhh*," I vaguely hear Sam murmur over the drumming in my ears. In disbelief, we watch with hammering hearts and fear unlike any I've ever known. The black bear steps once, twice, and then sits on the bank of the lake no more than fifteen feet away.

I'm shaking violently, silently praying. Sam is breathing slowly. In. Out. In. Out. Everything is happening in slow-motion, and I have a fleeting thought of this being what life is like right before death. It's outrageously peaceful in an extremely terrifying way. A phenomenon I cannot explain.

The bear paws at the water and then its face, splashing everything in the vicinity. I really, *really* want to run. Samantha senses this, and her fingers dig further into my skin. If I weren't so petrified, I would argue with myself to admire how magnificent this creature is. If we make it out of this alive, I vow to honor this animal for life.

His shaggy coat is cinnamon, not black. He's at least six feet in length with broad shoulders. His eyes are small, beady, and his ears are round. His muzzle, grizzled with brown, is long and narrow.

The bear glares at us then looks up. Again, to us. Then up. Neither Sam nor I am brave enough to look away from the bear to wherever "up" seems to be. He repeats his motions. With remarkable courage, Samantha looks up in the direction of the bear's interest. I gasp and close my eyes when it stands and moves. Sam steadies me with a death grip. When I open my eyes, the bear is gone, disappearing into the woods.

"It's a sign," Sam says, mesmerized by the peak to the northwest.

"*What…the…fuck…*just happened?" I screech, with hot tears on my cheeks. The magnitude of emotions swarm me—relief, panic, terror, gratitude. "Why are you not freaking out?" I jump up. "Sam?!"

"I don't know," She says, snapping from the spell. "I am. I was. But now I'm not. Don't laugh, but…"

"I can assure you I am *not* laughing. I'm freaking out!"

"Do you believe in spirits?"

"Holy crap, Sam! *Really?* You're choosing *now* to have an epiphany?" I shake my head. I'm so worked up I'm sweating. Adrenaline is pumping through my veins. I have the urge to swim swiftly across the lake to get further away from the bear that's shaven ten years from my life. I breathe deeply, inhaling as much oxygen at once as possible. "Okay," I say, as calmly as I can manage. "Tell me what you mean?"

"I was scared to death. My life was flashing before my eyes, and I kept picturing Ava, and when I saw Jordan…I can't explain it. I just knew we were going to be okay." Unable to drag her eyes from the spot, Samantha points to the mountain top. It's higher than anywhere we've been so far. "How did I not see it before? How did I not know?"

"Sam? Hello? I'm over here!" I say, dragging Sam's attention from the rocky peak to me. "Tell me."

"There," she points again. At the very least, it's a thousand feet higher than the crash site. "He's up there, Ryan. That's where we'll find Deacon."

I lift my eyes to the bald mountain top, daring us from afar. We had hiked the entire area around the site where the

73

Jeep had yet to be pulled from. We'd never gone beyond timberline where little to nothing grows, the air is too thin, and shelter is nonexistent.

"Alright," I say, believing her. The pounding of my heart reinforces what we both now know. "We need to get to the road and hitch a ride back to Dean's. We're hungry and tired. You need to get the cut on your neck looked at and see Ava. We'll sleep in real beds, take hot showers, eat decent food, and head out first thing in the morning."

"You're right. Of course, I know you are. I just don't want to lose him now that we're so close."

"Sam, we can't get to him today. It'll be dark before we can even get off this mountain, let alone make it to the base of that one. I need to ice my ankle," I add. It's not a complete lie, but the manipulative tactic works. Sam accepts we need to rest if we stand a chance against the climb that may take more than a day.

"Do you need help getting your boot back on?"

"I'm good, but Sam? I peed my pants."

"Me too," she admits, laughing.

By the next morning, the beginning of week three, we are achingly close. We've been in the same spot for several hours. There can't be more than five hundred feet between us and the top of this chiseled mountain that's become my nemesis, but we cannot advance any further. Every move we've made throughout the day has been calculated and thoroughly discussed. We can't risk being impulsive to get to closer, only to scare him off.

With overwhelming astonishment, I'm dazed by the reality, the magnitude of the moment. In a state of utter bliss, I swallow hard, tasting weeks of grime. I push aside the

74

exhaustion with the realization of what exactly we've sustained only to receive the most substantial prize of all. We've done the impossible. We have found Deacon.

Upon seeing him, which is why we haven't moved in hours, Deacon continues to run away. Cautiously, he returns to peer over us and then thousands of feet below to the crash site. He's traumatized. It's exceedingly upsetting. Samantha continues to call to him in a gentle tone, acquainting herself to him. Deacon is curious but fearful. I can only imagine what he's gone through and wonder if his mind will ever be right again.

What happens next is entirely Samantha: her tenacity, tender soul, and forbearance for animals brings Deacon closer. Very timidly, he's beginning to trust her. She has demonstrated such patience and placidity that her demeanor also spellbinds me. My faith in humanity has been completely restored while we sit together and wait him out.

Samantha eventually leaves me, asking with such compassion to let her proceed alone. I understand. I'm not hurt that we've come so far only to be left behind now. I feel nothing but respect as sheer pride surges through me. I'm overwhelmed by the gains she's made these past weeks, all while ensuring my safety and comfort throughout.

Samantha is no longer an acquaintance I met in a sleepy mountain town, no longer a fellow Texan in the cabin next door. She's more. So much more. She's my best friend, the second half to a whole, the sister I never had. A sister I've gained by choice. Just like that, in the span of four hundred and eight hours, we're bound for life. A bond built on the foundation of trust during these seventeen days of never being apart, learning all there is to know about one another.

I feel as much a part of this moment as the woman and dog within my sight, but it's evident the two of them must meet in the middle and alone. I can't help the tears staining my face as I witness each painstaking slow step closer together. I feel so much at once. In my head, it's worth repeating a thousand times: *We've found him!* Together, against unbelievable odds, we've done it. We are on the brink of rescuing him, and all I can do is lift my eyes to the beautiful blue sky and thank God.

For extra measure, and because Sam is so important to me now, I can't let this moment pass without also thanking Jordan for guiding our way. "So, yes, Sam," I whisper, although she can't hear me. "I do believe."

Samantha is sitting on a jagged rock with her hand stretched out. She has nothing to offer Deacon but time. His reluctance continues. He's inside of ten feet before withdrawing. It's a methodically slow process, but Sam isn't quitting.

He's near enough now to see he's matted and malnourished. I hold my breath when he's within reach. I don't know how Sam can hold her arm out to him for so long. Her resolve is inconceivable. Everything about the situation feels surreal. I have not dropped tears like these since I ran away from Silver Valley. I blink and then focus in to see Deacon is there, inside Samantha's embrace, as she mutters reassurance and love to him.

#

In my wildest dreams, I never imagined a dog would change my life so completely. I wonder why I feel different, so changed. Why nothing went our way for weeks? Why it took us so long? Is that's how life works? How lessons are learned? Does the universe take it's time teaching us the things we need to know?

Walking, I think about these things and more. I'd rather think about anything else other than leaving Deacon behind, which is what we're doing now. I can't bring myself to look back after the tearful goodbye until I hear Caren call after us. Sam leans into me for support. This goodbye has already been hard enough. Being a bystander to Deacon and Sam parting ways was painful. Their connection is transcendent, and all I want is to rush back to Buena Vista to hug Bodie and never let him go.

"I can't do it," Caren says. "Promise me you'll take good care of him," she pleas, pushing Deacon's leash into Sam's hands. "You...both of you, you saved him. That's everything. I have a long road and too many changes ahead of me to be fair and good to him." She wipes her eyes.

"It's a hunch, but part of me feels like you need him as much as he needs you." Caren's looking at Samantha. "It's enough. To see him again, to know he survived. It's enough." Weakly, Caren kneels, wrapping her arms around Deacon's neck. "I love you, boy. I love you so much. Live long, my sweet, brave boy." Caren stands, balancing on her crutches then spins away, never turning to look back.

We drive the hour and a half back in silence. Swallowing the lump in my throat, I turn my head to see Samantha sleeping in the passenger seat. Deacon, who is not small by any means, is curled in her lap and also asleep. I reach for

77

my phone to snap a picture. I never want to lose this moment and want to share it with Ava.

Spending almost three weeks completely off the grid with nothing more than friendship to get me through, I discovered the importance of hope. It's more than a bright star in a hopelessly dark universe and much more than an emotion. It's a promise to ourselves to never give up.

CHAPTER SEVEN

Buena Vista is not the sleepy mountain town I said it was. While Samantha and I were away, the entire area had swapped every calming attribute for the storm. The Arkansas Valley is thriving and multiplying in occupancy. Summer in the Rockies is no joke. It's no wonder that in our final days during the search for Deacon, we ran into multiple backpackers and bikers when emerging from the backcountry onto trails.

Unlike the vigorous activity around me, I could sleep for a month, but I'm wide awake, and my mind is reeling. Everything has changed. I'm different. Sam is different. We are both tethered and tired yet renewed. I'm learning it doesn't have to be scary to care. For me, it's a first, but for Sam, it's more like again. Not necessarily for people only, per se, but certainly for life.

It's after ten when I hear tapping on my front door. *Dean.* There was a party in the form of a BBQ waiting for us when Sam and I returned. I had only talked to Dean briefly here and there before sneaking indoors for a hot shower that promised to wash the funk away.

I'm unable to move for several long seconds longer, lying on my back and feeling nostalgic. It's strange, but it feels wrong to be staring at a ceiling instead of millions of stars and to be warm, fed and clean. I'm beginning to think this feeling is a stint of depression. It's like when a hostage starts developing a psychological alliance with their captor as a survival strategy during captivity. The San Isabel Forest has been my captor, and I most definitely feel the alliance.

"Hey," I say, opening the door. Dean peeks in, glancing around. "I'm alone," I add.

"Every light is on." He steps inside, sizing up the flames inside the fireplace. "And that's going to burn for hours. Aren't you tired?"

"I am. Even my eyelashes are yawning," I admit. I sit on the sofa and watch as he takes a seat in a chair across from me. He lifts his boots to the coffee table and crosses his legs at the ankles. Bodie is quick to climb up beside me and rest his head in my lap. "How are you?"

"Wired but bushed. It's been an eventful week."

"Same. By tomorrow morning, I'll want to kiss whoever invented the snooze button."

"Hitting snooze is like resisting your day. Why would you want to do that?"

I groan. "I'm too tired to punch you. If the next thing out of your mouth is something encouraging about how to set the tone for the day, I might hit you anyway." With his eyes on me, I stretch, needing a distraction. "Where's Colby?"

"With her mom." He smiles when Bodie stands on the cushion, circles once, twice, and settles in next to me exactly as he was before. "He missed you." I break eye contact with Dean and look down at my dog.

"I should have taken him but worried about other...animals," I say, remembering the bear.

"I'm unsure who *they* actually are, but they say fear is the best motivator. The more something scares you, the more you have to face it. I know what it's like up there on the mountain, so I think it's true. There are times you have no choice but to face the adversity. I can tell just by looking at you that it's changed you. How's Sam?"

"Stronger than I expected." It's the first thought that comes to mind. "I was worried how she was going to react, or worse, afraid she would relapse back into misery once we dropped Deacon off. Before that changed, too."

"People get hurt, then heal, and then get hurt again. It's the way of things."

"Well, that's not depressing at all," I joke, picking up a magazine from the coffee table and hurl it at him. Dean catches it with one hand and laughs. "Tell me about your week. Business is booming. Is that why you look beat?"

"Mostly."

"What's the other part of mostly?" I pry. "I've got all night," I add, prepared to wait him out. That, and I know it will be hours before I'm able to fall asleep.

"We almost lost someone earlier," he says. I tilt my head, wanting to know more of what that means. It's hard for me to measure "almost" because I learned a long time ago that almost never counts.

"Browns Canyon is the most rafted whitewater in the world. Just north of it is a thirteen-mile stretch called the Numbers. Easily the best Class IV run in Colorado. Runoffs been good, so the water's high. It's been cranking at about twenty-six hundred CFS. That's max adventure and high intensity. Every summer there are always intermediates who think they're experts and drop in where they shouldn't."

"You allow that?"

"Not my outfit. There's a handful of rafting companies throughout the valley. I was called in to assist, but to be fair, it was a private group out on their own."

"Why you?"

"Special Operations, Search and Rescue." *Okay, wow!* I had no idea. "The rainstorm that rolled through at dawn didn't help. A downpour like that creates problems. The river was insane, running close to three thousand CFS for a short while. Toss in a little debris with a thrill seeker and…" Dean shrugs his shoulders.

"What happened?"

"That section of the river drops quick. It's narrow and rocky with continuous whitewater throughout the route. It's physically demanding and easy to get caught under the rapids in the rocks. I got a call there was a swimmer."

"Swimmer?"

"Raft capsized. A kid, no more than seventeen, got his foot trapped by an undercut rock chiseled away by the power of the water. The raft hit the rapid with its side instead of the nose. Normally we'd set up a live bait rescue. It's a risky exercise where one of us swim the river clipped to a rope and held by people on shore, ready to pull. There wasn't time or enough feet on the ground for that, so I improvised."

"Dean—"

Dean waves me off then continues. "The Numbers have six major rapids. The first is the most technical. We were at rapid four, which is generally the most carnage. It was a battle, but ultimately, I was able to get the rope around him. It took too long for me to swim out, in any case. By the time I did, I had run upstream along the bank as far as the rope would reach then jumped in and pulled.

"It worked, freeing his foot from the rocks just as his head started bobbing in and out of the water. TC showed up just in time, snatching the kid then administered CPR. Thank God for that, because I got hung up wrestling a broken rock wall and crashing waves."

I'm so stunned that I can't think of what to say other than, "what's wrong with your shoulder?"

"Nothing."

"Liar. Take off your shirt." Dean's brow spikes and his lips twitch then spread into a smug smile. "Ha! But seriously, let me see what you've done to it." Reluctantly, he pulls his blue shirt over his head.

Wow again! I should have known. I'm captivated by his physique and gawking. He's broad, defined, and his skin is glowing from the firelight. He's also badly bruised. "You're sure nothing's broken?"

"Dislocated. TC knocked it back in." I cringe. *Men are so deranged.* "It's late, want me to stay so you can get some sleep?"

"You think I need you here to fall asleep?"

"I like how it feels to be with you, Ryan, and want to make it a priority. That, and I think I do want you to reach a point where you won't be able to sleep without me." Dean enjoys challenging me. My blush brightens, but I try desperately not to let it show. I honestly don't know what to do with this man.

"For now, I only meant you have the cabin lit up enough to rival Vegas. I'll bank that fire then sit here until you fall asleep in there." Dean nods toward the bedroom. "Without all these lights on."

"Really, I'm okay," I add with emphasis. "Thank you for the offer. You're a teddy bear under all that manly macho stuff. Oh! That reminds me! It's been decided!"

"What has?"

"My spirit animal," I answer, compellingly. "Is a bear!"

Dean rolls his eyes. "Mine's an owl."

I scoff. "*Please!* My spirit animal will so eat your spirit animal." Dean laughs, and together, we stand. Hesitantly, I walk him to the door. I want him to go and want him to stay. The battle between my libido and moral compass is confusing. He bends, and I close my eyes. He's going to kiss me. Except he doesn't. Surprised, I open my eyes, forgetting to be embarrassed. He is, however, less than an inch from my face, taking up every bit of air between us.

My heart is racing. There's no sense in denying it. I want him to kiss me. I'm practically begging for it. I have no idea how my hand ends up in his, but he's rubbing his thumb against my palm, featherlight. Without intending to, I lean in but then stop and step back, glancing down at my feet with wonder. There's more going on here than sparks of interest.

"Careful," he says. "Expectations lead to disappointment."

"Let me know when you touch down," I reply, deflating his ego even if he's right. I am disappointed.

84

"You know, behind every light, there's a shadow," Dean says at the door. "Turn a few lights off, Ryan McCray, you're safe here."

#

"Good morning," Samantha said, handing Juliann Jenson a gift bag of dog toys. "I wanted to swing by to say hello and introduce my daughter. Ava this is Juliann Jen—"

"Jules," the woman interrupted with a megawatt smile that melted Sam's heart. Jules set the gifts aside then waved them inside. "Come, I was sitting on the patio. It's not every day I get company."

The brief encounter with Jules weeks earlier, along with hearing about the loss of her daughter, had stuck with Sam. Common ground, Sam had thought, understanding what it was to lose someone so young. She'd made a promise to herself, a promise to engage with Jules, or attempt to be her friend.

"We have our dog with us," Sam said, hesitating at the door.

"Oh, that's fine. He's welcome here too." Samantha entered with Ava's hand firmly in her own, anticipating a cocker spaniel freak out, as Deacon followed behind them on a leash.

Sam quickly second-guessed her decision to bring Ava. Jules' living room was a shrine with framed photographs lining the walls, resting on shelves, and covering the entire surface of a sofa table and mantle. In every frame, there was the same young, blonde-haired child. Luckily, the remainder of the house was like any other, ordinary even, without evidence of the missing girl.

"Would you like some ice cream?" Jules asked Ava. "I have Rocky Road."

"That's my favorite!"

They waited on metal chairs in the shape of tulips for Jules to return. Sam pulled Deacon to sit between her legs and rubbed the edge of his fluffy ear between her fingers. She looked down, heartened by his progress.

Once Jules returned, she didn't exactly apologize for the shrine but explained. "I made a promise never to forget, although sometimes that means it may be uncomfortable for others to see."

"What don't you want to forget?" Ava asked.

"A long time ago, I had a little girl."

"What happened to her?"

"Ava—"

"It's okay," Jules assured Samantha. "Children say and ask what we should but don't." Jules patted Ava's hand. The simple touch moved Sam. She longed for Ava to have a grandmother, although that was no longer in the cards for them. Her mother had passed, and Jordan's mother was, well, never going to happen. "After all the years, it helps to talk about her."

"She was beautiful," Samantha said, hoping Ava picked up on her cue to let it drop.

"Where'd she go?" Ava asked, instead, shoveling a spoonful of chocolate ice cream into her mouth.

"No one knows. We never had any trouble 'round here. The kids...the lot of them...they all just ran. All day, every day. I see now she was just too young to be out the way she was. One minute she was here, and then the next…gone."

"Do you think she was stolen?"

"Ava!"

"I think that's exactly what happened," Jules answered, then moved her hand from Ava's to cover Samantha's. "It's been a long time since anyone's talked to me about this. Talking about Dawn is more helpful than hurtful."

"I work most days," Sam began, eager to steer the conversation to a new direction. "But I am taking an afternoon off next week to have lunch with Ava in town and show her the school. Would you like to join us?"

#

"Ryan, I need a job," Colby shouts, walking into my cabin like she owns the place. In a way, I suppose she does. "It's my daddy's birthday, and I got nothin' to give him."

I almost correct her grammar and quickly think better of it. Somehow, I'm still earning my cool points. "What would you like to give him?"

"A new truck. Another blue one."

I laugh. "Let's shoot for something smaller. What's your favorite thing?"

"My rocks," she answers. I can almost hear the "duh" she wants to add but doesn't.

"Right. What's my favorite thing?" I ask.

"Bodie."

"Well…true. But what else?" I try again, poking her in the belly.

"Pictures."

"Exactly. What do you say we make a frame with some of your favorite rocks and put a picture of you inside of it?"

"Yes!" Colby jumps into my arms and hugs me with all her might.

One oddly wrapped present later, the door rattles from Colby's hasty departure. Shaking my head, I decide not to procrastinate any longer. It's time to get back to work. With that in mind, I reach for my phone. The display indicates I've missed several calls from Darien. It isn't like her to call back-to-back without leaving a message or firing off a text with half a dozen demands.

Nonetheless, the sunlight is perfect for a photoshoot at Agnes Vaille Falls, and I need to get moving. The waterfall is on the southern slope of Mount Princeton just above Chalk Creek. I'm cocky now about my hiking ability, so the short half mile trek up Chalk Creek Canyon should be a breeze. It isn't until after I load Bodie and my gear that I see a note on the windshield held by the wiper.

We're having a party tonight, and you're coming!
Location: Dean's
Reason: Dean's birthday
More Reasons: I hired a stripper and got a keg
See you at 8:00
Jenna

Agnes Vaille Falls is a no go. My phone buzzes while I'm reading the notice which marks the area off-limits to the public. My previous research proves to be outdated. The trail to the waterfall has been closed for some time as a result of a deadly rockslide, tragically killing five people. A local high school coach and family. With another quick search on my phone, I read it was a catastrophic accident that rocked the community. There're more than a dozen articles that pop up on it, but before I can read further, my phone vibrates again with a call from Darien.

"Hey," I answer.

"Three words."

"Answer the phone. I know, I know."

"There's a lecture whirling with your name on it, something fundamental about deadlines, but…" Darien's voice trails off, so I wait patiently for whatever bomb drops next. "You need to go to Silver Valley, honey. Your aunt died."

<u>CHAPTER EIGHT</u>

"You didn't have to do this," I say, looking at Sam. "But thank you for doing this." Samantha glances at me then looks over her shoulder to her sleeping daughter in the back seat. Behind Ava, in the far back, two sleeping dogs are snoring. "By the way, I almost killed a park ranger today."

"I'm guessing it had something to do with your burning desire to fish in places you shouldn't?"

"No," I answer, feigning offense. "My work itinerary was being sabotaged when I got the call. Afterward, I decided to go for a walk and ended up taking a detour to avoid the crowded Arkansas River Trail. Apparently, I missed the event barricade that Paddlefest was underway. I was scolded for being on the wrong side of the trails then lectured about fishing. I was *not* fishing." Sam looked at me skeptically. My need to catch a fish isn't necessarily a secret. "At least, not yet."

"If it were anyone else, the fixations with bears and fishing would concern me," Sam says, handing me a cup of coffee. She's careful not to spill from the HydroFlask to my cup, determined to keep me caffeinated. Our goal is to drive all night. "I can't believe we managed to escape that party without any of them talking us out of it. And why are you so indifferent about going to your aunt's funeral?"

I had been late to Dean's birthday celebration by an hour. I wanted to congratulate him for another trip around the sun, but before I was able to pin him down, I was met with observant eyes. Leave it to Sam to know when something is off. I continue to discover things about Sam, and her ability to read me so well. There's a connection between us, one I share with only few, possibly only two.

I can't say how it escalated so quickly, but we left the party soon after I arrived. Now we're driving to Texas with a child and two dogs in tow. When I came out of my cabin with Bodie and a small bag, Sam, Ava, and Deacon were waiting. Sam was relentless about not allowing me to go through the next few days alone. Fortunately, Jenna agreed, easing my concern. The road trip happened to fall on the few and far between days Sam was scheduled to be off. I'm not entirely sure that was true.

"Not indifferent, just a long story. But more importantly, back to the park ranger." I roll my shoulders, uninterested in discussing my aunt, her death, or how I feel about either. "I saw him at the party, the park ranger. He avoided me like the plague once he recognized me and saw I was friendly with Jenna and Dean."

Sam snorts. "Friendly. *Right!*" I eye her. "You're dancing around your feelings for Dean."

91

"Am not."

"Are too." Sam rolls her eyes. "You like him."

"Do not."

"Do too." Sam tightens the cap on the thermos and stuffs it under her seat. "How'd your aunt die?" Sam asks, letting my Dean issues rest.

"My uncle found her on the kitchen floor with the water running and a sponge in her hand," I answer matter-of-factly because I honestly do not give a shit. At least, that's what I'm trying to convince myself.

"It's good timing. Sorry, I don't mean your aunt. Ava misses her cousins," Sam explains. "My nephew's birthday is next week." We're dropping Ava with family in Texas while we attend the funeral. Sam has decided to let Ava stay with their family for the week. Again, I glance at Sam. Her expression is blank. "Jordan's brother's son," she adds. "Mike offered to fly back with her." The subject is closed.

We left Ava in Dripping Springs, Texas, but not before an emotionally charged reception. Beyond anything I identify with when it comes to family. The love between Sam and her family is intense. Jordan's beautiful sister-in-law had a difficult time releasing Sam from a profound embrace. Mike, who Sam has shared bits and pieces of here and there, made a genuine effort to meet and talk with me. It was clear Sam had mentioned me before. I felt welcome and included, touched by the regard and warmth in the affectionate exchanges.

Afterward, we swung by my condo in Austin that I hadn't seen in the better half of a year. My mother resides in Austin which explains the location of my permanent address. A mile from my place, Mama is institutionalized in a large yet private facility for the mentally ill. Her home since I was four-years-old. It's the first time I've been able to sign her out. And I'm doing it now to take her with us to Silver Valley to bury her sister.

To her credit, Samantha is unfazed. She's yet to question how my mother communicates, which is responding to most everything with lyrics. We've crossed miles and miles of Texas, and all I can hear is Mama humming, and all I see in the horizon is baked earth. Sam sleeps while I replay the conversation with the supervising nurse who argued my mother was too unfit to travel, too self-destructive and mindless to cope reasonably in public. I took her anyway, not buying any of it. My mother's diagnosis as schizophrenic is circumstantial, and I hate labels.

"I was in seventh grade when I found a shoebox filled with pictures of you. You were on stage singing to a big crowd," I say to my mother who was strapped into the passenger seat with Samantha behind us. "You looked happy and so beautiful in those pictures. That's when I knew I wanted to be a photographer."

"A picture of me without you," Mama sings, courtesy of the late George Jones.

We stop for food at the Kuntry Korner in Zephyr, Texas. The young girl uninterested in taking our order has yet to make eye contact. That changes once Mama breaks it down with liking hers with "lettuce and tomato, Heinz 57 and French-fried potatoes." Thank you, Jimmy Buffet.

"A cheeseburger," I clarify.

We sit in a corner booth where I carefully explain to my mother why we're going to Silver Valley. Mama begins hugging herself then rocks forward. The sudden movement sends her Styrofoam cup of Sprite flying. Mama freezes then looks at us through fearfully wide eyes. Samantha doesn't hesitate to knock her own drink over, saying, "See, no big deal."

#

Silver Valley, Texas

"Nice resort."

Perched on a plastic recliner beside a pool sans any water, I glance up. "Darien!" I jump from the malfunctioning chair and tackle my friend. I'm so thrilled to see her that I forget to care we're staying at a single star motel. Our lavish accommodations are a hop, skip and jump away from the Village Tub, Wash 'N Dry and across from Wynne's Wigs.

"How did you find me?" I ask so loudly I'm practically shouting. I'm heartened that she's here, in the middle of nowhere, at an establishment we would typically never be.

"Small town. Not hard to find the dead." I laugh because Darien's true to form, completely unaware she's unintentionally morbid.

Darien Shay, for all practical purposes, is actually the kindest person I know, definitely the smartest. That's not to say her kindness extends to others. She's a testament to Corporate America with a tendency to be deficient in social delicacy. In short, Darien is the poster child for success in a cutthroat industry. Basically, a badass. The woman will

94

eviscerate anyone who gets in her way. And still, compassionate and protective where I'm concerned.

She's a stunning, fire-cracking redhead with dark eyes and perfectly aligned teeth set into a smile the size of the free world. Not to mention a body that makes the word 'namaste' pop to mind. I fantasize about her closet, confident I've never seen her wear the same thing twice. Even now, she's in a sheer black blouse buttoned low, tucked into black slacks with heels. Around her neck, there's an assortment of chains and pendants, and though she would never say, I know they're ridiculously expensive. And because I know her so well, I lift my sunglasses to glance around. Sure enough, I spot it in the parking lot. I burst out laughing.

My friend, in the shape of my boss, is strikingly polished with a fondness for fine wine and the F-word. She also tends to have an unhealthy obsession for sports cars, which brings me back to the source of my amusement. Darien has flown into Texas and somehow arranged the rental of a Maserati to be with me in the one place I hoped never to see again.

I size her up. She's here and looks completely out of place yet wonderful. Darien has never made me feel less than her equal, especially now when I'm back where I started. Instead, she's notorious for placing me on a pedestal, always encouraging, and always proud whenever I achieve a smidgen of success on my own. It's always been Darien, not philosophy, and certainly not my aunt or uncle, who taught me to rise by lifting others. It's always been Darien, who continually demonstrates there's plenty of sunshine for everyone.

Darien has firsthand knowledge that I grew up in a single-wide trailer with relatives reaping the benefits of the

Social Welfare System. The information only invigorated her to push me harder, trust me more. Until recently, she was the only person I've ever let my guard down enough to build a lasting friendship with. She's protective like I'm her daughter, or her sister, or her closest friend, or all the above. For these reasons, it's Darien who I've chosen to be my family—a family I feel is gradually growing.

"This is where we're sleeping?" Darien asks. "Let's find a store and buy disinfectant by the fucking gallon. Why are you laughing?"

It occurs to me that two of my favorite women on the planet are about to meet as Samantha steps out of room 6A, catching sight of Darien Shay. More accurately, it's the other way around. Samantha barely acknowledges the newest member of our entourage while Darien's locked in and speechless. An absolute first.

Darien anticipated swooping in and saving the day only to access she's been beaten to the punch. *Oh, yeah*. I see now that Darien has enjoyed the perks of being my only friend up to this point. By her expression alone, I'm getting the impression she's never had to share a single thing in her life before now.

"Darien, this is Samantha. You recognize her from the footage with Deacon?" I ask. "He's here. You can meet him! Deacon that is. He's with Bodie, watching over Mama while she naps," I finish, wondering why I'm rambling on when she's not listening to a word I say.

"Add tequila to our shopping list," is all Darien replies.

#

96

"Still can't believe you both came all this way just for me," I say this and more, feeling the effects of whiskey and wine. After the funeral, and once Mama was fast asleep, Samantha and Darien decided to get me drunk under a starless night in the Lone Star State. This is now my life. Bury an aunt then watch the sunset with a buzzing sense of relief.

Uncle Jim tried getting close enough to talk to me before the service, but Darien stepped in front of me like a human shield. "Not on your life," she warned, as we watched his broken body hobble away. He didn't dare glance in Mama's direction. I cringed at the thought, then stole a glance to my side to see Samantha. I haven't told her, but it was clear by her bold stance beside me that she knew. Now that they've realized they have a common purpose of coexisting, Sam and Darien have joined forces to safeguard me. Uncle Jim didn't stand a chance.

"Ryan has a boyfriend," Sam teases when my phone chimes, forcing me back to the present.

"Does she?" Darien asks, playing along.

I don't even bother with the two of them. I stand, fetch my phone from the table, and walk away, leaving them to quarrel out their fake animosity toward one another. The truth is, I need a timeout. I can't shake my uncle's cold stare from my mind. A shower didn't help either. I still feel dirty. If that weren't enough, I keep hearing my mother's voice throughout the service singing Eric Clapton's "Tears in Heaven."

I was surprised by the number of people at the memorial. It's intriguing how people flock together more out of curiosity than reverence. I regret not having the chance to visit with and thank Mrs. Ames. I've wanted to do that for years, and that alone would have been worth the trip. It didn't matter they were hand-me-downs. Because of Mrs. Ames, I always had a pair of decent shoes growing up.

There had been a vast number of floral arrangements delivered but not all of them for my aunt. Chili Freeman, a childhood acquaintance who earned the nick name honorably at a cookoff, handed me a bouquet midway through the burial ceremony. I kept the card then placed the flowers from Dean on my aunt's casket.

"Hey," I say, smiling into the phone receiver after deciding to return Dean's call. "I hear you've let critters into my cabin."

"Only ones with sharp teeth," Dean answers, then it's quiet for several fleeting seconds. "You sound like you could use a hug."

"One from you sounds pretty nice."

"Where are you?"

"Five minutes from insomnia," I answer, honestly. Then, "Still here. Silver Valley. We'll head back tomorrow after I take my mother to Austin." I sigh, dreading the thought of returning her to the hospital. The legal battle has gone on for years, but, as always, I silently vow to get her out of that place eventually.

"Sam still with you?"

"She is. Darien, too." Another comfortable silence passes between us, and then another, before, "I got flowers."

"Yeah? Flowers are good."

"Flowers are beautiful. Thank you."

"It's only fair you know I miss you."

It's quiet again. Like *really* quiet. I almost start counting the passing seconds when I decide to break the silence instead. "I should probably try getting some sleep, but I wanted to hear you tell me goodnight first."

"I'm not done talking."

"You're not talking."

"I'm thinking," he admits, making me smile. "I should have kissed you."

"*Hmm*," I manage, needing another second to catch my breath. "Who says I would have let you?"

"Want me to tell you what else I'm thinking? What else I should have done?"

Okay, I'm totally turned on. I'm also nervous that I'm about to have an introduction to phone sex before I've even kissed the man. "Why don't you tell me about your day instead."

"Chicken."

"A smart chicken."

"No such thing."

"A hen."

I hear Dean laugh and the sound warms my heart. "It's beautiful here tonight. The stars…they're incredible. Get some rest, and then you and Sam get back here to us."

"Good night, Dean." I start to end the call then remember. "Wait! Are you still there?"

"I'm here."

"I'm sorry, I almost forgot to ask. Has everything been okay there?"

"We'll talk once you're back."

<u>CHAPTER NINE</u>

Buena Vista, Colorado

Forgiveness. What does it mean? The process is a marvel, and the word itself is a spiky thorn digging into my side every time I think of my aunt. I try to dismiss it and think of something else but can't. It's intrusive and demanding. I'd even asked Sam her opinion on forgiveness on the drive back to Colorado, but that was days ago. "For me, it's the opportunity to give someone else a new beginning," she had answered, simply.

I remain torn, stuck between feeling it can be a self-serving act we use to free ourselves or a psalm I vaguely remember. Something about being rescued from the darkness and brought into the kingdom of the Son He loves, where we have redemption in the forgiveness of sins. Despite specifics of my upbringing, I want to be a compassionate person, to be empathetic and merciful. In other words, I want to forgive my aunt.

"What are you doing?" Dean asks, disrupting my thoughts.

"What's it look like?"

"Trying to unsnag your line."

"Funny. I've had several bites, I'll have you know."

"I bet. Those bites wouldn't happen to be the spinner bouncing off every rock on the bed of the creek, would they?"

"I feel like I should be offended."

I'm sitting in the middle of the creek a few hundred yards from my cabin on a large, smooth boulder protruding from the water. I've been fishing and pondering. That and I love watching the river slice through the forest like a smooth harmony, flowing like time, always onward. The tranquility I feel overwhelms me, and the man moving closer makes me feel things I'm not used to feeling.

I quickly decide the moment is mine to cherish. For the first time in my life, I think I've found the place to hopefully one day call home. It doesn't matter that the creek ranges from calf to knee high or that Dean's in jeans as he walks directly into the current, wading toward me. My feet are dangling in the water, my hiking boots submerged. I have a denim jacket on with a red long-john shirt beneath and a smudge of river mud on my cheek. I may have stumbled a time or two unsnagging my spinner here and there.

"Keep the tip of your pole low and at an angle. You want the stream's current to spin the lure. Reel in a bit quicker but not too fast. If it's too slow, it drops from the weight and drags along the bottom." Dean reaches for the rod and sets it

101

on the rock beside me. Somehow, he's maneuvered himself to stand between my legs, directly in front of me with little effort.

"Hi," I say, enjoying the smell and sight of him. "It's my shirt color. I need to camouflage myself more. Then look out. I'll catch dinner for everyone."

"Okay," he says, adding nothing more. His eyes lock on mine. His stare is so hypnotic that I don't see his hand dip into the water. He lifts it quickly, splashing water on me and laughs. I splash him back, nearly tumbling into the creek.

His playfulness is an anchor, the bedrock of who he is, and how I long to be. With him, I make sense. I also tend to stop breathing, and everything slows. I fall into the moment, feeling our exchange, responding to the connection between us.

It almost feels as if there's an ocean between us, not centimeters, until he leans in and the world around us fades. With his mouth a breath from mine, everything weighing heavily on my mind evaporates. All I can think is Dean. I want this. His name falls from my lips like a breathless prayer the instant he touches me, pressing his mouth to mine.

It's a kiss that draws sound from my insides, though its only just begun. My senses are on overload, already seduced. His lips against mine are not innocent. He's fiery, passionate, and demanding. I think to push away before I lose myself completely, but I'm powerless to do so. I feel his hands on my neck, below my ears. His thumbs caress my skin while I run my hands down his back, pulling him closer. There's no space left between us and no denying the rapid beating of my heart against his.

I'm unprepared to feel so much or to respond so wantonly. Until this instant, I didn't fully understand how right his body would feel pressed against mine or how much I need it. Heat is spreading through me, everywhere. This kiss is a mixture of salvation and torment, a yearning for more.

When it's time to either breathe or die, Dean chooses to extend our first kiss. Behind what should be the darkness of my eyelids, I see lights exploding. My entire body is tense, seized by overwhelming relief, panic, and lust. Tangling my fingers in his hair, I deepen every emotion I'm pouring into the kiss, relaying what I feel but won't say.

Reluctantly, I pull away. My breathing is labored. Dean magnetically gravitates forward before I have a chance to catch my breath, but instead rests his forehead against mine. My eyes are shut, clinging to the intensity a little longer. When I open them, Dean is looking at me like I'm the mysterious answer to a question he hasn't been able to find the answer to. Until now.

I lean forward and brush my lips against his. "Just checking."

"Checking what?" he asks.

"To see if kissing you again makes me want to climb inside your skin. It does. Take me somewhere. Show me your world, a place around here you love."

"This is my world, Ryan. All that was missing was you." He kisses my neck, driving me insane, and then I feel the vibrations of laughter against my skin. "That came out well-worn, but it's true. Too soon?"

"Kind of scary, but nice to hear."

"Gross, Daddy." Colby emerges from the pines, splashing through the rapids without a second thought before climbing easily into my lap. "Are you gonna kiss on each other all the time now?"

"I hope so," Dean answers. "On you, too!" He picks Colby up, planting loud, smacking kisses all over her scrunched up face. "Come on, girls. I'll take you both somewhere."

#

"Ever seen a river otter?" Drew asks. Although he's in his mid-twenties, I find him boyishly charming and enjoy being around him. I don't question his enthusiasm to tag along on many of my outings. I can smell Dean's influence a mile away.

"Not that I know of."

"They love to play. I've seen them manipulate rocks and sticks, play tag, hide-and-seek, dunk each other, wrestle and slide on mud or snow banks."

"Cute," I say, wondering if this is leading somewhere.

"Reece would be the one to talk about how rare spotting them is. Or list facts on endangerment. He's all serious, that one. Me? I just like how playful they are."

We're walking through the first of four tunnels just north of Buena Vista along the Arkansas River. The Midland Tunnels were built by the Colorado Midland Railroad back in the day for travel, though the railways are long gone. We're here because I was told my chances of spotting a

104

Great Horned Owl in this area are high, and it appears to be true. I'm very aware of the large, long ear-tuft, silent hunter across the river.

"I'm probably not supposed to tell you this." Drew removed his baseball cap, ran his fingers through dirty blonde hair. "Hell, I know I shouldn't."

"Too late. Spill it."

"Not too far from the house, Colby knows of a pool in the river where a female otter and her pups live. I'm a little worried, is all."

"Wait, back up. Did something happen to the otters?"

"No, no, they're okay. Colby got lucky though. Looked like there was a small explosion just before she got there. It could have been worse than it was. Dean said it was a contained spread of some type of poisonous vapor or aerosol."

"Colby? She's okay?"

"She's fine. As I said, timely and contained. Whoever did this, knows what they're doing. Colby's smart, and Jenna was quick to the rescue."

#

"You okay?" Samantha asks quietly, leaning toward me so the others won't overhear.

After a strenuous climb—initially proposed to be an easy walk to Hartenstein Lake which turned into a hike to the cliffs above—Dean insisted on taking everyone out for dinner. Everyone includes Jenna, which of course means

105

Garrett is also here and Colby, Reece, Drew and TC with the added pleasure of having Nana Sterling join our motley crew. Samantha and I have somehow become part of this family-like ensemble. And for good measure, Dean's gone as far to extend an invitation to Jules Jenson.

"Headache," I answer, fibbing slightly. My head does ache but so does my stomach and most every other part of my body.

I glance at Dean, remembering our afternoon. How he'd encouraged Colby to keep an eye out for mountain goats, which I called rams. Sure enough, it wasn't long before he pointed to several bighorn sheep, the correct classification, camouflaged against the rocks. I listened closely as he told her why there weren't many left, teaching her about hunting, disease and habitat encroachment. When she acted upset, he added they'd probably come back, that he'd seen the herd multiply over the past couple of years.

"You don't look well," Sam continues.

"Talk to Ava today?" I ask, dodging her concern.

"I did. She's having fun, but I miss her."

"Have you two ever been this far apart before?"

"Never," Sam answers. "Well, once. Jordan surprised me with a trip to the coast for our anniversary. Other than that, we liked having her with us." I notice Samantha lift her gaze to Jules. I see it, if only for a second. Being so near Jules, Sam feels guilty to have a daughter to miss. Nana Sterling is also observing before catching my eye and winks.

Under the table, I feel Dean's leg brush mine, and then his hand covers mine for all to see. It doesn't last long before his phones chimes. TC's phone does the same a second later. They read their displays, share a look, then resume eating.

106

I've seen this before. There's a Search and Rescue alert, and if they reach for their phones again, they'll leave. Dean's already handed Jenna his credit card to cover the meals just in case.

Samantha elbows me. I ignore her long enough to finish telling Nana Sterling about the bear we encountered which I continue to dream about. "Dreaming about bears means you need to go in the woods and feed them tacos. Then offer foot rubs before one tries to eat you for lunch," Drew informs me, jumping into our conversation, making no sense. Still, he always makes me laugh.

Nana Sterling chuckles, then says, "or…alternatively, it may symbolize the term bare. Perhaps it's an invitation to bare your soul and get everything out in the open."

"You should get a colorful bear tattoo," Reece adds, pouring a mountain of gravy on his mashed potatoes. "Did you guys know that bears are one of few mammals with color vision?"

Sam jabs her elbow into my side again, this time earning my attention. "Dude! Ouch!" She's nodding emphatically toward the glass window. "What?" I ask, peering through to see a group of girls standing in the parking lot.

"It's her! The doctor."

"What doctor?"

"The bear! Weren't you just talking about it? The bear. Deacon. The sign!"

"Sam, what's in your tea?" I ask.

Samantha rolls her eyes. "The day the bear told us where Deacon was, don't you remember?"

I remember, although I'm not sold the bear actually told us that. "What about it?"

"You made me go to the clinic to get the cut on my neck looked at. She—" Sam points through the window to a lanky girl with brown, shoulder-length hair "—said I was probably anemic and took blood. Remember now?"

"I do." It dawns on me. "*Oh*…that's the cute doctor you told me we should try to set Reece up with!" Reece stops chewing and looks to see the girl on the other side of the glass. We're gawking until only I look away, feeling nauseous, and reach for the glass of water. It's insanely hot in here.

"Holy—" Drew says, as Reece's chair screeches backward, he stands and then walks out of the restaurant.

"Who is that?" Dean asks.

"That's Brittany Saben. Diane and Joe's girl," Nana Sterling answers.

"Wow, *that's* her?" Jenna chimes in. "Not a tomboy anymore, is she?"

"That guy," Drew starts, using his fork to point at his brother through the window, "has pined away for her since she left but would never admit it. He never said two words to her when she lived here. Now look at him."

"Didn't Reece get in a fight over her? Garrett asks. "He got suspended for knocking the shit out of Bobby Clark for making fun of her? Sabens didn't have much money, she was always in her brother's hand-me-downs." This gets my attention. Once, I figure out why the room is spinning, I'll make an effort to befriend the good doctor.

"Brittany?" Reece asked, standing behind a group of women talking. The taller one standing in the middle of the group turned to face him. "It is you."

Reece knew most of the women but didn't acknowledge them until one, a relatively good friend of his, cleared her throat and slightly nudged Brittany forward. "We'll wait by the car," she said, speaking to Brittany but smirking at Reece.

"Reece Young, how are you?" Her voice was smooth and confident, letting him know she was no longer the shy, little girl who used to shadow him. "You look good."

"You look the same. I mean..." Reece shook his head. "Last time I saw you...it's been a long time." She smiled, as Reece fumbled his words. "Can I start over?"

"No need."

"You do look the same, Brittany. You have the same color of hair, not too brown and not exactly red but somewhere in-between. Your eyes, they're big, and sometimes like the color of honey and other times darker like now. You've still got a dimple, but only on the left side. It's been a long time, but I could spot you anywhere." Embarrassed, he added, "Where have you been?"

"School. Northern Arizona."

"For nine years?"

"Medical school. I wrote you a few times." She closed her eyes, silently cursing her barefaced honesty.

"Letters?" Reece asked, stunned. "Wish I had, but I never got any."

"In that case, I have a drawer full of them," She added, relieved that he thought she was kidding. "My friends are waiting." She hitched her thumb toward the window at the faces of his friends and family inside the restaurant, "And from the looks of it, yours are too."

"Never mind them. Are you around awhile? Will I see you again?"

"I'm back, Reece. Working at the medical center. You should drop by sometime," Brittany said, before turning and walking to join her friends.

Interesting. It's surprising how much one can learn from people who don't realize you're listening so closely. *The Saben girl, that's a new twist.* She may come in handy, he thought, pushing a toothpick deeper between his teeth. He slid a twenty to the edge of the table to cover his meal, stood, and then walked around Dean Sterling's table of family and friends.

CHAPTER TEN

I'm sick. Like *really* sick. The banging on the door isn't helping matters. Knocking like that only ever means one thing: Dean Sterling. When the knocking stops, I crack one eye into a little slit, making out the figure floating somewhere above me. I groan, dying a slow death on the couch.

"Ryan?" I feel the pressure of the backside of Dean's hand against my forehead. For a brief second, it feels good, nice and cool, and then the pounding inside my head resumes. "You're burning up." I can hear his heavy footsteps move away before the door squeaks open. "Colby!" Dean yells. "Run get Samantha and bring her here."

Dean's lifting me. I don't have the strength to open my eyes and too tired to ask where he's taking me. I hear rushing water just before I feel him peeling away the clingy, sweat-soaked t-shirt I'm wearing. I don't even care that I'm partially naked in his arms, somewhere, with the sound of running water nearby. Then I feel it. The biting ice water inside the tub jolts me awake.

"How many times have you thrown up?"

"Nine hundred thousand times."

He's not amused. "How long have you had that rash?" he asks, seeing the spots on my leg around my knee and moving toward my thigh.

"Don't know. Wasn't there yesterday."

"Ryan, stay awake. We need to get you to a doctor."

"M'kay. Just let me rest a minute."

"You'll sleep, trust me. For now—" he splashes cold water on my face "—I need you awake." I feel his gaze, and somewhere in the far back of my mind I scarcely comprehend his struggle. He's trying not to look at me, trying not to let this be the first time I'm exposed to him, or notice the scar across my hip.

"*Uhmm*," I hear from the doorway of the bathroom. It's Samantha.

"Thank God," Dean says. "Grab me a towel." There's a pause while they rustle around the small room. Then, "Sam, did Ryan ever find a tick on her when you two were out looking for Deacon."

"Yes. It was disgusting, but it wasn't then. It was after Silver Valley. She was fishing here in the creek. She made Drew pull it off her leg just under her knee and gagged the entire time. Oh, God, is this Lyme's Disease? I knew she didn't look right at dinner last night."

"It's Spotted Rocky Mountain Fever. She'll be okay, but only if she gets treatment."

"Not...going...anywhere." I slur, drifting in and out of a very uncomfortable slumber.

"I can't stay," Dean explains, his expression dark and regretful. "I was coming to tell her I got a call. They found a woman. A climber. She's fallen down a couloir west of Ptarmigan Lake. Can you stay with Ryan? I'll radio Reece to see if he can ask Brittany to come up."

"Of course, go. I've got her."

"Bye, Blue," I grumble. Surely, I'm closing in on my demise because I've let an endearment slip through my lips. It was only yesterday, I loosely remember, that I teased him incessantly of his obsession with the color.

"Alright," Sam says, rolling her eyes while lifting me from the unsympathetic, cold water. "Let's get you in pajamas and to bed." Hazily, I realize modesty is no longer a concern.

"Is Brittany coming to put me out of my misery?"

"I'm betting Dean makes sure of that."

"They look cute together. Brittany and Reece."

"Mhm."

"Sam?"

"Hmm?"

"Am I hot?"

"Smokin.'"

I laugh despite enduring the plague of a parasite. "Dean said I was burning up. Am I? Because I'm freezing."

"You've got a high fever. Help me get this sweatshirt on you. Lift your arms."

"Is Darien here yet?"

Sam's brows furrow. "She's coming here?"

"For the weekend. Proofs, edits, layouts."

"Ahh."

"You can't "ahh" me, Sam. Why don't you like her?" I squirm to find comfort while every muscle in my body cries. "My feet are cold."

"I like everyone," Sam responds, rummaging through a drawer for fuzzy socks then slides them on me. "I'm sorry you feel so awful."

"Except for Darien." I manage to groan and yawn at the same time. "My hours on earth are numbered," I whine. "My final wish is for you to be nice to each other. Give her a chance."

"Sure."

"By that, I don't mean disappear when she's around."

"We'll see. Come on, little cub, get under the covers."

"Maybe Reece was right. We should get matching tattoos to honor our bear."

"Why don't we buy matching charms instead?" Samantha's smiling now. *Good.* Even in death, she's my work in progress.

"We still owe them a night on the town to thank them."

"I remember. You do realize that translates to many hours and a hefty bar tab?"

"We should do it this weekend while Darien's here."

"Says she who's sporting a rash, a fever, and vomit breath."

"Right...*that*. Soon then."

"Close your eyes. I'm going to call Ava and grab a few things. I'll be right back."

"Okay," I mumble, as Samantha retreats. "Hey?" I call after her, my eyes fluttering open. By the door, Samantha turns to face me. "I'm so glad we're here together. In Buena

114

Vista, I mean. I never knew I could miss a person I'd never met before."

#

"Ryan will begin improving by tomorrow, and she'll feel a lot better within seventy-two hours. Even then, it'll take a good week to get completely out of her system. I've started her on Doxycycline. Make sure she takes another one tonight with food, then only one a day for ten days. If she'll do it, have her take Oracea on an empty stomach an hour before she eats to help with nausea."

"Got it. Thank you, Brittany. Really, I can't thank you enough for coming up here."

"Not a problem. Oddly, I was going to have a nurse call you this afternoon to arrange an appointment."

"Me? Why?"

"Perhaps the clinic—"

"My daughter's physical for school? Everything's okay?"

"What? Oh, yes. She's perfectly fine."

"O-kay," Sam draws out the two syllables.

"I don't think it's appropriate to discuss here, like this, with people wandering around."

"Is it something with my lab work?"

"You're fine."

"Then, I don't understand."

"Not here, Samantha," Brittany responds, firmly.

"Do you ride?" Sam asks.

115

"Ride?"

"Horses."

"I have, yes."

"Fine, let's go. There's a place I like to go where no one will bother us."

"Uhm, alright. I need to run to town and change. I'll meet you back here, in say, an hour?"

"At the stables, yes. I'll have a horse ready for you."

An hour after meeting at the stables, Samantha cued her horse to stop in a narrow meadow hugging the high climb to the peak. "I like it here. You can see the entire valley. And there—" Sam pointed south "—the Chalk Cliffs skirt the peak with craggy white stone unique to the state. This place is as good as any, whatever you need to say to me, you can do it here."

"Why here, Samantha?" Brittany asked.

"The view is beautiful."

"I mean Buena Vista. Why are you in Buena Vista?"

"Why is anyone here? Look around."

"I grew up here. That's why I'm back. It's my reason for being here."

"You haven't been paying attention if you think BV is a secret. At this point, you may even be outnumbered by transplants in the area from other places near and far. What's with the inquisition? Does it matter?"

"Under different circumstances, no."

"My reasons are personal."

"There are beautiful places all over the country, so I need to ask again. Why Buena Vista?"

"Are you sorry you came back? Is that what this is about?" Sam asked, puzzled by the interrogation.

"This isn't about me, but I have unintentionally found myself in a unique situation. I'm trying to navigate how to handle it, trying to figure out what you know, if anything."

"So, the question has nothing to do with you being a doctor."

"It does, actually, subsequently I need for you to trust me. I think you should get off the horse, and I think we should find somewhere for you to sit to hear what I have to tell you."

#

"A Porsche," Samantha said, talking to herself. *Un-freaking-believable!* With her cabin in sight, she crossed the creek on horseback in a hurry to get back. Next to her place, she sees Ryan's lights burning brightly, and a black Porsche parked in front. Rolling her eyes, she remembered Brittany on horseback behind her. Samantha shifted in the saddle to see the doctor over her shoulder, entering the water.

Fallen branches splintered apart from a deer dashing deeper into the woods after spotting them. Startled, the quarter horse Brittany was riding stumbled over slippery rocks in the creek, knocking her foot loose. "Stay calm." Samantha quickly unmounted, jogging back.

Slowly, Sam stepped into the creek with her arms held high and her voice soothing. "Horses can be flighty creatures, Brittany. I need you to listen carefully and follow

117

my lead. Unexpected smells, sounds, and movement create fear. If he thinks he's in danger, he'll react. His instinct is to flee. You're prolonging that process, so he wants you off and quickly."

"Samantha!" Brittany screeched, feeling his hind legs dip deeper into the water."

"You're okay." Sam stepped forward. "Come on, boy. *Easy*, you're all right.

"My boot's stuck," Brittany said, with one foot loose and the other trapped while gripping tightly to the saddle horn with both hands.

"I see that. I'm coming."

"Samantha, what can I do?" Darien asked, from the riverbank.

"Stay back," Sam answered, then turned back to the horse. "Brittany, breathe. He's vibing you." Samantha was thigh deep in the current, reaching for the horse named Harvey. She knew Harvey's back leg was stuck between boulders, knew they were already on borrowed time before Harvey began thrashing his body through the water.

"He's high-headed and jiggy. Any second, he's going to rear up to try and free his leg. When he does, the saddle will shift, giving you a nanosecond of leeway. When that happens, I need you to press down as hard as you can in the stirrup then push out and jump away as far as possible. The hobble strap tore. I'm telling you this because he has no clue what I'm saying only that I'm calmly doing so. The straps hold the fender extension and stirrup leathers, so the rider doesn't catch a foot between and get hung up."

Sam pointed at Darien. "See her? That's Darien. Once you're free, get away from the horse and get to her." Sam turned her head. "Darien, move downstream about twenty feet. It's shallow there but be ready to grab her just in case she's injured."

Harvey reared, exploding through the water. Brittany shot up and out, and Samantha dove. Behind Harvey, Sam reached between rocks, wrapping her hands around the cannon bone of his trapped leg. She pulled against the current, receiving a blow to her shoulder from a belting hoof. Harvey was loose and leaping from the river.

With her knees to the bed of the creek, Sam was submerged up to her shoulders. Using a boulder, she pulled herself up, breathless after having the wind knocked out of her, and then waded to shore and collapsed.

"You drink tequila, right?" Samantha asked, eventually, looking up at Darien.

"Like a rock star."

"Great. Let's go."

#

After carefully examining Harvey, Samantha secured the horses, and then showered and changed while Darien medicated and tucked Ryan in for the night. *All that was left to do*, Sam thought, *was forget*. Brittany had assured them she was fine and able to drive after politely declining an invitation for drinks.

It was early in the evening. Early for the tavern to be wall-to-wall busy with patrons. But then again, it was summer in Colorado. Darien finagled two stools near the end

119

of the bar, waiting. Sam pushed through bodies, wishing she was able to push aside the events from the afternoon just as easily.

"You're very blasé about saving that girl's life. Wave it off all you like, but if it weren't for you, things could have taken a deadly turn." Darien kept her eye on Sam, looking for a sliver of emotion, seeing nothing. Sam was quietly stone-faced, staring at their drinks sitting side-by-side on the bar top.

"Only you would order a glass of wine in a small town that cost more than every beer lined up on this counter combined," Sam said, finally.

"Then kudos to me for having taste. Are you hurt?"

Samantha couldn't help but laugh. *Hurt? Yeah, you could say that.* "I'll be fine."

"I was there. I saw that horse kick you. The air was knocked out of you, and you didn't give up. I've never seen anything like it." Darien let her eyes roam the room then settle back on Sam. When Samantha tried to hold a flood of tears at bay, they came anyway. Darien leaned in, shielding Samantha from the view of others wedged around them.

"Have you ever felt like all the good was behind you? Like you've already lived your best life with someone, and now you're just killing time?"

"I've never loved anyone that much, so no."

"See. There's no use talking about it. Any of it."

"What I can tell you is nothing I say will make you feel better if all we're going to do is scratch the surface. Peeling away a layer or two may help. *Talking* does help. As you know, Ryan is unapologetically trustworthy, so anything I know is limited at best."

120

"This is bigger than my broken heart, if that's even possible."

"Lucky for us, we have all night."

"She kept pushing, asking questions."

"Who did?"

"Brittany. She asked to talk in private, so it was either the medical center or…" Sam trailed off, remembering. "It's starting to sink in," Sam admitted, wiping at her face with shaky hands. "It can't be true. But it is true. I feel sick. I feel like if it weren't for Ava, I'd surrender once and for all and just be done. How am I supposed to react? How can I be happy about one thing and not mourn another?"

"I don't know what that means exactly. It might help for you to understand it's not a punishment to have one thing and not another, to be one way and not another. What did Brittany want from you?"

"Answers."

"Be specific?"

"She asked why I was here and about my family."

"Your family?"

"She wanted to know if my parents were alive. Why does she care, right? I kept wondering the same. My dad died when I was in my early twenties. My mom eight years later. How is that her business?"

"I think you're about to tell me."

Samantha dropped her head into her arms resting on the counter. "Darien, look, you should run fast, far, and quickly because I'm on the verge of losing my shit. Right now, I don't know the difference between insanity and denial, but I do know I'm seconds away from a complete breakdown."

Darien raised her hand, holding up two fingers. "Shots. Your best tequila. Keep them coming," Darien ordered, pushing a hundred-dollar bill toward the bartender.

"I was adopted, but my parents were my parents, you know? I never had any reason to go looking for my biological...whatever. I already had the best."

"You're lucky."

"I had blood drawn to test for anemia when I had a cut on my neck looked at. And because I did, I'm somehow a match, Darien. *The* match. The only possibility on earth. Undisputable DNA proof."

"You're the daughter of a serial killer?"

"Worse." Samantha lifted her head, her eyes brimming with fresh emotion. Inhaling deeply, she was on the brink of saying the truth out loud for the very first time. "I'm the girl who went missing from here thirty years ago."

CHAPTER ELEVEN

On the second day of a two-day backpacking trip, Dean hung back, letting the group set the pace. It was a trip TC would usually guide, but the Caldwells were regulars who requested Dean every summer for the past eight years. The family of four with their two friends put their group at seven. *Seven*, Dean thought, including himself, yet counted tracks for eight.

Someone had come around the campsite during the night while they slept, quiet enough not to wake anyone. The tracks were apparent, left for Dean to find. He kept the information to himself, trekking behind the others to keep an eye out for anything unusual. Twice, he thought he saw someone but couldn't be sure—shadows and sounds were the way of the forest.

"You've got a good eye, kid," Dean said, kneeling beside the Caldwells teenage son, Caleb, recognizing another kind of track. He lifted his head, catching the boy's gaze. In the distance, they could hear the pitch of the waterfall cascading over the steep ridge ahead. "Elk," Dean confirmed, brushing his fingertips against moist soil stamped with fresh prints.

"How can you tell?" Mrs. Caldwell asked, falling back from the others to see what her son had discovered.

Using his index finger, Dean drew two sets of tracks. "These on the left resemble a whitetail deer. The hoofs are like two crescent moons touching at the tips." He gestured to the drawing on the right. "Antelope. Their imprints are larger and wedged. The tips seldom touch." Moving his hand, Dean pointed at the original imprint Caleb found. "An average elk, regardless of gender, has hoofs wide and round and usually no less than four inches long."

"What about bears?" Caleb's friend questioned. The bear inquiry was expected, the most popular question of every tour, every summer.

"Here and hungry," Dean teased. "Black bears. For the most part, as long as we avoid them, they steer clear," he added, losing sight of Mr. Caldwell. "Let's get moving."

At twelve-thousand feet, Dean dispatched TC. Half an hour later, and after Rangers received word that Bruce Caldwell was separated from the group, Dean heard the chopper. He didn't know how it happened, but Mr. Caldwell was below them, clinging to a shallow overhang, stranded on the eastern side of the peak. Bruce Caldwell had slipped and fallen, Dean presumed with a sick feeling in his gut.

There wasn't a quick or easy way to descend. Dean had no choice but to backtrack, running the direction they'd come from, leaving the others with strict orders to stay put and together. Once he was beneath the tapered edge, Dean climbed quickly, passing the first pitch between belaying, anchoring himself along the way.

He shouted to Bruce reassuringly, keeping the conversation light. His priority was to keep everyone calm. "Look at that sky, Bruce, it's a bluebird kind of day, so we're feeling good, right?" Dean asked steadily, though his psych was through the roof.

The ear-piercing shrieks from Mrs. Caldwell above weren't helping. "Caleb!" Dean hollered. "Take care of things up there for me, buddy. See to your mom." Dean hesitated only a second, relieved her screaming ceased. There was an instant of silence, and then Dean hollered again, "Mr. Caldwell, you okay?" but heard nothing except the whipping wind in response. *He's passed out*, Dean thought, coming into view of the ledge covered with generous helpings of gravel and loose babyhead boulders.

A skilled medic was lowered a hundred feet from the helicopter in a basket, but the wind was proving to be problematic. Dean could see Bruce's leg dangling over the ledge, unconsciously sliding closer to the edge. It would be dark soon, but that didn't matter either. He had to act fast, or Bruce was going to fall to his death with his family watching from above.

"Climbing can be dangerous, isn't that part of the fun?" Dean said, slicing his finger wide open while jamming it into a tight pocket when his foot slipped. "Then there are days shit really hits the fan," he continued talking to himself, pulling his weight up with one arm, his legs stretched and straining. "Another fine mess you've got yourself in, Sterling," he mumbled, pulling himself higher to belay and ascend.

When he reached Bruce, Dean used his shoulder as a barricade, enduring the weight of Bruce's limp body. He didn't want to do it, but with little choice, Dean hit Mr. Caldwell. The shock and light force of the blow worked, rousing Bruce conscious. He needed Bruce responsive to get the closed loop through the friction hitch he'd knotted before attaching to the rope to hold the heavy load.

Apart from a likely concussion, Bruce's broken leg was the only concern Dean was able to identify other than fear. "Listen, man, I know it hurts. It might even feel like you've got nothing left in you. You do. Look up, Bruce. That's your family. They're watching. I don't have the equipment we need, do you understand?" Bruce didn't respond, only looked wide-eyed and dazed. "I need you to grab on to me and use all your strength to swing around to my back and hold on like your life depends on it." *Because it does.* "I'll get you down."

"Dean?" Trembling, Bruce blinked, clearing his vision from the searing pain in his leg.

"What's up, Bruce?" Dean asked, taking a deep breath while he assessed their surroundings.

"I'm not crazy. I didn't see anything or anyone, but something pushed me off that ledge. Something tried to kill me."

#

"Dean saved him?"

"According to the text I got from TC, yes."

126

"Is he back? Have you spoken to him?"

"Dean? No. They should be back anytime," Jenna answers, putting a glass of hot tea on the nightstand with graham crackers. I'm still confined to bed although feeling like a human again and ready for this infection to be behind me.

"Was it an accident?" I ask.

"One would hope."

"But?"

"I can't shake it. I've got a bad feeling about this, Ryan." Jenna grabs a throw blanket from the bottom of the bed and begins folding it. "You live in Austin?" she asks, changing the subject.

"I have a membership to a gym there I've used twice. Killed my share of houseplants trying to give life to a sterile and highly over-priced condo, and a mailbox with my name on it. Other than that, I live on the road, one place to the next." I reach for her arm. "Jenna, stop cleaning. What's up?"

"Will you leave soon?"

"I've got some time. I need to be in Seattle by the first of September."

"Will you come back?"

"The project here wraps in another two to three weeks."

"I'm not asking about your work. Will you come back for Dean?"

"Jenna—" I want to say more, but nothing comes out.

"Sorry, I'm out of line. Things are…so crazy right now. I think what I'm trying to ask is, is he worth it? Is what's happening between the two of you worth considering coming back to find out?"

"I've never considered settling down anywhere before—"

"Fair enough. It's none of my business."

"I was going to say I've never considered settling down anywhere before I came here." I let that sink in as her eyes lift to meet mine. "Now I have a hard time picturing myself anywhere else." It's warm in here, and it's got nothing to do with having a fever, at least I hope not. "Where's my helper been?" I ask about Colby, desperately wanting to talk about something else.

"She's staying with Nana Sterling while Ray's in town."

"Dean's dad? I got the impression they don't speak."

"They don't, not really. We tried having dinner all together before my mom passed away, but when the subject of Dean's mother came up, things got heated, per usual. They haven't spoken since. He's going to need Ray's help but would rather cut his own arm off before asking."

"It's worse than he lets on, isn't it?"

"I've told you about Cripple Creek? It's a small town in Teller County, eighty miles southeast of here. In the early nineties, an amendment was added to the Colorado Constitution permitting gambling in Cripple Creek. What I'm getting at is over a hundred years ago, Cripple Creek mines paid out one hundred and fifty million in gold. Last year, Cripple Creek casinos paid out three hundred and sixty-three million in gold. Prescott will receive pushback from locals, the town, and more. However, it's Dean's lineage, the backstory and ownership, the territory itself where Prescott interests lie. A vision, per se."

"Jenna, how much does Dean need?"

"Two point three million," she answers, quickly. Unable to swallow that many zero's, I lace my fingers together, staring at the slightly chipped polish on my index finger. "Some of it, the lowlands along the highway, he can sell. They'll have to physically drag him away before he would consider putting a price tag on the rest. We do well, but we aren't millionaires. The custody battle inevitably coming for Colby won't be cheap either. He needs his dad's help. He needs Ray."

"Is there anything Dean can do? Anything without having to seek Ray's help?"

"By court ruling, the Treasurer's Office cannot refuse partial payment on property tax when delinquent, although the interest and penalties are gruesome. He'll be denied leniency. It's a lengthy process, which is why his arm is being forced in other ways. Prescott doesn't seem to be very patient now that my mom's gone."

We hear the front door then heavy footsteps before I see Dean in the doorway to my bedroom. He's beautiful. The sight of him continues to surprise me each and every time, growing in intensity. There are small, dark spots on the shoulders of his baby blue shirt. I hear it then, the soft patter of rain against the window. "Hi," he says. "You look better."

"She wants to go fishing," Jenna tells him, laughing. I'm relieved he's here, instantly putting an end to an uncomfortable conversation and lightening the mood.

"No chance, you're in this bed for at least one more night."

"I don't like this bed anymore."

"Easy enough. Let's get you in mine," Dean offers, grinning. He's procrastinating. The so-called mood may appear light, but the tension growing inside this room is thick. Jenna is waiting for answers. He turns to her. "It's okay. A badly broken leg looks to be the worst of it."

"What happened to your hand?" I ask, as a low rumble of thunder announces the arrival of the storm. I can almost feel the vibration of its power.

"Nothing more than a few stitches. Bruce Caldwell wasn't so lucky. That leg of his is pretty gnarly. Jenna, he's in Salida and having surgery tomorrow morning. I don't know much more. I stopped listening when rod and screws were mentioned." Dean cringes, as I learn something new. In addition to the bat phobia, he's squeamish with medical procedures. I smile because I can only imagine how he behaved while getting his finger sewn back together.

"Should we send something, or take it over?"

"You should make an appearance, but I'll handle the rest." Jenna is back to fiddling with the blanket. *And, here we go!* "Tell me what really happened?" she asks, forgetting I'm in the room with them, listening to a conversation I shouldn't be hearing.

"There's no evidence to indicate he was pushed or that anyone else was there. The authorities deem it an accident." Dean reaches for my hand, holds it in his, something he often does. "I don't think Bruce slipped. I think he was pushed."

There's a light tap on the open door to my bedroom. It's Samantha. Her hair is damp, and she has a peculiar look. I sit up higher with my back against the headboard. I'm already worried, ready to battle whatever has put that look back into her eyes. Even if it means going to war in a nightshirt with the might of nothing more than soup and crackers for days on end.

Sam lifts her hand, halting me from catapulting from the bed. "I'm fine," she says, walking to the edge of the bed and sits. The bedroom is closing in with four adults inside its small quarters. "How do you feel?"

"Like I need a shower and a change of scenery. Sam?"

"Relax, Ryan, I'm working up to it."

"You're not leaving," I demand, ready to argue.

"Why would I?" Sam turns away from me and faces Dean. She sighs, then, "I'm glad I found you all together. It makes what I have to say easier if I only have to do it once. I'd feel better if you sat down."

"Ryan, I'll check on you in the morning," Jenna says, retreating.

"Jenna, please stay," Sam says. Jenna leans against the doorjamb while Dean moves to sit in a reading chair across from us. I stare at the bandage wrapped around his hand, holding my breath, listening to my gut which warns me something significant is about to go down.

"Everything all right, Sam?" Dean asks.

"I know this is awful timing." Sam looks at her clasped hands in her lap then looks to Jenna. "But now that I know, it can't wait. You both deserve to know the truth. We were friends once, I think. A long time ago."

"College?" Jenna asks, scrolling her mind for memories.

"Way before then," Sam explains. Dean shifts in his seat. I glance up from his hand to meet his eyes. He's tired, and I have the urge to wrap my arms around him, but this is about Samantha, so I shift my attention to her. "I'm so sorry."

Essentially, Samantha should have been an engineer of sorts. She's logical and strategic in most everything she does—behavior, thoughts, words—with one exception. She's deficient when it comes to thinking and doing for herself. Seeing her now, like this, is like watching the guilt she carries burst around her like a giant soap bubble, but the result isn't clean. She's a selflessly beautiful yet wonderous mess, taking the brunt of every storm.

"It's important to start by saying I had no idea." Her voice quakes. "I don't have any answers or understand any of it, especially the why and how." Sam swallows. "After losing Jordan, I had my doubts. My view on religion blurred, and I was no longer convinced. It all felt so cruel and unnecessary. But how can I question it anymore? Especially now. It's clear I've been led here, and not just this time, but all the times before."

"Are you tangled up with Prescott? Is that why you're here?" Dean asks.

"No. It's nothing like that." Sam stands then begins to pace the width of the bed. "I had lab work done. It was all so random, and all because of a cut on my neck." Sam sat, stood, then sat again. "The afternoon Ryan got sick, Brittany asked if we could talk. That's how I found out." Sam stands again, paces once more. "Jenna, did you have a purple bike with a basket?"

"A million years ago. I was five."

"Four," Dean corrected, scooting to the edge of the chair. "Why?"

"It's vague, but it's the only thing I remember. For years I've had recollections of that bike but never knew why until now."

132

"Sam, sit down," I suggest, reacting to her anxiety. My back is up and not because of the strike of lightning. I'm torn. I feel the need to be protective of Samantha because Dean is feeling the same for Jenna.

"I don't have specifics," she offers, ignoring me. "I'm sure we can get them, but—" Sam hesitates. She turns and is facing Dean now. "I believe the two of you were as close to a brother and sister as I ever had until I was taken."

"What's she saying?" Jenna asks Dean. Dean stands. I stand. I'm in front of Samantha, shielding her but there's no need, especially with Dean's eyes beginning to gloss with moisture.

"You're Dawn Jenson?" he asks, in disbelief.

"No, I'm Samantha." A tear escapes her left eye, rolling the length of her cheek. "But I was Dawn before someone stole me from you all and took me away."

"Oh, my God!" Jenna cries, lunging to embrace Sam.

I see a flash of movement and look away from the two women hugging to see Dean quickly on his way out. I hear the thud of boots against wood as he descends the steps of the porch then the weight over gravel. Sam pulls away from Jenna then rushes after Dean. "Dean!" Sam hollers, while Jenna and I are quick to follow. To hell with being inside this room, restricted to this cabin.

Samantha spins him around from the death grip she has on his arm after running to catch up. The rain is no longer light, it's swift and pelting, and assaulting us all. "It's not your fault!" she yells at him. "It was never your fault!" Sam's no longer timid and gutless in the situation. She is not going to let this discovery slip them somewhere between disaster and destruction. She's stronger now, clutching on to

133

this harsh development like maybe it's an opportunity to re-erect and reunite.

"I looked away. For thirty seconds, I looked away." Puddles are forming around Dean's boots, while his wet shirt clings to him. "When I turned back, you were gone."

"Whatever happened would have happened even if you hadn't."

"Jules Jenson," Dean says, his eyes wide with acknowledgment.

"Is my mother." Samantha closes her eyes. "I have to tell her before someone else does." Lightning strikes, a brilliant white-hot bolt flashing with blinding brightness.

"I'll go with you."

"I'll let you drive me to town, but the rest I need to do alone."

"How will you get back? How will you get home?"

"It's Buena Vista, Dean. I am home."

CHAPTER TWELVE

"Which is your favorite?" I ask.

"This granite." Colby points at a coarse-colored stone of varying colors. "Sometimes there's gems in granite. It's like a two for one."

"It's pretty. Are you excited for Ava to come back today?"

Colby looks away, suddenly concentrating on the untied, fraying laces of her Nikes, and then biting on the inside of her cheek, she looks me straight in the eyes. "Yeah, me and Rutger have been waiting out here all morning. It's just…"

"What's wrong, Colbs?" I ask, skirting her imaginary dog.

"Sometimes Ava lies," Colby tells me, unhappily. I think about this for a second. There're so many ways to respond, a million directions I can go, but I choose to stay quiet and listen, instead. "Ava pretends her parents are still alive. Both of them." My heart cracks. Ava is like her mother—fiercely loyal and protective of a person who no longer exists.

"One time we were hiding, and once it was all clear to climb out of our fort, I saw Ava was dropping tears. 'Cept just like them other times, she said she had a tummy ache or stubbed her toe. I knew it wasn't true, 'cuz Ava's strong like me. Before she left, I heard her tell her mom during our sleepover that she'd said her prayers already. That wasn't true either. She told me she was angry at God, so she wasn't talking to Him anymore."

"Was that scary to hear?"

"I mean…kind of. Nana Sterling says we're all God's children, and He takes care of us no matter what. Then stupid Stanna Truitt told me people who question God go to Hell."

"You're right. Stanna is stupid." *So much for taking the high road.* "And before I say anything else, please don't tell your dad I said that." I wink at Colby, sealing our secret. "Listen, kiddo, there's times…many of them actually, when people let their fear get in the way of their compassion. Ava's faith is intact. But you're right, she is confused right now, and it's because she's lost someone she loves. It feels unfair."

"Is compassion like common sense?"

"I've never thought of it that way, but yeah. In this instance, it's caring for someone suffering." I give Colby a second to digest this information. "Ava doesn't mean to lie. She's hurting, and while she is, let's hope she's healing. It takes a lot of time and understanding from people who care about her. Like you do. It's not always easy being a good friend, is it?"

"Do you think I'm Ava's best friend?" Colby asks, hopeful.

"I would bet ten bucks on it. Know what else? I think this is God's way of helping Ava. He's working through you and needs you to be kind and supportive. Isn't that what best friends are for? I mean, besides painting rocks, building forts and riding bikes?"

"I guess so. It kinda sounds like it. Is this what Nana Sterling meant about trees?" Colby asks.

I know what Colby is referring to, I remember the conversation from the restaurant well. Nana Sterling's metaphoric description of friendships had gone as such: People, like leaves, are seasonal, going whichever way the wind blows. The branches, though, they'll fool you. They're strong until a storm pushes through, and then they break, leaving you high and dry. But, if you're lucky enough to find a few friends like the resilient roots at the bottom of the tree, you're blessed. Those people aren't worried about being seen, and they aren't going anywhere.

"Yep, you're a root, kiddo." I decide not to include that Nana Sterling's insight came from an episode of *Big Momma's House*.

Colby and I look up at the sound of a screen door slapping shut. Jenna is taking the steps several at a time from the office near the main house. "Colby!" Jenna hollers. "Come on, I need to run you by Nana Sterling's for a bit, and we've got to hurry!"

"Oh, jeez," Colby groans, unalarmed by Jenna's acceleration as if it's the norm. "Can't I stay here? Ava's gonna be back soon."

137

"Sorry, Colbs. Let's move it. Reece got in a fight with a kayak, and the kayak won. He's at the clinic getting stitches. Sutures seem to be the latest trend." Jenna pauses, glances at me, and adds. "Met your friend." Jenna nods towards Darien's car. "Drew tried to hit on her," Jenna explains, and suddenly I feel anxious. *Uh oh, what has Darien done?* "Hilarious," is all Jenna offers, and I can only imagine.

Just then, as if on cue, Drew pulls in quickly, coming to an abrupt stop near us in a Chevy pickup as dust fills the air. We all cough and cover our eyes.

"For fuck sakes, Drew Young! You're a five-year-old with a driver's license," Jenna turns to Colby. "Okay, okay. I cuss too. But only sometimes, and I'm an adult!" *Jeez*, I repeat in my head what Colby grumbled only a moment ago.

"Just got the text about Reece. I'll go, no need for us all to rattle the cage," Drew says to Jenna while I watch. I see movement from the corner of my eye and notice Darien walking from my cabin toward Samantha's. *Hmm, the morning continues to entertain*. I turn back in time to see Jenna concede and the gigantic smile spread across Colby's face. Colby sprints off before her aunt has a chance to change her mind.

"Don't give that girl a hard time, Drew!" Jenna demands. "Let her sew him up and kick him out without rattling her cage." By this, I gather they are referring to Dr. Brittany Saben. Drew's moved on to taunting Brittany now. Although he's obvious with his flirtations, I've noticed he's overly ornery, and beneath the surface a smidgen surly. *Jealousy*. Either that or envy. It's never easy watching your best mate fall in love when you've been their number one for as far back as you can remember.

"We'll see," Drew responds, blowing Jenna a kiss and punching the accelerator, leaving us showered in a veil of dust as he waves goodbye.

It's a perfect opportunity to escape. Jenna's already retreating toward the office, and I've got hundreds of slides to go through. I don't need to be in the crossfire between whatever is brewing between Samantha and Darien. I can't seem to figure out whether they've reached a truce and tolerate one another for my benefit. Or if they're bonding in a way only polar opposites can sometimes do.

#

"Hey," Samantha said, eyeing Darien's wayward approach. Sam held a coffee mug loosely in her hands that rested atop the wood railing.

"Regrets?" Darien asked.

"Yeah, about that. Everything after 'bartender, I'll have another' is a blur."

"Understood," Darien accepted and let it drop, earning a curious look from Samantha.

"What's with you?" Sam asked, almost laughing.

"It's nothing, Sam. I'm adapting. Normally I'm not accustomed to such things," Darien answers.

"Such as?"

"Being dismissed."

"You surprise me. I didn't take you for someone who requires reassurance."

Darien pondered that, standing beside Samantha, leaning against the railing. "Momentarily stunted. Rarely happens. Consider me resolved."

"You're so weird," Sam offered, shaking her head. "Was that supposed to mean you're at a disadvantage because I'm acting like an asshole?"

"Not at all, I'm good at asshole. What I'm not used to, however, is sentimentality, and something about you softens how I normally react toward conflict. You've been through enough, so I'll respectfully back off while I can."

"Morning, Ryan," Darien barely acknowledges me as she walks efficiently by, ignoring the mug of coffee I offer. One glance toward Samantha's cabin and I see why. Sam's sporting a 'what-the-hell-just-happened' look. It must be in the air around here as things continue to escalate and quickly. I'd only been inside long enough to pour two mugs of coffee, ignoring the work waiting for me.

"You okay?" I ask, climbing the steps of the deck toward Sam. I look over my shoulder in the direction of my other fleeting friend. Darien's already disappeared back inside, no doubt to bury herself in work she brought with her. A task she's perfected.

"Dandy."

"*Hmm.*" It's a word Sam and I have started using often.

"I'm not the nicest person right now."

"Okay, I've been warned," I say, not budging. "What's up?"

Sam turns on her heels to face me. "Who am I?" I'd like to answer but don't get the chance. "What kind of person

140

sinks so low they're willing to sleep with someone else just to forget everything else for a while?"

"I think that probably happens a lot, actually."

"Not to me, it doesn't. Am I trying to torture myself even more? As if the past fifteen months haven't been hard enough? Who am I, Ryan? Seriously? A widow? A victim of kidnapping? A whore?"

"You're not a whore, Sam, you're—"

"I was married to a man before I met Jordan. Did you know that? I struggled for the better part of a year coming to terms with a part of me that upended my entire world. Before Jordan, I had no idea. *None!* I doubt I would have ever gotten there on my own if she hadn't walked into my life out of nowhere."

"Samantha—"

"I can still feel the ghost of her," Sam continues while I watch her splintering apart. "I knew instantly, Ryan, and it had absolutely nothing to do with *what* she was but everything to do with *who*. I knew it the second I laid eyes on her the same way you did with Dean but try to deny it. I did the same. It's no different."

I stop trying to intervene and listen as Samantha's memories begin to drench her cheeks, and my eyes water from the sight. She's letting me in, letting me be part of her breakdown—a breakdown that is long overdue. As her pain spreads, I can feel a fraction of the torment as my heart tightens around the words she's crying. Carefully, I wrap my arms around her and pull her closer, feeling her body shudder with sobs as we sink to a bundle on the floor. I have never felt a person shatter in my arms before.

141

"Sam, we're all different shapes and ways. Our happiness...mine, yours, everyone's...they're unique. You don't have to defend what you had together."

"I'm not, Ryan."

"Good," I say, not meaning to jump into any of this, but the door was *finally* open. "Besides, aren't regrets a privilege from people with free will? When have you or I ever had that luxury?"

"I'm not ashamed either. I didn't choose to be this way, but I did choose to be happy." Sam's eyes glisten. "I'm not ready to let go."

"I don't think you'll ever be ready. I don't think you'll ever love anyone else the way you loved Jordan. The way you still do. That doesn't mean you can't be happy again, Sam."

"If this is where you tell me to start unfollowing old dreams to chase new ones, I'll dump your body in the creek," Sam says, sniffling at the same time she halfheartedly laughs. "Jordan was the exception to every rule, who patiently waited for me while I fumbled through, wasting time. I wasted time, Ryan. That's what hurts the most. All the time I can't get back. I just..." she breaks more, her voice cracking "...need more time. A chance to say goodbye."

"You're finding ways to do it. There's no right or wrong way to do it."

"Really? Well look at me now. I was horrible to someone trying to be nice. If that weren't enough, I can't bring myself to go back and sit and talk with Jules either. Not yet. It's cruel to ask for time to wrap my brain around it when she's waited a lifetime for me to find my way back home."

142

Samantha is tacking on additional shame where it doesn't belong. I need to stop her and help put her heart and mind at ease. With her arguments of time aside, her alleged betrayal is the real culprit for this meltdown. Her loyalty to the life she shared with a person who is gone has not diminished and is once again leaving her in disarray. My thoughts are interrupted as Sam stands, breaking free from my hold on her. "I need to find your friend," she says, determined to go after Darien. "I need to apologize."

"*Whoa!*" I say, getting quickly to my feet. "Let that fire simmer a little first. I know Darien very well. She gave you a pass, and I've never seen her do that before, so maybe let bygones…"

"But—"

"How much tequila did you drink?" I ask, bringing Sam out of her stupor.

"Tequila? Why?" Sam wipes her eyes, removing the wet proof of grief. "Too much. Never going near the stuff again. Jose and Sam are a no go!"

"Good. I'll remind you of that next time you feel like strolling down memory lane. Sam, listen to me, please. Nothing happened between you and Darien. She got you home in one piece and stuck around only long enough to make sure you didn't get sick before you passed out."

"She told you that?"

"No. She hasn't said a word about you and won't. I saw it all from my place. Neighbors and all," I add. "I wasn't being nosey."

"Right," Sam says, relaxing, then thumps the back of her head against the log beam. Within seconds her eyes widen as she remembers something. "Wait here. I got you something."

"Me?" I ask, but Sam's already gone, disappearing into the cabin. She's back almost immediately and hands me a wrapped package the size of a shoe box. I tear away the giftwrap and lift the lid. Emotion slams through me. In her darkest hour, Samantha is giving me light.

Sam blinks, letting one final tear escape her expressive eyes, although mine are now cascading my face like a waterfall. *She gets it*. I've never shared my past, only tidbits of information here and there, but she knows. What have I done to deserve her?

"Maybe," Sam begins, "we have to understand darkness to appreciate the light." I drop the box full of individual night lights and hug her. Again. It's clear, Sam and I are in a state where we require human contact. We stay that way for a long while until her sadness slips temporarily away, and I'm able to comprehend the extent of her generosity.

"My uncle raped me," I say for the first time in my life, the truth spilling out like a flood.

"I know."

"I haven't slept with Dean because I'm afraid I'll react to something he does, and…" I trail off.

"Dean's a smart man, Ryan. Trust him to know when and how to be with you."

"I'm tired of the grip the past has on me. Tired of losing out because of it."

"We'll figure it out. Let's make a promise to one another, a promise that we'll either win or learn, but we're done losing. I don't want you to lose out on anything anymore."

"I don't want *you* to lose anymore."

Sam sniffles. "God...it feels like we've swallowed a copy of *Eat Pray Love*."

I laugh. "Enough already. Aren't you sick of this? I am. It's time to move forward."

"Okay," Samantha says, simply.

We hear the crunch of tires first and then see the car pulling in. Samantha transforms before my eyes, joy radiating like a burst of something new and fresh. Ava is home. Before she's up and rushing to her, I reach for her arm, stopping her. "Sam, you're the absolute best person I know. *That's* who you are."

CHAPTER THIRTEEN

"A lot of people turn their backs on a guy like me," Drew confesses. "The odds of not falling off the wagon aren't in my favor, but Reece got me through AA. He never lost faith in me."

I'm getting a glimpse of Drew Young minus the flirtatious and wisecracking demeanor, so I willingly remain silent. His admission comes after a scuffle only moments ago with Reece during an unceremonious fish fry that assembled on a whim. Not that I contributed any fish to the fry. Luckily, I was closer than Garrett and quickly jumped between the brothers and convinced Drew to walk it off with me by the creek.

"Ryan, there are some things brothers just do. Knocking into each other's fist happens. There's no love lost because of it."

"Why are guys so mentally defective?"

"Are we?" He laughs. "We're hot-headed, is all." Drew moves a branch aside, sparing me from getting scraped. "You probably haven't noticed because my brothers and our friends don't tread lightly around me. They trust me not to slip, and I repay their confidence by staying sober." I think back to all the meals, poker games, and more and surprisingly attest that I don't recall a single instance of Drew drinking.

"Then why are you so salty?" I finally ask. "Are you jealous?"

"*Jealous?* Me? Hell no, I'm not jealous. Of what?"

"*Hmm*," I offer, unconvinced. "Reece is splitting his time between work and Brittany, which has you wondering where you fit in. Do you deny that?" Drew eyes me narrowly. He wants to disagree but is wise enough to recognize the truth when he hears it.

"Reece has the look," Drew says, dodging my question. "It's different from the way Dean looks at you, but it's still a look all the same. He's serious about her."

"How does Dean look at me?"

"C'mon, Ryan, some things can't go unseen. When I catch Dean watching you, I see a look a man only gets once in a lifetime, and that's if he's lucky. You're the only woman, or person for that matter, I've ever seen Dean lose his edge around. You're capable of bringing the strongest guy I know to his knees." Drew shakes his head, uncomfortable. He's not a regular with displays of emotion, and neither am I. I can feel the blush shading my skin.

"We should go get our poles," I say, and point to a deep pool of slowly moving water in the creek where there are fish to be caught.

"Want to hear something crazy?" Drew asks, snubbing my idea.

"Crazier than everything else you've said?"

"Yeah." He grins, and we start walking again. "One afternoon last fall we were all bundled around a campfire. Nana Sterling had been studying the significances of names and whatnot. When she got to Dean and revealed the meaning of his name, none of us believed her. I did a quick search while everyone waited to call her bluff. She was right. I'm betting that once I tell you, you'll research it later to see for yourself. Go ahead. It's there. Dean's name means Supervisor of the Summit."

"You calm your tits yet?" Reece asks Drew from behind us, close enough to hear the earth crunch beneath his boots along with the gurgle of the creek. I tilt my head, extending an exasperated sigh in Reece's direction. He smiles, his good looks capable of quickly defusing anyone's irritation. "It would be embarrassing for you if Ryan has to watch me drown your ass in the river."

Drew snorts. "My ass? That's funny. I was just thinking how envious yours must be from all the shit that comes out of your mouth."

I roll my eyes not even trying to hide the amusement spreading across my face. Their brotherly banter is back to normal without any clenched fists. "If this is what sibling rivalry is all about, I want to be part of the family," I say, and whack Reece on the arm.

"You already are," Drew says, flaunting his signature wink. "And if Dean gets his way, you'll be filing a change of address soon. But, back to this guy," Drew points at Reece. "Sex or love?" he asks Reece.

148

"Both."

"Fine, then man up and tell your ball and chain you're going with me Wednesday on an expedition to locate your balls. We can hit up some pocket water."

"What's pocket water? Can I come?" I ask, hoping it involves fishing.

"Every crack in Colorado's high country holds clear water pockets, brimming with wild trout. They're not large, but they're aggressive. Fun to catch," Reece explains. "Sorry, not this time, Ryan. We're going on a lone voyage into the wild west." I scowl. "I've got something I need to run by Drew before I tell the rest of you," he includes, softening the rejection.

#

"Here's another." Jules Jenson handed Samantha a black and white Xerox copy of a letter written to the Chaffee County Sheriff's Department. One of hundreds of letters inside a metal box the shape and size of a cereal box.

"How'd you get these?" Samantha asked.

"Well, I wrote them, so it would have been easier to copy them myself, but I wanted confirmation that they had been received. I sent letters weekly reporting your disappearance. Copies of police reports can be obtained from the Records Office three to five days after the date of occurrence. Or in this case, being received. Aside from a request form, there's a five-dollar fee for the first five pages, and a dollar for every page after that. I was careful never to get too lengthy."

149

Jules reached for a pair of reading glasses, smiled at Sam, and then put the glasses on.

"My name is Juliann, and I am the mother of Dawn Jenson," Jules began reading aloud. "I would like to share the feelings and reactions resulting from my daughter's kidnapping and subsequent treatment by her captor, law enforcement, the news media, and the public.

"While getting ready for work on the morning of October twenty-seventh," Jules stopped reading and peered over the rim of her readers at Sam. "I'll skip specifics. She scrolled to the next paragraph. "Accusations of my neglect—"

"Jules, please don't," Sam says, reaching for Jules' wrist, stopping her. "I can't listen to you blame yourself for what happened."

"If only—"

"No, Jules. We have a long road ahead, but it's the one thing I won't allow. It wasn't your fault. All I want right now is to get to know you and spend time together. There is something I need to ask, and I'm sorry, but I need to know. Was my biological father in the picture when it happened? Is he around?"

"We were never a couple, if that's what you mean. He was a young, handsome man. A tourist."

"Got it."

Jules drops her readers to the table with a thud. "Since finding out, I can't eat or sleep. I have so many questions, so many things I want to know about you, about Ava, that I forget you must have questions too. I'm treading lightly, so nervous I might lose you again."

Sam stood and walked around the table to kneel beside Jules. "Some things can't be explained. Things we may never know. I had loving parents who are both gone now. I have to believe they adopted a little girl without any knowledge of a corrupt adoption agency, or worse. I have lawyers and friends all over the country, people who will look into all of it. Chances are, those responsible are long gone, but if there's any hope whatsoever at getting you justice, I'll go to whatever length necessary to do so."

"I'm not sure there are any answers to be found. It's been so long."

"That might be true, so you need to believe me when I tell you this...I am so happy to know you. To know that of all the women who could have been my biological mother, it's you. You've also given me something special that I can finally give my daughter. A grandmother."

Wiping her face, Jules meets Sam's eyes. "I've got a little bit of money I've saved over the years. You can use it to—"

"You keep it and do something fun for yourself. I'm going to tell you something else, something no one else knows. I don't want you to ever worry again about this or your future, and I think the time for you to retire has come. Besides, I'm going to need help with Ava. What I'm saying is, I have money. I'm not fond of it because most of it has come to me by losing things and people I've loved."

"How do you mean?"

"Life insurance for one. Jordan took care of us in many ways, in addition to an inheritance from her French grandmother. My ex-husband, a story for another time, bought me out of a lucrative business. My adoptive parents weren't wealthy but were good with what they had, which I've used to invest in endeavors with a friend...my brother-in-law, Mike. He's someone very special I want to tell you about someday when we have more time."

#

Colby and Ava want to get a jump start on Christmas in the tail end of July by making snowmen out of rocks to sell during the Fall Fest. I step over a small mound of freshly painted white stones they're currently gluing together, three at a time.

"Wow, I bet you sell out the first day," I say, admiring their crafty work.

"We'll have more for Christmas Opening, too!" Colby informs. "Nana Sterling already put it on my calendar at her house for special stuff. December seventh," she noted, proudly.

"Is it like a party?" Ava asked.

"A big one for everyone. It lasts all day with lotsa fun stuff to do. There's a chocolate walk, caroling, a chili cook-off, pictures with Santa, a Christmas movie, and once it's dark there's a Parade of Lights."

Although these little people are a source of daily entertainment and I enjoy being with them, it's back—the melancholy that's been clinging to me for days. Summer will soon fade to fall, and I'll be leaving for my next assignment in Seattle.

"Can you take us in the woods to collect sticks 'n stuff? We need arms for the snowmen." Ava asks.

"Sure," I answer quickly, eyeing TC circling the dumpster. "Give me a minute to grab my camera." I have every intention of heading into my cabin but curiously angle toward TC instead. Walking closer, I notice the knife on TC's belt. It's no different than what I've seen on Dean or Drew, except for size. TC's is excessive, and his hands are covered in blood. My feet are no longer carrying me forward. He hasn't seen me yet, and I think if I move quickly enough, I can retreat without notice.

"Ryan?" TC calls. *Shit!* "Can you please get Samantha. And if it's not too much trouble, I need you to hurry." I hear the urgency in TC's tone along with a low growl inside the large dumpster. *Growl or groan*, I wonder, moving quickly to fetch my cell phone charging inside. Instinct, warranted or not, has me calling Brittany right after I call Sam.

Within minutes, while sitting on my porch steps, Sam runs down from the stables toward me. I point in TC's direction. Surprisingly, I've managed to keep a safe distance. I watch as Sam slides the side door that looks more like a window and peers in. *She's absolutely crazy!* In the time it takes to blink, Sam is climbing into the dumpster. TC tries to call her back, but there's no use. Clearly, he doesn't know her very well.

One by one, I see Samantha handing TC one of two small bear cubs. Nervously, I swallow hard before remembering the girls. I leap up, racing to them. Of course, they're watching it all go down. Luckily, it takes little effort to steer them inside. "You can watch through the window but do not come out." I look at Ava to verify she understands under no circumstance is Colby allowed out. Ava, of the two, will listen.

Where there are cubs, there is almost always a huge, very protective, mother bear in close proximity! Then I remember TC's hands. Why are they bloody? I'm not half as brave as my body is pretending to be, but I'm on the move again to get to Samantha and help, whatever the cost.

"Where?" I hear Sam ask TC, as I approach them. The next few minutes blur together as Dean fishtails his truck to a stop and jumps out. Already, he knows more than I do and runs behind the dumpster. I'm two strides ahead of the others to follow Dean. The cubs, however, are ahead of me only to find their mother in a bloody heap between the large metal receptacle and the woods. Inside a tangle of barbed wire wrapped tightly around the dead bear, there is another cub still clinging to life and it's mother.

"I tried cutting the cub free before hearing the others inside the bin," TC says.

From where I stand, there are three sizable gunshot wounds that I can see on the dead creature lying before us. There may be more I can't see. Two are embedded into its right side and a third through the neck. Even still, she's beautiful. Gruesome, yet I can't help but admire her splendor and consider what she must have suffered to protect her cubs. She'd been shot a minimum of three times and rolled in barbed wire, roughly hauled, and then dumped with her cubs by a dumpster. None of it makes sense but it's a message for Dean, nonetheless.

Together, Samantha and Dean carefully unwind the wire and free the third cub. To do so, they are both in direct contact with the mother bear and the blood she's lost. Like TC, they are now damp and colored in deep red. Sam stands

154

to assess the cubs crawling all over the corpse that was their mother.

"They're around three to four months," Sam tells Dean. "Most bears give birth in February, but from their size, I don't think that's the case here. I'm guessing March, maybe even early April." Sam wipes above her brow with her sleeve, leaving a smear of blood above her eye.

"Can they make it out there?"

"Not without her," Sam nods to the mother bear. "After seven or eight months, maybe, but not before. They can't go back up there alone. They won't survive. Even if we were able to find their den or another, it's of no use. We need to work fast."

"You want to make an enclosure? You want to look after them?"

"Until they can make it on their own safely, yes."

Dean looks to TC and TC nods. TC walks away quickly with his phone in hand, gathering the troops. Within the hour, many people will be scurrying around to help build an enclosure to protect the cubs from other animals, elements, or permanent captivity. The melancholy I felt before is nothing in comparison to the sadness I feel now. I'm sickened by the meaningless death of such a spectacular animal. She did nothing wrong but live within her means inside her natural habitat, protecting her own.

Brittany and Reece are quick to arrive, and after addressing the wounds on TC's hands, Brittany asks me for a ride back to the medical center. It strikes me odd that I notice Drew's truck parked outside the tavern in the middle of the day. I don't mention it to Brittany, not that Drew's done well with being discreet. I'm baffled why he would park at a bar in the middle of town for everyone to see.

While driving, Brittany continues to get calls. The town is alive with adventurists, the medical center calls her incessantly. "Tired?" I ask, noticing her yawn yet again.

"Worked a double. Fourth one this week and filling in when I can at the hospital in Salida."

"So, not Reece's fault?" I joke.

"He wants me to move in with him," she answers candidly. I'm not prepared for this, not that it's overly shocking, but it is unexpectedly soon, and none of my business. *Poor Drew*, I think, he's certainly not ready for this. "I can't remember a time in my life, even when I was gone all those years that I didn't want to be with Reece Young. Now, I have him."

"Are you worried it was all too easy? That you're moving too fast?"

"Ryan, I *was* easy. He didn't have to try very hard. I had never been with anyone before him. I was too busy with school and…" she waves her hand in the air. "One minute he comes to see me and the next we're in his bed. There hasn't been time for anything else."

"Like what? A date?"

"I sound stupid."

"Not to me, you don't. It didn't take me long to know I wanted to be with Dean. I think I knew it the first time I saw him. When you feel something so strongly, everything else seems trivial."

"But you didn't sleep with him right away, right? That's the difference."

"No, I didn't." *Still haven't.* "But it's not because we set a stopwatch to it. Dean and I had things to work through. I have...*had* a few problems."

"You're better now?"

"Getting there. In a way I can't really explain, I think coming here has saved me."

Brittany's small smile turns unstrained as we approach the medical center. "Thank you," she says, and it feels like it's for more than just the ride. She hops out and waves, jogging inside. I decide to check on Drew despite the nagging inner voice in my head to leave him be. It's an unnecessary argument because Drew's truck is no longer in front of the bar. He's gone to join the others. Sighing, the weight on my chest lessens, and I feel a massive sense of relief.

#

He sat in another bar, a new distillery one on South Main, peeling away the local label on a longneck he would not drink. He enjoyed the power of being able to sit amongst other patrons with a tight grip on his addiction and not indulge. He didn't bother looking up when a man occupied the empty stool beside him. He knew it was the same guy who'd been tailing him throughout the day, waiting for an opportunity to approach him.

"Buy you another?" the clean-cut, nicely dressed man asked.

"I'm good."

"You've kept me on my toes all afternoon," the man acknowledged, understanding Drew had bounced around from one establishment to another purposefully. "Drew Young, right?"

"Who wants to know?"

"Henry Prescott," he answered, lifting his hand to the bartender.

"Why waste time cutting to the chase," Drew began. "What do you want?"

"I think we both know the answer to that."

"If that's true, you're talking to the wrong guy."

"Not necessarily. I'm interested in offering you a job."

"Not interested."

"We've got big plans for this town, Drew. Plans you can benefit from, should you oblige."

"Oblige? Who says stuff like that?"

"As I said before that, big plans."

"By ruining it?"

"By putting it on the map. I make things happen, Drew, not all of them are good."

"You're threatening me?"

Henry smiled. "I'm informing you."

"On me," Drew said, standing and placing several bills on the bar top to cover their drinks. "Thanks, but no. Take care, Henry."

Drew had gotten the text, and then several after to head up the mountain but held off long enough to get the identity of the tail. Now he knew. The time had finally come, they're moving in. He needed to tell Dean, needed to get up the mountain and join the others.

Heading west, Drew overshot the turn for Cotton Creek Expeditions and drove past Rainbow Lake after spotting a silver pickup following closely behind. A new tail, he realized. This vehicle was nothing like the G-Wagen, otherwise known as the Mercedes-Benz G-Class, Henry had driven.

Drew shook off his paranoia once the pickup turned into a lot leading to the Denny Creek Trailhead. At the turn for Ptarmigan Lake, he turned his truck around and headed back down Cottonwood Pass. He couldn't help but glance in the parking area as he passed Denny Creek. It wasn't surprising to not see the truck. The lot was deep and mostly out of view.

When approaching a private turn, Drew caught a slight reflection. At his speed, on that particular bend of the pass, he had no time to react as the silver vehicle darted out, ramming into him. He squeezed his eyes closed, praying, as his truck rocketed over the side of the mountain into a deep gully of rock and timber.

CHAPTER FOURTEEN

Black. The word circles not as a color but a void. It's continuous, repeating itself as Reece drops to his knees in a black suit while the fine-grained walnut casket lowers into the earth's fresh grave. "Angels" by Robbie Williams is playing lightly in the background. From where exactly, I don't know. We're at Mt. Olivet Cemetery owned by the town of Buena Vista with an exceptionally grand view of Mt. Princeton.

The space between what's right and wrong is nameless. How has this happened? It's as if everyone has been anesthetized for days, letting the shock sink its wicked teeth in. It's all over us, this tremendous loss. Even me, and I'm new to this pieced together family.

Dean is holding my hand tightly, and on the other side of him, he holds Colby close. In the days since the accident, Dean, Colby and I have spent little time apart. He doesn't need to say why he keeps us closer than before. Weeping,

Jenna is beside us. I hear the rustle of material and from the corner of my eye see Brittany wrap a consoling arm around Jenna's shoulders. Reece refuses to speak to Brittany, to anyone for that matter, but especially her.

I haven't told anyone. I can't. What good would telling anyone that I saw Drew's truck parked outside a bar just before he died? It's a secret that's eating me alive. But I have to have faith even if it's blind. I owe it to Drew to trust he didn't do this to himself, to believe it was an accident, nothing more.

An altercation snaps me from my thoughts as Garrett tries to help Reece to his feet, only to have Reece shove him roughly. I tighten my grip on Dean, holding him still. What's happening is between brothers grieving their brother. Their scuffle is over quicker than it started, and the service continues.

Through dark sunglasses, I scan the faces of so many people, easily the majority of the town. People Drew had known his entire life, people who had either watched him grow up or grown up beside him. All of them waiting for their turn to toss handfuls of dirt onto a wooden box expertly crafted to offer comfort to the living, not the departed. It's clear. His death will hang over the town like a hooded veil for years to come.

"Goodbye," Garrett says, choking on the words. Goodbye. I swallow the word and turn to look for Samantha. She's behind us with Ava and Jules. Dark sunglasses also block her eyes. I can't read her, but I know. Her mind is elsewhere, someplace painful.

Colby leans against her dad. Dean picks her up and holds her tightly in his arms, close to his heart. He looks at me, and whispers what I think is, "love you." He doesn't mean to say it, not to me, not now, not like this. I'm confident it was intended for Colby as she rests her head on his shoulder. Still, it feels like cement and guilt are being poured into my heart, helping it sink, because I could have but didn't say those three words back. Even if they weren't meant for me, I want to comfort him.

I stare off, allowing my mind to wander. I harbor too many fleeting thoughts. The crazy kind everyone has in moments like these. The kind where it makes sense to interrupt the service and scream. The sort where you're brave enough to tell everyone not to wait to do it, that thing, everything, whatever it is. It doesn't matter what it is as much as it matters to make it count. Only I'm not courageous enough to ever really do it.

There's movement. It's Dean. He hands me Colby and steps forward to deliver his eulogy. I brace for it. Taking a deep breath, I look at Reece. He's barely able to remain upright. Jenna moves away from Garrett, closer to me, occupying the space where Dean had been. I think nothing of it. She needs to be close to Colby and places her arm around us both.

"The strongest of friendships are those that turn into family. A family by choice. And so, I am both destroyed and privileged to stand here today. It's correct, Drew may not have been my brother by blood, but he was by devout devotion. I never questioned his friendship, nor did he mine.

"As I look around, I see many faces, old and new, expressions of discontent and grief. There isn't one among us who can doubt the love Drew had for this place and all of you. For the differences between us, the balances and discords that make our community unique and empathetic for our own. He understood that together we weather storms. He would never accept anything less, and for that, we will help one another pull through.

"If you're here, chances are you've been on the receiving end of his good-humored manner a time or two. If you knew him well, you would agree that this clear and beautiful day is Drew undeniably consoling us from above, proving Heaven is closer than it seems.

"With that, I'd like to share that Drew Young, the son, brother, and friend of Buena Vista gave the ultimate gift the night of his death. Organ donation is both courageous and selfless, and even though our prayers for his survival were not answered, other's prayers were. Where one life came to an end, three others will go on."

#

Journal Entry 405 / Letters to Jordan

Things aren't much different from when I wrote yesterday. In the wake of the funeral, life on the mountain is quiet. Because they're all so close, I believed the loss would bind them together even more, but now I worry invisible rage is wedging them apart. Death has a way of doing that. I would know.

Please give me a sign. Or is this where faith is called into action, and I'll have to wait and see? As you know, I'm not religious anymore. I was getting there, but that was before you died. Lately, that's changing too, reverting back to where I was when things were good. I'm beginning to wonder about the premises that setbacks are opportunities for growth. Not that your death or Drew's were setbacks. I understand that my progress won't come automatically. I have to make use of it, and that's what I'm trying to do.

I was going to start this entry by telling you it's been a terrible week, but who am I to say? In the long view, does anyone know how the week will be judged?

With her pen in hand, Sam glanced up. She weighed her options, balancing the journal on her knees. By the looks of what was happening next door, she needed to act fast. Rising, she took a deep breath, setting the journal aside, and then walked the short distance between cabins.

"Leaving?"

"Looks like."

"Alrighty then," Sam said, backing away. "Safe travels."

Darien tossed her laptop along with her purse into the passenger seat then turned, swiping at choppy, auburn bangs. "Are you hungry?" she asked.

"Hungry? It's like my middle name. Why?"

"Let's grab burgers and have lunch in the park."

"That sounds deliciously suspicious. Is it code for 'let's talk?'"

"Milkshakes, too."

"*Hmm*," Samantha murmured, tilting her head. "Will the real Slim Shady please stand up."

Darien chuckled. "It's true. I like junk food. It's perfectly normal."

"Fascinating, I would have never guessed." Samantha stepped back, relaxing her shoulders. "On a side note, it was nice of you to stay for Drew's service, and for the food your company sent."

"Yesterday was rough for everyone. Can I ask you something personal?"

"Why not, I knew the greasy food invite was a farce."

"Are you okay here? I mean truly okay. After everything that's happened and with the amount of time that's passed since you left Texas."

"I'm holding up. Besides, is anyone ever 'truly' okay? Life happens, and we roll with the punches."

"Right, so what you're saying is we all love, smile, cry and die? That's reasonable. I suppose the only difference is some do it with more poise than others."

"And the others?" Sam asked, feeling she should be offended but wasn't.

"Some hide, some run."

"I'm not running."

"I believe you. It's only...never mind. Let's go eat."

"It's only what, Darien?"

"The night in the bar, you had a lot to say. Not all of it was about finding out what happened to you when you were a little girl. You talked about your family in Texas. There's a lot of love there."

"There is. Sure, sometimes I feel I'm in the wrong place at the wrong time with the wrong people. I'm not. I'm exactly where I need to be."

"Then let's go. I'm starving."

165

"Are you trying to irritate me?"

"Was that a yes? I couldn't tell," Darien asked, smirking.

"I'm not getting in *that*," Sam pointed at the Porsche. "Plus, you drive like a maniac."

"Your loss. I'll meet you there in ten, and I'm feeling generous. I may even spring for your lunch before I'm out and you don't have to dodge me anymore."

"I'm not—"

Darien lifted her hand, her palm facing out, effectively cutting Samantha off. "Save it. Dipping salty fries into a chocolate milkshake is all I'm after."

They ate lakeside, in McPhelemy Park, on a picnic table of metal and wood. The burgers were from a place across the highway, a legendary stop for tourists. Also notorious for assigning customers with iconic names instead of numbers when their orders were ready. When Darien's order was ready, the girl working the counter called loudly into the microphone for Lady Gaga.

"You're so out of place here," Sam said, eyeing Darien in slacks, a silk blouse, and heels with copper hair curling loosely around her shoulders.

"Straight from here to the office."

"Do you ever slow down?"

"I'm here, aren't I?"

"You are, which gives me an open to apologize. I was a jerk. I'm sorry. Nothing happened between us, so *whew*, crisis avoided. Besides, this whole angsty thing is exhausting, dontcha think?" Sam asked, admiring their tasty spread across the table. She looked away, reading a wooden

166

sign, announcing the park had been donated in 1880, then back to Darien.

"Would it have been so bad if something happened?"

"Not ready or interested. No offense, if I was on the make, you'd be the first person I'd call to watch NASCAR with."

"I don't drive *that* fast."

Sam arched a brow and stopped chewing. "How many tickets have you gotten?"

"In the past month or year?"

"I rest my case. So" Sam set her burger down "we're friends now?"

"You can count on me to speak Tequila whenever I'm around."

"You'll be back then?"

"With or without Ryan in the area, yes. Always. My grandparents had a second home here. We came every summer. I love the city, but a place like this never leaves you."

"That explains Ryan's assignment here. Thank you for that, by the way."

"Life has a funny way of tossing people at us when we need them most." Darien crumbled the wrapper and surprised Samantha by hooking it ten feet to the garbage can and sinking it. "But, you're right, I did choose to conclude our project here. It's something I've wanted to do for years. Professionally speaking, I don't often let sentiment interfere with what I do. This has been the exception."

"You have people who do this sort of thing for you? I mean, you don't drop in on people the way you have here, with Ryan, do you?"

"Never. I make a point to check on her."

"I've got a feeling there's more to your ongoing concern. I suppose Ryan will tell me when she's ready."

"Samantha, there are things about Ryan that Ryan scarcely knows. Your bond is unique, so please, continue to champion for her, even when she's wrong. She'll need someone in her corner. There's also something pretty significant happening between her and that little girl."

"With Colby?" Sam thought about it. "I see it, too." Sam set a fry down, no longer hungry. "Why are you sending her to Seattle then?"

"It's Ryan's choice where she works. We have a contract. It's important. She signed on for it over a year ago. It's possible it will nudge her toward what she wants, even if she doesn't know that yet. She'll question everything, especially her feelings until she's gone. Then she'll know, and I believe she'll do what's best for her."

"Interfering gets messy. I'll never forgive you if she doesn't come back."

"Trust her. It's going to be hard to see her go, but you have to believe in her."

"And you? We'll see you around from time to time?"

Darien leaned in, lacing her fingers together. "I purchased property here five years ago. I come up whenever I can manage to get away. It's undeveloped but on the water, so there's that." Darien smiled. "In the past, I've stayed at cabins on the outskirts of town. The WiFi is good, and the location is ideal, but we both know how persistent Ryan can be. She insists I not stay alone and bunker with her instead. Can I tell you how much I detest sleeping on a sofa sleeper?"

"I think you pretend to dislike things more than you actually do."

"Anyway, I try to tackle projects while I'm here, a personal pact I made with myself. The first summer I planted trees. One day when I'm ready to build, there will be a driveway lined in beautiful pines. These past few days, I've been working on a garden, which is a challenge due to the fucking deer."

"That's where you disappear to? *You* get dirty?"

"I'll do you one better. It may even knock your socks off." Darien straightened, offering a million-dollar-watt smile. "I own a pickup."

"Mind blown!"

Darien laughs. "I like you, Samantha."

"Since when?" Sam smirked. "Seriously, though…don't. As you know, I have more issues than Heinz has pickles, including a dog who requires more therapy than I do, and bear cubs who think I'm their mama."

"Speaking of, how's yours?"

"*Ahh*, and there's also that. Jules Jenson really is my mother, isn't she? Just when I start to get my bearings, something else knocks me over. This town may be heavy-hearted right now, but whatever went down thirty years ago isn't over. I'm going to find out what really happened.

#

Sometimes I pretend I come from a normal family where my mother is a taskmaster, mission maker, and decider of everyone's general direction. Not something I read last winter in *The Carousel*. If that were the case, I would be on the right path, or at least have a blueprint of the direction my life is going. Instead, I'm watching Dean between limbs of a juniper, and craving maternal guidance on what to do.

I knew from the first time I saw him that there was something even then. I may have pretended otherwise, but deep down, I knew. All these weeks later, and I'm no longer curious about the butterflies that take flight in my stomach every time I see him. I want to go to him and ask if he feels it too, but then think better of it. Maybe it's true, maybe it takes meeting the right person to figure things out, and I don't need motherly advice after all.

I have no idea how long Dean has been by the creek. I can only guess it's as close to how long Jenna's has been sitting at her desk, staring into space. Their grief comes in waves, engulfing and overwhelming. Drew's death has brought on an awful hollowness for all.

Dean's wrecked yet resilient. It's bewildering. Here, when he thinks he's alone and no one is watching, he's noticeably broken. If only I could break my own heart and use those pieces to fix his. It's clear he desires isolation, even if his idea of that is in the middle of a forest, thick with wonder. Quietly, I retreat, leaving him within his element to work through this devastation.

It's not long, a couple of hours at most, when I hear movement inside my little bungalow. I have just crawled under the sheets after a hot, soothing shower, determined to get through the night without dreams. Listening to him approach my room, I feign sleep. I feel the weight of him

170

drop beside me on the mattress, and then feel his breath against my skin. I open my eyes.

"Are you going to make a habit of breaking into my cabin after dark?" I ask.

He doesn't answer and kisses me instead. I can't take it anymore. I need him. I roll over, straddling him. It doesn't matter that I'm in a ratty t-shirt, we've overlooked music, and there are no candles to be found. My mind is made up.

"I saw you earlier by the creek," he says, with his lips against my neck. I can't respond with his hands moving up my body, leaving fire trails everywhere his fingers touch. "When I see you, Ryan, especially there, things snap back into place," he says, lifting the t-shirt over my head. He catches the curve of my breast, his palms are hot, and it feels like the temperature in the room has gone nuclear.

Suddenly, I'm on my back with Dean above me. I lift my hand to sift fingers through his dark hair, urging his head to mine for another kiss. Except, Dean resists. I open my eyes to see his clouded with hesitation. I lean forward, removing every inch of space between us.

"Whatever it is…it can wait. Block out the noise and focus on me."

I can tell he's struggling, but in the end, he disregards my plea and sits up, pulling me with him. His concerned expression jolts me to back reality. He releases my hand and wipes his across his face, attempting to swipe away his frustration. "You know those things that keep you from saying things you shouldn't? I can't think of them. What are they called?"

"Filters? Yes, I know them well. Mine are usually broken."

"There's something we need to talk about, and I'm trying to figure out how to tell you. Information Ray found out."

"Your dad?"

"Yes, he's here." Dean reaches for my hands again, although this time he's doing so nervously. "I asked him to look into a problem of yours that's going to upset you. I wanted to help you, and now…"

"What did you do?"

"I don't want you to leave, Ryan. If you do, I have to know you'll come back, and not for work, but for this…for us."

"Dean, what did you do?" I repeat each word slowly.

"I'm getting there, but here's the thing…it's not anything I saw coming until it hit me, and then *wham*, I was in it. It's difficult and messy and amazing. It kickstarted my life back into full throttle and breaks me in ways I didn't imagine possible. And forget fighting it because it's the impossible force."

"What are you talking about?"

"Love."

"Dean."

"I thought if I could do this one thing, give you this one thing, then you might stay. I asked Ray to look into court-ordered records keeping you from getting your mom out of the hospital so we could bring her here."

I leap from the bed in one fluid motion, yanking the top dresser drawer open and reach for a different t-shirt, and then pull sweatpants up my legs. "Please leave."

"No." Dean stands, moves closer, and stops an inch away. "Why are you so afraid to let me in." I shove him

172

aside and go to the small closet and grab my duffle. "You're running now?"

"It's called work. Time to go."

"Ryan, look at me." I do. It's a mistake. The hurt and fear he feels break me. I lean against the doorjamb of the closet, defeated. "We'll get through this. Let me help you."

"You tried getting my mom out of the looney bin? Thanks, but I could have spared you the effort. Next time you want to go digging in someone's personal and private life, I suggest you talk to them about it first."

"There's a way to get her out, Ryan, but there's something you need to know first to have a fighting chance to do it."

"What's that, Dean? What could you possibly know that I don't already? She's crazy. I know. I've heard the diagnosis over and over again. She requires specific management. Care that I seem unfit to provide."

"She's not crazy, Ryan." I look at him. *What nerve!* I'm shaking with a mixture of shame and fury. "We have to go after your uncle first. He's got power of attorney, and he's been persuasive with everyone about her mental state to protect himself."

"My uncle?" *Screw this. I'm out!*

"Ryan, please. Stop packing and sit down."

I spin, looking directly into his eyes. "Why?"

"Because he isn't your uncle. He's your dad."

PART TWO

Winter

CHAPTER FIFTEEN

The wind is piling snow along the edge of the road in drifts, blinding the day in white dust. It's the beginning of December, and already the wintry weather is a blunder of ice and regret. But what is regret? Is it like residue? Something I try to get rid of, but it continues to stick because I've done something I can't take back?

It's been four months since I lashed out, backed away, and fled. That, I do regret. I left Buena Vista when my anger was a flash of fire, bright but brief, protecting me from the truth. Or maybe I went to face my demons. Either way, I'm done running.

I'm no longer looking over my shoulder or answering calls from the past. There's too much in front of us, and by us, I mean Mama and me. She's with me now, and we're back. I have no expectations other than wanting the chance for a life here—a life I'm going to have to fight for.

Mama's sitting in the passenger seat singing "Change," giving Taylor Swift a run for her money. I'm not the sole answer to her needs, but she often reassures me through lyrics that nothing other than love is enough to help us through. In her own odd way, she's helping me too, teaching me to never give up on anything I can't go very long without thinking about.

If I want a fighting chance, I can't keep pretending. Before, I worked at keeping my feelings at bay while Dean wore his on his sleeve. Confronting him will be difficult, possibly the hardest thing I've ever done besides leaving, and he may not believe what I have to say. My actions have always been driven by impulse when I'm scared or uncertain, so I'm vowing never again to make decisions when I'm afraid.

I'm ready to go to him, directly up the mountain, but can't. Not yet. There's no magic pill here. It's going to take time. If I want to win him back, and I do, I'll have to pace myself without causing more damage.

It's not only Dean but also Colby. I want her. I want them both, equally, to be my family. And the list goes on. A list of people I need to make amends with for leaving behind, starting with Samantha. I have missed her and am despondent without her friendship. Nothing else will work until I bridge that gap.

Sam is the only person I've responded to, but those interactions were brief at best. For the past two weeks, I haven't heard from her, nothing of substance anyway. I've hurt her, too. Or, worse. Maybe she was right in one of our earlier text exchanges: *It's the ones who disappoint you who need you most*. That stung because there's no maybe about it. Nothing hurts more than being disappointed by a person you never dreamed would hurt you.

I gape through the windshield at trees bare of leaves and at an angry sky while the harsh wind howls against the frosting glass of my 4-Runner. I shiver, glancing at the digital thermostat on my console. It's five degrees.

I used the time away, all one hundred and twenty-seven days of them, to accept the things I can't change. Ultimately, I'm at peace with that. I accept there are two aggressive parts of me in constant competition with another and both are hungry. The bigger and better part of me is my heart which craves the love and faith the people in this town have to offer. My mind, however, feasts on resentment, and not for me, not anymore, but for others, beginning with Drew.

The first thing I need to do is deliver a message. I didn't believe it then, and I definitely don't believe it now. Drew Young's death was not an accident. On one of many sleepless nights, I occupied my time by writing, so I've sealed those sentiments in an envelope. Held by the weight of a small rock, on the edge of the road at the sight of the crash, I'm leaving a letter.

Dear Killer,

Hi, my name is Interested, but I'm sure you know who I really am. We've crossed paths a time or two. I'm the one who stumbles upon your messes and who you watch from afar. Let's not forget the times you've followed me.

You killed a friend of mine. You could argue I didn't know him long enough to care as much as I do. That only fuels my fire. Although, I'm more confused than anything else. Mainly about why. Why him and not me? We both know you've had the chance.

I want to tell you something about him. You may not care, but you should know he meant the world to many good people who didn't deserve the tremendous loss. It's as if you snatched crucial pieces of each of them when you killed him, and there's no way to coax them back.

I won't lie, I've wished you dead and then had to ask myself what's the point in that? It won't bring Drew back. I don't expect you'll ever write, nor am I foolish enough to assume your remorse or guilt. I merely thought it was fair to say my piece before you return. Because let's face it, we both know you're coming back.

And when you do, understand this: I'll be ready.

Interested

#

With a stroke of luck, I no longer have to orchestrate an encounter with Dean. We're standing in the same small line at the pharmacy. He's with Nana Sterling and obviously running the same errand with his grandmother that I am with

180

my mother. Prescriptions. He doesn't see me, nor does he know I'm back. No one does.

It can go one of two ways, except it won't because I'm not giving up. With her arm hooked through Dean's, Nana Sterling turns, and there's nothing left for me to do but take the first step. When she notices me, a hint of reluctance flashes through her eyes before it disappears, and she promptly spreads her arms widely for me to walk into.

Nana Sterling's embrace is just as I remember: warm and comforting. I feel Dean's presence all over me now, not that he's anywhere near touching me. His eyes are locked on mine with a message I can't read. It's a first. Slowly, I pull away enough to introduce Nana Sterling to my mother. With subtle grace, Nana Sterling guides my mother to the front of the store to browse through locally made trinkets and other merchandise while Dean and I talk.

He isn't budging, not even an inch, only standing gallantly and waiting. Everything I say and do here will count, so I silently instruct myself to be brave. I can't afford to screw this up. Instinctively, I reach out to touch his arm, but he's quick to move out of range.

"Hey, Blue," I'm first to say.

"Ryan," Dean responds, curtly. I take it back, I can read him perfectly. He's surprised to see me. He's also angry. "Passing through?"

"Taking some time off." *Baby steps*, I remind myself. I'm stuck between revealing too much or too little. All I can think is, *please talk to me*. "I wanted to see you."

"Tying up loose ends?"

"Can we go somewhere to talk?" I ask him, tempering the sting of his accusation. He swallows. My eyes follow the dip then rise of his Adam's apple before lifting to eyes that always remind me of whiskey. "Please."

"I think…" Dean looks over my head, looks everywhere but at me "…I need to say no." I nod, unable to find my voice. "Take care, Ryan." He passes me, and it takes everything I've got to watch him go. He stops long enough to look over his shoulder to see me standing despairingly, and then he's gone. If only I could turn back the clock to last summer, freeze frame it, and have a redo. *Fight for him.* I will. I'll do everything I can to fix what I've broken between us.

Jenna rounds the corner, and I'm caught off guard almost bumping into her. I should have known. They're a close family, and it's Wednesday. It's the one day of the week they always have lunch together. "Ryan!" She says, stunned, "I knew you would come back."

I reach out and pull Jenna into a hug. She's hesitant at first, and then I feel her arms tighten around me. We stay that way for at least a full minute before she backs away. "I need to catch up with them." She takes steps backward. "It's good to see you."

And just like that, it's over. I've seen them. They know I'm back, and Samantha will know soon enough. Like everywhere, news travels fast. I need to call Sam before she hears from anyone else. I also need to get Mama back to the lodge to rest and give myself a few minutes to digest what has just happened.

On the outskirts of town, I've rented one of nine log cabins at a place Darien suggested, and I'm so glad she did. It's perfect. It helps that it sits along the northern bank of Cottonwood Creek. Our accommodations are cozy, affordable and equipped with everything we need, including two bedrooms and a fireplace. Not to exclude Bodie, who certainly appreciates the pet-friendly policy.

I unlatch and crack open the front door, mistaking the knock for the friendly manager, only to come face-to-face with Samantha. So much for easing into it. She's cut her blonde hair, not much, but enough for me to notice.

"Hey," she says, and breezes by, slightly bumping into my side as she passes with Deacon on her heels.

I close the door and lean against it with my hands clutching the knob behind my back. We use the awkwardness to observe Bodie and Deacon share in a sloppy, wet reunion. "Hey," I say, finally.

"It's hard to be unsympathetic when I did pretty much the same when I left Texas, hurting everyone I left behind."

"Sam—"

"Let me finish." Sam's acting as cold as the creek behind my cabin—frozen on top but the water still flows beneath. Sam starts to remove her jacket then decides better of it and leaves it on. Not a good sign. "A lot has changed."

"You think?" I blurt the words sarcastically, without thinking. I'm in self-preservation mode for whatever comes next.

Samantha inhales, deeply enough to see the rise and fall of her shoulders. She does this once. Then twice. "I'm just saying the ground isn't very solid right now." She sighs, and I take it to be an indication that she's softening. "You look good," she says, though she's not looking at me. Thus far, none of them have been able to really look at me.

An uneasy feeling begins to take root in my stomach. "Thanks," I offer lamely, needing some water and walk to the kitchen which is part of the same room. "How are things?" *What am I saying?* I wonder, hating the small talk.

"Things are circular. No real movement, no change, no improvement. Just round and round in circles we all go."

I hand Samantha a glass of water and sit on a chevron patterned loveseat across from her. "I don't know what that means."

"Me either," she admits. She sets the glass of water on the coffee table and stands. "I need to go." I stay seated, saying nothing. It's happening, and I figured it would, knowing the rejection would hurt. Three times in less than an hour feels excessive and a bit harsh. I wait for Sam to turn and offer me a glimmer of hope by looking over her shoulder, but she doesn't. She calls for Deacon and shuts the door behind them.

I close my eyes briefly then jump to my feet and quickly check on my mother. She's napping, completely undisturbed. I walk briskly to the door and swing it open, ready to chase after Samantha, but come to an abrupt stop instead. Sam's leaning against her Range Rover, waiting.

"I hate you," she says.

"I know."

"You can't vanish on people, Ryan. You don't just get to leave without a word."

"I know," I repeat. "I'm sorry." I lower my head, ashamed. "I'm so many things, Sam, but sorry tops the list. I mishandled everything." I look up and into her eyes. "Did Dean tell you what he found out?"

"Dean? You're kidding, right?" she scoffs. "I can't even say your name around him without him pulling a disappearing act. You did a number on him, Ryan." I gnaw

184

my lip to keep my teeth from chattering. I've come outside in socks and without a coat. My socks are wet, and my toes are numb. "Yes, he told me the night you left. Ava and I came back from dinner with Jules to find Dean standing in the driveway, staring down the road at nothing but darkness." I shrink at the image. I did that to him.

Samantha leans over, grabbing a fistful of fresh snow and throws it at me. Before I know it, we're in a full-blown snowball fight in the courtyard. I don't stop to think much of it. I can only imagine how it looks to the other tenants, watching as two grown women chase one another. Not to mention, we're both screeching with two barking dogs knocking us over.

Just like that, the thick fog between us has lifted. She remembers how we are together, the rarity and strength of our bond. "You brought her here with you?"

"I did." As I answer, we hear her first then see Mama in the doorway, humming "Let the Good Times Roll."

Sam gets to her feet and goes to my mother. "I like The Cars too," she says, giving my mother a peck on the cheek before going inside the cabin, tracking snow along the way. "Come on, Ryan, we have a lot to talk about."

#

"My boyfriend is a good man, he's not a monster. It was only the one time. The time I found her in the basement, tied to a wooden pallet beside a dirty mattress. She was pitiful

185

and naked, trying to scream but gagged instead from the bloody rag shoved into her mouth.

He didn't mean it, he even apologized. Besides, it wasn't his fault. She tricked him, playing mind games, using his anxiety against him. He thought they were pretending. Role-playing, he called it. She was his hostage."

He pressed the arrow on the display, pausing the audio testimony streaming through the speakers of his truck's upgraded sound system. He enjoyed satellite radio, enjoyed hearing statements from eye-witnesses to heinous crimes. It was fun listening to a podcast while watching Ryan McCray and Samantha Devon reunite. Away from Dean Sterling and his beloved property. At long last, all the chips were back on the board, exactly how he hoped it would be.

He brushed his thumb over the letter in his left hand then carefully reached for the envelope resting on the dash. He smirked, folding the letter in thirds then stuffing it back into its place.

"I'll see you soon, girls," he said, and then drove away.

CHAPTER SIXTEEN

"But, Daddy, it's a friggin' Christmas tree not a—" Colby lifted her arms, crooking her fingers to make air quotes "—winter tree! 'Cuz, *duh*, we've got those kinds of trees all over and not just when it's winter."

"I don't know, kid, not everyone celebrates Christmas. Your teachers are probably trying to keep that in mind," Dean argued, but glanced at Samantha and rolled his eyes. "And, Colby? Knock it off with the friggin' and freakin' or anything else remotely close."

"*Well*," Colby continues, not skipping a beat. "And why so early? Christmas break isn't for like two more weeks."

"No clue, but we're rolling with it, so behave."

According to Jenna, who was repeatedly on the receiving end of their pranks, Ava and Colby were "thick as thieves." Fortunately, their teachers were wise enough to split the girls into separate homerooms. Little else kept them apart, and thankfully the holiday party was grade level. Relieved that it was, Dean and Samantha prepared to endure the ordeal together as they walked the school hallway, rounding the corner to the first and second-grade wing.

Amid Pin the Carrot on the Snowman, Stanna Truitt decided there was no better place than a party to perturb Colby Sterling. "What do you mean Santa isn't real?" Colby shouted. Dean stepped forward, noticing his daughter clenching little hands into tight fists before Samantha grabbed him by the shirtsleeve and pulled him back.

Ava stepped out of the line and raised her hand, impatient to be called on. "Mrs. T, Stanna is disrespecting my religious beliefs!"

Laughing, Sam pulled Dean away from the games to the back of the classroom where they discovered a table decorated with an assortment of treats. Biting into a sugar cookie slathered in red icing, Dean caught Samantha watching him. "What?"

"You can't avoid her."

"I know, I keep telling her I'm going to ground her the next time she cusses, then don't. This parenting stuff is hard."

"Dean, you know who I mean. How long do you plan to let Ryan wallow in the dark corners of her mind?"

"Let's not go there."

"We're already knee-deep." Samantha handed him a blue napkin with white snowflakes on it to wipe the cookie crumbs from the corner of his mouth. "She came back for you."

"Or for you."

"That too." Sam shrugged. "I'm part of the equation, but it's completely different. I'm her…" Sam stopped, pondering

188

what exactly they were. "In some other life, we were sisters. Maybe even twins because we are *that* parallel. We're best friends, ride or die's, or whatever else they use these days. But get real, Sterling. It's not easy for her, but she's here, and she is here for you."

"That ship has sailed."

"Really? Can you look me in the eye without lying and tell me you've thought of little else since bumping into her at the pharmacy?"

"It'll pass."

"Right. So, loving someone is just something people do until what? They find someone else?"

"Below the belt, Sam."

"True, and not my style, so I'll ask differently. After someone like Ryan, can there be anyone else for you?"

"There might be," Dean answered, looking away. "But not like her."

"Exactly. And you can say her name, you know? It won't kill you."

"That's just it, Sam. It does."

"Dean…you're *killing* me." Sam smiled, not expansively nor exposing any teeth, but instead with compassion. "Do you have any idea what I would give to have another chance with the one person I loved most and lost? Or how much I regret the time I wasted being apart from that person because I was too busy thinking instead of feeling?"

"You know as well as I do, I won't be able to stay away from her. It's as if every minute that's passed since I saw her has tripled in length, but I can't forget how easily she left. It's been almost four months. Four. She never called, not once."

"I know. I do, but let's be fair. And sorry, buddy, but with a pretty heavy dose of betrayal on your part, you blindsided her with shattering news. She probably spent the majority of her time away angry and the rest of it thinking you might think differently of her now because of it. Try imagining how she must have felt. How dirty. How unworthy."

"I have. I've gone over every possible scenario again and again. It doesn't change the one thing that stands between us."

"Which is?"

"Her lack of faith. She can be leery about everything else, Sam, but not me."

#

Denver, Colorado

Ray Sterling stepped from the elevator on the fifty-third floor into the reception area. Henry Prescott was waiting, prepared to escort Ray into the Senator's office. Intimidatingly handsome in tailored suits, they entered the high-rise suite to see Senator Jonathan Prescott engaged in conversation with a younger man taking notes.

Ray marveled at the view. He turned to Henry, the son of the Senator, briefly sizing him up before turning back to the splendor beyond the glass. His sister Joyce had been married to Jonathan Prescott, a disappointment that made Henry his nephew.

190

"From up here, it's like standing on a Goliath's back, looking down at the world in awe," Jonathan said to Ray, dismissing his assistant.

"Senator," Ray greeted, taking a seat in a leather high back, facing his stealthy opponent.

"No need for formalities, we go too far back." Jonathan nodded to the vacant chair beside Ray for Henry to sit down. "If you don't mind, I thought it prudent for Henry to observe. Learn the ropes, so to speak."

"I don't believe Henry is new to debt collection," Ray offered, earning a chuckle from the Senator.

"You're a clever man, Ray, I give you that. On the other hand," Jonathan paused, then stood. "Let's step out to the veranda, shall we? I'll have my secretary fetch your coats."

"I can't help you. I don't have proprietorship," Ray declared, buttoning a thick, charcoal grey, dress coat. He was aware the move outdoors was made for privacy.

"I suggest you either correct that or become influential."

"Dean and I are practically estranged, you know that."

"Yes, his choice. Certainly, nothing to do with your participation in the absence of his mother."

"A long-ago lapse in judgment."

"Oh, come now, how many callous choices can one man have without paying the piper? It's intriguing, really, how you were able to procreate through different women and essentially correct your mistakes by elimination. Fortunately, my marriage to Joyce conveniently placed me in a position to accommodate you."

"I was young, Jonathan. Naïve, for that matter, and desperate. Twice I let you convince me to listen to your advice and later consider your help to resolve my problems."

191

"Indiscretions, if memory serves. That's what you called them then."

"You were persuasive, ensuring me she would be placed out of state. There was no way for me to have known child trafficking and exploitation were part of the arrangement. I thought it meant her mother would be influenced to give her up, and that you guaranteed her safety and adoption into a good home."

"She was placed into a good home."

"How was I to know that? Furthermore, I thought you'd dismissed our conversation, terminating the idea altogether."

"Why would you think that?"

"Because she wasn't adopted at birth. Because her mother never identified me as the father. Because she was with her mother for several years before…"

"Ah, yes, a temporary glitch in operations. Tell me, what's it been like being privy to information on a missing child all these years and never coming forward? All that time you let poor Juliann Jenson suffer."

"I never asked you to do it, I never paid you."

"What you did was present a businessman with an opportunity to make money."

"Then considered yourself paid in full. And for the record, I really did believe she was kidnapped."

"Sure, you did," Jonathan lifted the collar of his coat, blocking the chill. "I've done you a solid favor. Several, in fact. Now I require one or two in return."

"Not this time. You can't get to me without implicating yourself. I spoke to you in confidence more than thirty years ago, no more than foolish talk at the time. The events that took place afterward were all by your own design, using your men."

"But you did pay, Ray. Remember that startup firm that went bust? The partner who vanished with your money? Those funds were deposited into an account of a known felon. Kidnapping laws classify the crime as a third-degree felony, a permanent mark on his public record. Not that you knew that or ever bothered finding out. Unfortunately, he's passed. A boating accident, I believe."

"You set me up?"

"Quite the contrary, I merely arranged an introduction. And before you attempt to lob additional allegations in my general direction, let me inform you that I'm well prepared. Keep in mind that it's not me who has a track record for taking his children from their mothers."

"I never did anything illegal to gain custody of Dean."

"Tell that to your friends on the jury."

"You're tied to every bit of it. If I go down, you're coming with me."

"Such a cliché, Ray, even for you. Nevertheless, any accusation made in your defense will seem no more than a personal vendetta. You take issue with my exposing your son's property tax evasion and more. Such envy, beginning with my rise in the political arena, whereas you're still practicing law. No evidence exists to implicate me, otherwise."

"Stonegate Center for Men," Henry reminds his father.

"You're quite right, Henry. I did forget about that. Indeed, there was that time we looked into the rehabilitation center after I disclosed your problem with substance abuse to Joyce."

"My *what*? You've compiled years of lies!"

"Quite effectively, wouldn't you say? If I remember correctly, that visit was recorded in the visitor's log. Oh, come on, why wouldn't I falsely document that and other incidences? I believe that particular notebook has been in storage for quite some time with other personal items, such as furnishings. Likely stored where monthly billing and cameras validate their date of entry. I'll have to look where. It's was all so long ago."

"All circumstantial evidence."

"Don't think I haven't got more. I can be a master of illusion."

"I still can't help you."

"What is the name she goes by now?" The senator looked up briefly to the clouded sky then snapped his fingers. "Samantha, am I right? Of course, I am. What would be worse, I wonder? Eating in the chow hall with other inmates or Dean finding out Samantha is his sister, and you've known all along?"

Jonathan scowled at the smirk on Henry's face. "Don't gloat, Henry, we're far from the finish line." Jonathan turned his attention back to Ray. "I don't see any reason for you to worry, Ray. Think of all this as encouragement."

"What do you need me to do?"

#

It's after eleven when headlights press through the drapes of the living area. I'm working on a business plan

194

inside my cabin, snuggled on the couch with my laptop and wrapped in a blanket with Bodie at my feet. Mama is tucked in cozily in her bedroom and has been sleeping soundly for well over an hour.

I'm keeping company with one of my favorite labels of Cabernet Sauvignon from Napa Valley. An overpriced bottle only Darien would send me. There's music, "Gloria in Excelsis Deo," streaming softly through the Bluetooth speaker on the counter. The fireplace is working mightily in conjunction with the thermostat to keep us warm, but I can't shake the chill clinging to my bones.

I think nothing of the headlights until I hear the sound of a vehicle pulling up close to the cabin. And not just any car. It's a big one. I don't realize I'm holding my breath until I hear the light tapping on the door. I'm not afraid for reasons most women would be at this time of night, I'm scared because I know who it is. Dean Sterling.

It's snowing, and there're small crystal-like snowflakes in his hair. God help me if I'm not captivated by the lone soft, white flake on his eyelashes. At first, we stand staring at one another, silently arguing. He's devastatingly good-looking, standing valiantly at my door, wearing mixed emotions. I'm so turned on I can't think to speak.

Briskly, he steps forward, and I step back. He closes the door behind him, and we repeat these steps like a dance until he backs me into the wall. He inches closer. There's nothing I can do but latch on to him.

We stumble into the end table, knocking over a lamp. His breath is hot against my neck. His teeth scrape my skin, forcing me to suck in an audible, ragged breath. Then he kisses me. There's nothing soft or sweet about his kiss. It's

195

steeped with both anger and passion, igniting me—everywhere. It's a full-on, open-mouthed, sexual kiss, and I love it.

We're backing and bumping into every obstacle in our path to my bedroom. His jacket is discarded and thrown somewhere along the way. As we cross the threshold into my room, he roughly yanks his shirt over his head. There's pounding in my ears from the blood surging through my body as he lifts me. I wrap my legs around his waist. One step. Two. Then he lays me on the bed, covering my body with his, determined to make us one.

My body melts into his, like wax to a flame. It feels so right to have the weight of this man on me, but I need more, need the power of him inside me. I reach between us, reach for the button of his jeans, then rake my fingernail against the zipper and hear him groan. He lifts his hips, helping with my task, and I feel the undeniable intensity of his desire.

His hands are moving now. All over me. Everywhere. The sensation rocks my head backward, engulfing my senses, robbing my worries. *Wait! Mama! Noooo! Stop thinking, it's fine.* My mother can sleep through a hurricane. Besides, there's a noisy space heater in her room she finds comforting. *And Bodie?* He's sleeping on the sofa. Everything is fine. But it's too late, Dean felt my brief freeze-up and stops. I could cry.

I rise enough to lift the ivory, V-neck sweater over my head and feel dark hair fall past my shoulders and down to the mid center of my back. His eyes glaze over. *It's on.* He's back on me with a vengeance, taking his aggressions out on my leggings, or more accurately the removal of them.

196

I bite my lip to keep from smiling when he grazes my panties with fingertips. His hands are made for chopping wood and saving lives, not silk. *Oh, my God!* Correction, his hands are made precisely for this. I gasp at the promise of those hands.

I'm completely naked beneath him, and we are yet to speak a word to one another. There's nothing to separate us but his jeans, and the friction there is mind-blowing, but they need to go. Before I know it, his mouth is on mine. His tongue finds mine as his hands tangle in my hair, holding me close. I crave more, crave every flavor of him.

Finally, he whispers my name, but nothing more. We're moving slower now. Dean's taking his time with every touch over my body. When his mouth moves to my breast and closes around it, I pant for air. A single, whisper-soft lick sends a bolt of pleasure ricocheting through my body.

Hips grazing hips, his mouth ghosts over mine. I push at his jeans, force them as far as I can reach before he lifts once more and does the rest himself. My heart's exploding to the rhythmic sound of our murmurs. He spreads my legs and sinks between my thighs. We're so close. He looks at me, silently begging for consent. *Is he crazy?* I am on fire.

I rock against him. Dean rises enough to kiss and slide into me all at once in one very sure, very wet move. For a heartbeat, we hold, savoring the moment before my breath catches when he begins to move inside me in a slow, arduous rhythm. We move together, rising then falling—the higher the high, the lower the low, with emotions mounting.

I don't even care who can hear or if they can. I cry out. Louder, I moan. He thrusts deeper. Movements become a blur. Our bodies explode.

Tangled around him, I listen to the beating of his heart thumping rapidly inside his chest. All I can think is, *please stay*. What we've just done was beautiful. But also, tragic.

His passion arrived unannounced and ended explosively, but he remains silent, unable to talk to me, to whisper the things lovers do. I want to pull the sheet over our heads and stay as we are. Together, hiding from the world. If only for the night.

Above my hip, at the small of my back, he's slowly caressing me, featherlight. I want to roll him over, crawl the length of his body, and do it all over again. Slower this time, forcing his surrender. I want more. Him. Again. Already.

Somehow, I have to reach him through this cold, winter night. As if in slow motion, Dean sits up, throwing his legs over the edge of the bed as he might stand. I lift my hand to stroke his back and feel him shudder. He's torn.

Dean looks over his shoulder at me, then gently rubs his thumb across my cheek, just under my eye. He tries smiling but can't. Suddenly, I'm watching him dress. I can't help it, I feel so rejected. The weight of the moment hits me hard. I don't want him to see me cry, so I get up, reach for a robe and cover myself. I look at him one last time before leaving the room for him to finish in peace.

My heart is broken.

I scold myself to stop it. *It's a start.* Even still, I can't bear to watch him walk through the door. I don't want to hear the sound of his engine come to life and then fade as it moves in a direction away from me. Instead, I go to the bathroom and turn the knob in the shower to hot. Under the spray, I close my eyes. When the water begins to run cold, I

turn it off. Reaching for a towel and stepping out, I know.
He's gone.

CHAPTER SEVENTEEN

"You're telling me he showed up late at night, stripped you naked, had sex with you, then left without saying a single word?"

"You make it sound like a bootie call," I respond, chewing. Sam arches a brow. "Shut up," I add, tossing an unopened, small cup of strawberry jelly at her.

We're at a café for breakfast after Sam dropped Ava and Colby by school and in the wake of my…I don't even know what to call last night. The café is in walking distance from the lodge where Mama and I are staying, and it's my new favorite place. Everything piled on my plate is deliciously comforting. For the first time in days, I have a healthy appetite. I groan, relishing in the indulgence while resenting my subconscious' nagging need to find a treadmill once we're done.

The café, much like the entire town, is decorated for the holiday season. It's no longer snowing, and the sun is out.

It's a beautiful morning, though cold. Through the window I notice long icicles, dripping at the sharp tips. The sun's reflection, the ice, and glass cast a rainbow prism on the wall above Sam's head. I laugh. *How perfect!*

Sam and I are at one of few tables occupied, so Mama opts to sit at a small table for two behind us to doodle in her spread-out sketchpad. Winter in town differs drastically from summer. For the most part, there are mainly locals now, minus those traveling through on their way to the slopes. Monarch, near Salida, isn't far south. Cooper, near Leadville, is also within an hour and north. A bit further and along the I-70 corridor are the bigger ones: Copper, Vail, Beaver Creek to the west with Breckenridge and Keystone to the east.

"How do you feel about it? You're okay?"

"I wasn't, not after he left. It was all so…amazing. Then sad."

"On a scale of one to X-rated, how amazing?"

"What are you, twelve?"

"Totally, which means I require details."

I flashback to last night and blush. "Forget it, and you really are twelve sometimes, you know?"

"What we are is thirty-something, and I need to live vicariously through you now that you have a sex life."

"I don't have a sex life. It was one time. *Ugh*, I was pretty easy…so very, 'hey, let's have sex before we rush into dating.'"

"Right. You've been together for seven months, you're such a slut."

"Known him for seven months, big difference."

"Trust me, you now have a sex life. He's waiting for you to make the next move. You should try sexting him."

"You want me to sex text, Dean? *Uhm*, no. Is that what you do?" I ask, jokingly. "Sext?"

"With men? Oh, yeah, I can see it now. I get a dick pic from a guy, and it's no different than when Deacon brings a dead squirrel in the house. They're both so proud, but I'm not touching it."

I laugh. *God, I missed her*. I reach across our little table and cover her hand with mine. "I'm sorry I left. I'll never do it again, and won't let you either. You're my Thelma."

"Why do you get to be Louise?"

"She had brown hair."

"Oh. Good point." Sam takes a sip of her coffee ridiculously diluted from the amount of creamer she uses. "You know what that mountain means to him, his house, the creek…all of it. It won't count until you go to him, until you go there."

#

Sam was right, and because she was, I'm driving with Mama to Cottonwood Creek Expeditions to find Dean. It's late enough in the afternoon that I hope to see Colby too. It gets dark earlier now. The sun is setting, and it's only 4:50 p.m. There's little to no chance Dean will be out on a snowmobile at this time of day.

At the turn, I have the impulse to drive on. I didn't plan to drive to the exact place I left the letter, but I'm here just

202

the same. There it is. A message, although it's not the one I left. This envelope is the size of a greeting card and is red. It, too, is weighed down by a small rock.

"Wait here," I say to my mother, and hop out of my SUV. At the edge of the road, I use my thumbnail to split the envelope open under the seal. Inside is a card. *Merry Christmas*, I read on it's cover. When I open it, a folded piece of paper falls out. Of course, he's too smart to handwrite anything. It's typed and printed in black and white.

Hello, Interested. It's okay for you to call me Killer, and you're correct, I do know who you are. But you're wrong about following you, that wasn't me. As for the friend of yours, my condolences. Some messages are meant to be bolder than others.

Why him and not you? Simple, I don't kill women. Or, at least - not yet.

When I return is the question. But when I do, please take your own advice. Be ready.

Sincerely,
Killer

#

Dean's house, the office building with Jenna's apartment above, the cabins, the workshop and more, are all strung with an array of colorful Christmas lights. It's charming and cozy with the white snow and the deep green of pines that surround every structure on the premises, including the newest addition: Sam's bear cub enclosure. I have no doubt it will be used for many animals in days, months and years to come, but for now, it's empty. Sam had mentioned earlier they released the cubs in late October.

Pulling further in, I see something else that makes my heart skip a beat. Colby. She's alone and in the midst of karate-chopping a snowman in half. With her leg mid-air, she freezes, seeing my car. I don't have time to pull into the driveway to park before she beelines toward me. I have no choice but to stop and get out. She leaps into my arms and wraps her little body tightly around me.

Hugging her, I look up to see Dean with Jenna on the porch watching us. The warm glow of light from the house behind them makes me yearn for my camera. Jenna pats Dean on the arm then retreats to her place with a simple yet sweet wave for me. Dean treks his way toward my car, helping Mama out and escorts her inside, leaving me with Colby. I have some quick making up to do.

I lift the tailgate and reach for a small box then hand it to her. Her eyes widen in surprise. "It's not Christmas yet," she says.

"It's not for Christmas. Open it."

Inside the cardboard box, there is a silver necklace. With it, there's an assortment of ten bullet shaped healing pointed Chakra pendants—aka crystals. Every stone is a different color. If she chooses, she can swap the pendants daily to suit

204

her mood. This gift appears to be the jackpot of all gifts, and I'm rewarded with a sloppy kiss on the cheek.

"While I was in Washington, I visited a place called Crystal Mountain. I got these for you in a gift shop there."

Inside, Dean is leaning against the counter in the kitchen while Mama closely inspects all the photographs held on the fridge by magnets. Colby pulls me to the family room to see the Christmas tree. It's massive, smells wonderful, and is brightly lit with hundreds of small twinkling lights. I feel a pang in my chest for missing out on the decorating.

It's apparent either Jenna or Nana Sterling have helped, the house isn't only festive, it's beautiful. It doesn't hurt that there's a crackling fire in the fireplace. Colby calls for Rutger, her imaginary dog, to join us while I continue to glance around. It's all so picturesque.

From close behind, I hear Dean approach. "Is your mother okay if we leave her and Colby alone for a few minutes?"

"Yes, she knows right from wrong. She won't venture out alone. Other than not having too much to say, there's nothing overly wrong with her that I can see. Why?"

"Come with me." He takes my hand and leads me to the staircase. Upstairs, we enter his room where he leaves the door open.

"Your mom…she's pretty."

"You should tell her that," I suggest, gently. He smiles. "We're talking now?"

"About that. Last night…I didn't go there for *that*."

"I know."

"When I saw you…and things…it just happened."

He's having trouble forming his thoughts into words, so I step closer and brush my fingers above his eye, over his brow. "I was there, I know."

"I really wasn't expecting…"

"Dean, I know," I say for the third time.

"Are you staying or passing through?"

"I want to stay."

"What about work? Your condo in Austin?"

"I'm working on an idea, and my condo's under contract. The couple buying it hope to close next week."

He bends enough that I think he's going to kiss me but instead presses his mouth to my neck. There's instant heat between us. It's mind-blowing how much I want to close the door and strip him down. "You've been busy." He sighs, breathing against my skin. "Every day you were gone, a little more of me died inside."

I make him look at me, lifting his eyes to mine with a hand on each side of his head. "I love you," I whisper.

His eyes close while his chest expands, filling with air, holding on to the moment. "Then I'll go with you," he responds just as softly.

"Where?"

"To get your things. You're coming here to be with us."

"Into my old cabin?"

"No. There's an empty room next to Colby's for your mom."

"What about me? Where do I go?" I ask, flirtatiously, arching a brow. He grabs me and hauls me forcefully against him, and I can't help but squeal. Wide-eyed, we both look at one another and laugh, wondering how we'll explain that to the two waiting for us downstairs. "Can I just say I love that you have a fireplace in your bedroom?"

"I know last night wasn't perfect—"

I shush him by placing my index finger against his lips. "It was really, *really* perfect." And I know he grasps my meaning. I kiss him, only a peck, and pull away. "The sooner we go…"

The next thing I know, I'm being yanked once again, this time to gather our crew to move us from town to the mountain. I halt, remembering. "Wait. I have to show you something first." From the pocket of my coat, I pull it out and hand Dean the red envelope.

#

"Who was that?" TC asked, suspicious of the man in a thin raincoat and khaki hiking pants—the convertible kind that zips off at the knees. Odd for the time of year and biting temperature. In Drew's absence, TC had been helping Samantha regularly. There was never a shortage of work with close to thirty horses and whatever else Sam routinely took in to nurse back to health.

"No clue," Sam answered, unconcerned. "Just another browser-by asking when we'll open."

"Strange time of year to ask that," TC added, lifting his hand to indicate the area around them covered by a white blanket of snow. "He say anything else?"

"Asked about hunting. Seemed interested in finding out if this was also private property."

"Also?"

"I'm just repeating. Why so many questions? I get this stuff all the time."

"About hunting?"

"Well, no, but—"

"He say anything about what he was hunting?"

"He did, actually. Friendly guy. When I mentioned I was an animal paramour not fond of hunting, he got chatty. Apparently, there are five animals you can hunt around here in the winter, and his interests lean toward mountain lions. It was hard, but I managed to be modest with my judgment. Still, I let him know my opinion."

"Which is?"

"They're hunted for recreation, for sport, and for trophies."

"Not always. Rancher's livestock is lost, pets disappear, people become afraid."

"Yeah, the power of the human imagination. Have you ever wondered if maybe that mindset is really just basic envy?"

"How so?"

"Because mountain lions yield to few? I'm not denying aggressive behaviors. What wouldn't be when being hunted right out of their own environment? You live here, TC. You're Search and Rescue, how many people do you know who have been attacked?"

"Personally? None. Not saying it doesn't happen, because it does."

"It does. I agree. And still, your chances of being struck by lightning are greater."

"That saying always makes me laugh, and as much as I enjoy your advocacy for animals, this time you're mistaken. Mountain lions attack. Bikers. Climbers. Other animals. It happens and more often than lightning strikes."

"*Hmm*. Okay, I'm not the kind of person who never changes her mind. Just don't ever let me see one hanging above your mantle."

"He wasn't dressed right," TC said, his attention jumping back to where they started. "It's early. We usually don't get hit so soon, but the storm we just got and the one on the way can paralyze hard-hit areas. Any hunter going out in that should be prepared for whatever nature brings."

"He struck me as the type to be prepared. I would have been suspicious, otherwise. Wait a minute! Is that what this is about? Has something happened?"

"No more than usual," TC answered, as he turned, looking in the direction the man had driven. TC knew he wouldn't get much further. Cottonwood Pass was closed at the Avalanche Trailhead. The movement opened TC's coat wide enough for Sam to see the Ka-Bar Knife strapped to his belt and the Pentax binoculars around his neck.

Sam eyed TC skeptically. "What's with all that garb?"

"That's *my* point, I'm always prepared. Alright, you win. Something has happened, but I'd appreciate you not mention it to Dean."

"Dean doesn't know?"

"He knows, but he wouldn't appreciate me telling you. And, Sam, with Ryan back…I know you two are tight, but maybe keep this to yourself until we have a chance to look into it."

"If you're asking me not to run my mouth, I won't, but I won't lie either. If she asks, I'll tell. What's happened?"

"Before the storm came through it was nice. You know, you were here. That's the thing about winters in the Arkansas Valley, one day it's sunny and sixty and the next we've got ice and road closures. Anyway, a woman was attacked."

"By a mountain lion?" Sam asked, adjusting the front closure of the twin buckle while rugging—blanketing—a quarter horse to protect from the harsh wind and temperature.

"No, by a man. She was taken from an RV campsite then stripped and strangled."

"She was killed?"

"No. We don't know if he decided against killing her or ran out of time. The group she was with went searching for her pretty quickly after she disappeared. She'd been gone only about twenty minutes from where they were camped."

"What kind of message is that?

"If I had to guess…probably 'get out while you can.' I didn't mean to frighten you."

"You haven't. I'm not new to this rodeo."

"What's that supposed to mean?"

"Long story. Some other time."

"That reminds me. I wanted to ask if you'd like to have dinner sometime?"

"With you? Like a date?"

"A date to dinner, yes."

"No to the date, but sure to dinner."

CHAPTER EIGHTEEN

"Alicia, my name is Jenna Sterling, and this is my friend, Garrett Dillon. Thank you for meeting us here, it's my favorite place to grab coffee and doggie treats for my friends." Jenna tried not staring at the colorful markings along Alicia's neck, but her eyes kept diverting between them and Alicia's red-rimmed and blackened eye.

They were seated in a coffee shop during the quiet time between breakfast and lunch with few customers or waitstaff to disturb them. Alicia and Andrew Paschke had cautiously accepted the invitation arranged by Brittany Saben, who had delicately suggested they talk after treating Alicia for her injuries.

It was also Brittany who reluctantly determined Jenna was the better of the two, between Dean and Jenna, considering the specific ordeal Alicia had survived. Garrett, however, had insisted at the last-minute Jenna not go alone and sat beside her, across from the Paschkes.

"As you can see, my wife…she's been through a lot. I want to take her and go home, but she insisted we do this first."

"I understand and do appreciate it. Where's home?" Jenna asked.

"Colorado Springs," Alicia answered, finding her voice. It was raw but forceful, clear she didn't want anyone speaking for her. She eyed Garrett, suspicious of every new encounter with every man since her attack.

"Colby, my niece, she loves Cheyenne Mountain Zoo," Jenna said, hoping to familiarize herself with them.

"We met there," Andrew stated. "Not at the zoo, but close. We both worked at the Broadmoor at the base of Cheyenne Mountain. We were in high school. She was westside, and I was a northeast kid who struck gold when I met her."

"Not so lucky now, huh?" Alicia attempted to joke, but it fell flat as the table grew quiet. "When I'm alone, I can hardly move, and not because I think he'll get me again, but because my muscles seize up. It's as if my body is struggling to recover. Then I look in the mirror and the bruises I see…I know they'll get worse in days to come."

"Nothing is broken?"

"No bones, if that's what you mean."

"I'm very sorry, Alicia. The incident took place extremely close to where I have a home and business with my cousin, Dean Sterling. There has been a string of events that we're trying to piece together to catch whoever is responsible."

"We've already talked to the police," Andrew stated.

"Yes, well, some things have occurred that don't appear to be tied to one another according to the authorities. We believe they are. I don't want to make you uncomfortable, so please stop me if anything I ask is too much. Did you give a description of him?"

"No. Nothing other than his build, which is pretty characteristic for almost every man I know. He was wearing a mask. A winter one that covered everything except his eyes, the kind skiers wear."

"Anything you can say about his eyes? Anything distinct."

"No, he had sunglasses on. Black ones."

"Did he say anything to you?"

"Yes, he said that he told her he didn't kill women. To consider myself lucky."

#

"M'kay listen, guys. I almost died today!" Colby starts, dramatically. "Daddy plowed for Ava and me to ride our bikes, right? We're riding super-fast and Ava skids and makes this pile of dirty snow like a big ol' slushy mound. So, I'm thinking...I'm gonna do that too 'cuz it would make a good jump, and we're practicing for our bike show."

"For you guys," Ava explains to her mother.

"But then I decided to pop a wheelie instead. And...*splat*! I was seein' stars! I looked away for like a second—" she lifts her index finger and waves it "—to see if Ava was watchin' and didn't see the tree, like at all. So, my helmet saved my life for real, but I still smashed my face. That's how I got this," Colby finishes, pointing at the cherry-burn on her chin.

"I bet that's how bugs feel," Ava adds.

"Yeah! And guess what else?" Colby asks everyone, with her arms working overtime. "I didn't cuss, not even one friggin' time!"

"*Ohhh* this my shit," Mama sings from the couch. *Thank you, Gwen Stefani!*

"Alright, you two, up to bed or this sleepover isn't happening," Sam says, and wraps her arms around both little people, giving them smacking kisses all over their faces.

We're at Dean's, lounging in the living room and swapping stories. Technically, I live here now too. Darien is visiting, adding to our girl's night, while Dean's at a SAR meeting. We've had pizza and are drinking wine in front of the fireplace. To Colby and Ava's delight, Sam poured them apple juice in wine glasses matching ours.

"What about the two of you?" Sam asks, once the girls are upstairs. "Any stories you're as profoundly proud of?"

"Lots," Darien says, and Sam rolls her eyes.

"High School," I say, responding to Darien. It's the first thing that came to mind. "Tell us one from high school."

"Easy." Darien takes a sip of the wine she brought from a resort she enjoys in Breckenridge. "I grew up in a small suburb in Denver called Capitol Hill."

"Of course, you did," Sam murmured.

"As I was saying," Darien continued, ignoring Sam. "I was in art and marketing, no surprise there. For an assignment, I had to design the wrestling team's uniforms. If you don't know, they're tight and suspender-like, so any

214

verbiage on the back is either small or abbreviated. I should rewind and preface all of this by admitting there was a guy. His name was Dave Gardner. We dated for a hot minute, and after I broke up with him, he told the entire team I had sex with him. Needless to say, I was the topic of gossip for months."

"Was he the one?" I ask, earning a spark of interest from Sam, not that she's overly obvious about it.

"No. That one was Robert."

"So, you do like men," Sam more states as if she's bored and more to herself than to us.

"She's flexible," I add, and give Sam a look to knock it off.

"I wouldn't say that. Anyhow, the big reveal of the new uniforms was during a match to see if they'd make State. The guys unzipped their jackets and took to the mat for warm-ups. As they jogged in circles in the middle of the mat, the audience got a glimpse. The backs of the uniforms were abbreviated for Capital Hill, except I left out the H. So, everyone saw C-MEN."

"Semen! I repeat a few seconds later, slow to the party. "You're awful," I say, laughing. "Did you get in trouble?"

"Nope. Unfortunately, they ended up winning and then winning State. Not only did they think it was funny, they thought they were some sort of good luck charms. The coaches, on the other hand, never asked me to design uniforms again. What about you? Any high school memories you're particularly proud of?"

"I'll take a hard pass on that," I say, because I've got nothing to say about my life in Silver Valley. Other than bolting five minutes after graduation.

215

"Don't look at me," Sam offers, "we'll be here all night."

I hear the buzzer and jump to my feet to swap laundry from the washer to the dryer. The laundry room is directly off the kitchen and also dark. The light switch is poorly placed by the door leading to the garage, and it's no secret I dislike dark rooms. Out of habit, I move quickly to flip the switch. Two steps into my launch, I'm roughly knocked over.

I scream, kicking and slapping against a stronger body that has tripped over me and was hiding behind the laundry room door. Adrenaline floods my system, pumping like it's trying to escape. In the darkness, my eyes are wide with fear. It's all so fast, and already I can taste the saliva thickening in my throat and feel the sweat trickling down my back.

His hand covers my mouth, trapping the air inside. My own hands are trembling as I reach to scratch at the dark shape latching onto me. I'm punched in the stomach and feel my fingers curl into a fist, digging into my palm as oxygen floods in and out of my lungs. My terror is like a knife slowly twisting into my gut.

Vaguely, I hear her. Samantha. She's with me, inside the small room and has jumped onto his back, slamming her fists furiously into the man on top of me. In the blunder of flight and fight, there's screaming, and then a loud pop—a firecracker but flatter—that echoes through the house before everything goes eerily still.

It's deafening, responsible for my slight disorientation. I can't hear anything beyond the ringing in my ears. It's so painful that I have momentarily forgotten what's happening. Until I look up.

In the doorway, with the kitchen light silhouetting around her like a halo, Darien is standing with her arm extended, holding a handgun. I don't have time to register why my friend has possession of a Smith & Wesson .38 Special J-Frame Revolver. I only know those specifics because, with a past like mine, I've been tempted a time or two and have done my research.

The weight of the monster on top of me lightens. As Darien stands trembling and paralyzed, he scrambles away, slipping on blood. He's clutching his leg below the knee, near the calf. He moves quickly with a heavy limp through the garage door and further away into the darkened woods.

#

Two days after the break-in, and many closed-door conversations with Sam, Jenna, Darien, TC, Garrett, and Dean later, I'm finally alone. The living and office quarters of the property are locked up and as secure as Camp David. No one is getting through the front and certainly not out. After a heated debate, Dean has reluctantly conceded to allow me to sit on the back porch to get some fresh air and sunlight. He gets how therapeutic listening to the creek can be.

I've endured forty-eight hours of discussions on everything from how a wounded man simply vanishes without a trace to Sam and I taking the girls to Denver. The worst of it was the argument between Sam and, well, pretty much all of them regarding guns. It took me jumping in

217

rather emphatically to remind everyone how Samantha had lost Jordan. In hindsight, Sam had listened. In the end, she'd even agreed that had it not been for Darien's gun, neither of us might not be here at all.

The blood trail, or lack thereof, disappeared no more than three hundred feet into the thickest part of the woods behind the house. The place Colby and Ava call the "thicket" where trees and brush are abundant. Although we hope only temporarily, it's disheartening to know they've lost that fortress as their prized place to play and hide.

I look up, and for one transcendent minute, I forget everything else. I laugh because a mountain bluebird is visiting again, drawing me from my trance. Dean and I like to banter over this little guy who is related to the western bluebird which is more commonly seen in these parts. This bird enjoys the feed I leave out, and I tease Dean that he's here because of Dean's love for the color blue. I adore this bird because like Darien, he's out of place here and belongs in wider, open spaces. And because he does, I've named him Dee.

Dee is a medium-sized bird with a light underbelly and black eyes. He's brightly blue, almost turquoise, and likes to show off. He swoops by then glides across the creek an inch above the water then soars upward over the bank and up. I follow his flight when my eyes land on a dark-haired woman. She's standing directly across the creek on the ledge of Sterling Point. *Holy Mother of all that is holy!*

It's possible I'm still disoriented, or better yet, having a phenomenal daydream. She's both tragically and beautifully surreal, and surreal because it's her. Dean's mother.

I know because...I actually have no idea how I know, I just do. There's little doubt, and I'm already up and ready to cross the creek, eager to go to her. Except I can't. If I take even one step off this deck, Dean will be out here in a flash. The same way I know that, is how I know it's her. There are no explanations other than instinct, and I trust mine.

There's also the matter of the creek. If I try to cross, I'll freeze to death. Even if that veers toward the melodramatic, I have no desire crossing where it's icy in spots. My mind jumps back to Dean. I'm amazed he's not hyperaware of another presence on his property and in such close proximity.

She's moving. I don't have to go to her because she's coming to me. I'm startled, hoping she's not actually going to try and cross the water. *And, hello?* How on earth does Dean and TC not know there's movement other than mine or Bodie's? One glance to the large picture window and there he is, looking through. Dean is locked into the figure approaching the creek on the opposite side of us.

"She's chosen you," Dean says a moment later. He's stepped out and is standing by the door, no further. It's a colossal, life-changing event for him, yet he's remarkably composed.

"Blue," I say going to him and placing my hands flat against his chest. "This is your moment, honey, not mine. Go meet her."

His gaze slices through me, and I feel the heat surge through my veins, setting my blood to boil. It's like this now. Whenever he looks at me, despite every circumstance and variable, I want him. Which is ludicrous, considering the time and place.

219

Suddenly, as if I've snapped my fingers near his face, Dean is over the shock. He's walking across the sprawling deck to the edge and rests one hand on top of the railing. With his other hand, he's pointing. He draws an invisible half circle, welcoming her to come around and through the front gate.

Ten minutes later, while Mama and Colby watch reruns of the CMA's, a black Sedan pulls through the front gates that Dean has opened. Dean's mother—presumably—is not alone. There's a tall and striking man with a mix of silver and jet-black hair opening the passenger door for her. He's wearing jeans and a steel grey sweater.

My breath catches. It's no longer basic instincts at work. From where I stand, much closer now, it's crystal clear. It's irrefutable, she is Dean's birth mother and not just because Colby looks so much like her, he does too. If I had to guess, Dean is thinking the same. And so much more. They're facing one another, no more than ten feet apart, in quiet awe.

Dean holds out his hand, a soundless request for me to join him. I do. Once I'm beside him, clasping his hand, the taller man steps forward to shake our hands. "My name is Luke Walker." Dean grips this man's hand and keeps it firmly inside his own. "I'm of the Weeminuche of Ignacio."

Over the months—before, during, and after—my hiatus, I've read everything I can get my hands on regarding Native Americans in the Rocky Mountain region. So much of it is beyond my scope, but I do recall a bit. Luke is part of a modern-day tribe currently called the Southern Utes who are mostly located north of the San Juan River here in Colorado.

"I've been married to Alameda Jey for twenty-seven years. We call her Jey." It's Luke's thoughtful effort for introductions. Luke steps aside as Dean and Jey timidly shake hands. The apprehension vanishes the instant they touch, and Jey is quick to pull Dean down to her height and into a fierce hug.

"We live near the water of Lake Capote, outside of Pagosa Springs," she finally says, her voice somewhat shaken. She's anxious and uncertain where to begin, so she goes with what's easy. "Luke's in software development, but also with the Tribal Natural Resources Administrative Branch. We're here to help you."

We all turn at the sound of the front door slamming behind a hasty exit. Jey takes one look at Colby before turning back to Dean. "There's plenty of time for all that later. Please, may I meet her?"

"Of course," he answers. "Come inside."

Inside the kitchen, we sit around the table, minus Mama who remains glued to the award show. It's times like these that remind me how easily children simplify a situation that could otherwise be awkward and difficult. Colby has effortlessly made her way to be the center of our attention. There are so many questions, so many unknowns, but for now, we're content.

Colby's rock collection, along with her pendants, are on full display on the table as she and Jey have a thorough discussion of each. Dean observes them carefully, and I watch him. Luke sits back, sipping coffee from a mug with a Denver Broncos logo stamped onto it. I smile at that because the mug is blue.

When Colby reaches for a burnished blackish-brown sedimentary rock, she lifts her eyes to meet Jey's and hands her the piece of coal. "I think Daddy knew I was gonna like rocks even before I was born."

"What makes you think that?" Jey asks, delighted by Colby.

"Because he named me Colby. My Nana Sterling told me it's Scandin...*something* from a place called Kol."

"It's sure pretty. Your name and the rock."

"What's your name mean?" Colby asks.

"Well, I'm lucky, I have two names. My friends and family call me Jey, but Alameda Jey is my full name." She smiles at Colby, then, "In my family—"

"Like your tribe?"

"Yes, exactly like that." Jey laughs. "Alameda means a grove of cottonwood, and Jey is what they used to call a blue crested bird, like a bluebird."

You've got to be kidding me!

CHAPTER NINETEEN

"I used to sit here for hours and watch them practice. You never saw one without the other," Brittany says, remembering Reece and Drew. It's the first thing she says after Sam and I find her sitting on the bleachers at the high school football field. We've sandwiched her between us, prepared to do and say whatever we need to get her to talk. That, and because it's cold.

We rarely see Reece. Garrett makes daily efforts, but other than Garrett and the arguments they have, only Dean is able to get close. Reece's grief is not in waves. The relentless surge continues to pull him under. When I saw him last, coming out of the store while I was going in, he was no more than an empty shell. He hadn't noticed me, let alone bothered lifting his head once I called his name.

Pushing that memory aside, I want to hug Brittany. She looks so lost and forlorn. I'm ashamed to admit that I'm also questioning the similarity of her heartbreak compared to theirs. Reece is alive, losing him can't be anything close to Reece's loss of his brother, or equivalent to Samantha losing Jordan. I chew on the inside of my mouth, reprimanding myself. That's unfair and who am I to measure someone else's pain?

"Do you know what we were doing when the Sherriff called looking for Reece and Garrett to tell them about the accident?" Brittany asks. I do know, but don't say out loud. We were all doing it together. Building an enclosure for bear cubs. "We were joking about how fast we were moving in together. He was teasing me about a shotgun wedding, saying that's what I'd want next."

"I definitely can't say from experience, but I do sometimes think some of the people who are loved the most are treated the worst," I offer, lamely.

"Everyone's different. We carry grief in many ways, none matching the other," Sam, who hasn't said a word, finally says. "I've whispered a thousand words and cried a million tears, and still, I need more time."

"How will he get through it? How do you?"

"I pretend a lot. I've gotten very good at it while I quietly cope."

"All my things, most everything I have, is still there. In boxes."

"I can get your things," I tell her.

"No, I have to do it." Brittany stands, pushing her hands deeper into the pockets of her coat. "Thank you for finding me, and Sam...pretending to be okay when you're not is just another way you're proving how strong you really are."

224

#

He leaned against an Aspen tree, knotted with scars that Ava says look like eyes, watching the creek cut through the forest like a ribbon. The river always talks, always speaks to those who listen. And he was listening, waiting for the flowing wisdom to clear his conscious. It was time to go all in or walk away. Time to listen to the demands of his heart which required more, because the middle ground guilt was getting them nowhere.

"Boo," she whispered against his ear, sneaking up from behind. He smiled at the feel of her arms slipping around his waist. *She's mine*, he thought, his boldest prayer answered.

It wasn't any different for Jenna, wearing her guilt like an ugly scar that never went away. In subtle ways, she would make amends, but enough already. It was time for her to leave the 'what could have beens' behind and move on. Time to stop trying to talk herself into caring for a man she didn't love and be with the one she did. Time to tell Garrett it was never going to happen.

"Look there," TC said, pointing to six mid-sized pups taking turns peeping into the rotting Spruce's hollow trunk.

Resting her head on his shoulder, they watched the coyotes, better known in the area as prairie wolfs. "Did you ask Samantha out?"

"Yes," TC answered, feeling Jenna's breath against his neck as she sighed.

"Why do you do this to yourself?"

"Because I knew she would say no."

"What if she would have said yes?"

225

"Then I would have spent a little time doing what you always do."

"Being with someone else while thinking of you? You know the truth, I'm not with Garrett."

"Maybe not, or not anymore, but everyone in this town thinks you are, including Garrett."

"Only because he paints that pretty picture. It's not even his fault, really. People believe what's easy, and Garrett and I are fixtures in this town. Childhood sweethearts. If fault needs to be assigned, it's probably mine. I should have made it very clear I didn't come back for him after college, even if we haven't dated or touched since high school. He's my best friend and has been for as long as I can remember, but you're who I want."

TC turned, exchanging their spots, then pressed into Jenna leaning against the tree. "You shouldn't come out here by yourself. It's not safe."

"The only person who knows these woods better than I do is Dean. And he knows about us. I don't keep things from him, which means Ryan probably knows too. There're no secrets between those two, not anymore. He's on your side, by the way. Apparently, it doesn't matter that Garrett is his closest friend and someone we've known our whole lives. Dean wants me to tell him. He doesn't understand why I'm so private...so protective of this."

"Then what's the problem? Is it me?"

That TC even had to ask her, stung. "No, it's me. Garrett's like family, so good to us all, and then everything with Drew. The timing is horrible, and...I'm just...I hate knowing I'm going to hurt him," she explained, knowing there was more. So much more. "Let's get through

226

Christmas, and then I promise I will tell him. Please don't doubt me on this."

"There are times I wonder if my warped idea of our relationship is a result of overthinking or denial. You, Jenna Sterling, are either going to drive me crazy or kill me because it hurts loving you so much."

"How about we shoot for a better scenario like my making you blissfully happy, instead."

"The way you did the other night?" he asked, moving in closer. Just as quickly, he stepped away, placing distance between them. He heard it again, the sound. More snapping of twigs beneath boots, more slushing of snow beneath the weight of approaching steps. TC turned a half circle then exhaled, relaxing.

"Hey, TC…Jen," Garrett greeted both, his eyes darting between the two.

"Hey. Get that transfer case looked at?" TC asked, casually.

"Yeah, hole in the back just like you thought. Had to replace the whole damn thing. Used that guy over in Leadville you told me about. Appreciate the tip." Garrett crossed his arms over his chest. "Jen, I got your message earlier about grabbing lunch. Came by to see if it wasn't too late before catching a glimpse of you headed this way. You shouldn't walk out this far alone."

"Just told her the same," TC agreed.

"Well," she looked at TC first then Garrett, "now neither of you have to worry, because look…here you both are. And please, I know my surroundings and my limits. Besides, I saw TC headed this way and came after him to talk. Now that you're both here, I'll kill two birds with one stone."

227

TC eyed her suspiciously, wondering if she'd suddenly changed her mind and was going to tell Garrett everything. A conversation, he quickly realized he wanted no part of.

"Relax, both of you. I only need advice. Garrett, I'm sorry I have to ask. I know none of us are ready to talk about it, but we're at a point where I have no choice but to ask. Because you're his brother, and TC because you stepped in when…" Jenna stopped. It had been months, and the words were still too raw, too hard to say.

"It's okay, Jen," Garrett said. "You and Dean have done everything you can for us…for the family. Do what you have to do."

"It's more than filling a position for Drew, it's also Reece."

"Reece?"

"Is he coming back? Can he?" She raised her hand stopping them both from impending arguments. "Let me finish because if there's even the slightest bit of hope he's coming back, we'll wait. For however long it takes. As hard as it is to admit, if he's not coming back, if you don't think he ever will, we have to know."

"He'll be back," Garrett said, convincingly. "And until he can pull his weight like before, you can pull guys off my crew to help wherever they can. I can help, too."

"I know you would do that for us, and for Reece. Thank you. It's just that Reece…he's not easily replaced. As much as your heart is in the right place with your offer, Reece has remarkable experience and knowledge.

"I'm with Garrett on this," TC said. "It won't be today and maybe not tomorrow or even next month, but he'll be back. I can help as well. We'll make it work. But, listen, I need to run." Without being overly obvious, TC looked at Jenna. "You two enjoy your lunch."

She watched him go, felt the tug in her chest, and then turned to face Garrett. "I hate I had to even ask you any of that. We love Reece, please tell me you know that?"

"I don't ever second guess you, Jen." Garrett looked in the direction TC had gone, then to Jenna to see she was doing the same. "Everything okay? Did he say something to upset you?"

"Who?" Jenna asked, blinking. "TC? No, no, nothing like that. I was just thinking how quickly and how much things are changing and trying to figure out how to defuse all these setbacks without triggering more damage."

"This is where you and Dean are so much alike, almost to a fault. You carry too heavy of a load Jenna."

"Is there such a thing as loving or worrying for your people too much?" Jenna asked, sliding her arm through Garrett's as they began their walk back.

"No, I don't think there is. We're all doing our best adjusting to the changes. I'm starting to think that I've spent so much time making plans only to spend more time watching those plans fall apart."

Suddenly Jenna stopped walking and looked at Garrett curiously. "Garrett, why aren't you working?"

"It's lunchtime."

"No, it's after two."

"Does anyone ever get anything past you?" he asked, smiling. "Alright, alright. Having a little trouble with my guys, nothing to worry about."

"What kind of trouble?"

"The kind where I've got two crews and one didn't show up for work. Word on the street is there's a new hotshot builder in town, and my guys were presented with an opportunity they evidently couldn't pass up. Prescott Engineering, Construction and Project Management."

"That sonofabitch!" Jenna said, shaking her head. "Garrett, I'm so sorry."

"As I said, I'm not concerned. My best guys are loyal ones who come from a long line of woodsmen. I'll have a new team ready to roll within a few days. As for the suckers who left, good riddance. I owe Prescott for the favor. He took the deadweight off my hands."

"We should tell Dean."

"Already did. And, Jen…" Garrett hesitated. "I'd feel a whole lot better if you wouldn't wander out alone with TC anymore."

"That isn't a conversation for today."

"It needs to be. There's something about him that doesn't sit right."

#

"What are you doing here?"

Startled, Brittany jumped from the sound coming from the dark corner.

The house was unfinished but livable. A two-story passion project with a grand view of both Mount Princeton and Yale. Reece had worked on and around it for the past three years. Most of that time with help from his brothers.

Brittany reached for a lamp no longer there, then ran her hand along the wall and switched on the overhead light. Using his sleeve, Reece covered his eyes with his arm as bright light illuminated the room. She looked away from him, unable to look at the desolate man sitting in a chilly and dark house completely alone.

Her belongings that were once packed neatly into boxes were strewn everywhere. The coffee table was turned on its side and broken. The television was missing. Where it was once plugged in, there was now a hole through the drywall. On the counter there were several upright and knocked over bottles of whiskey and beer. One was shattered from rolling over the edge to the kitchen floor.

When she refused to answer, he followed with, "how'd you get in?" Brittany tossed her key at him, then watched as it bounced off his chest then landed on the wood floor. He never so much as flinched. Her eyes lifted, meeting his. There was a cut on his lip and bruising along his jaw. Another fight, she guessed. She'd heard about them.

"I have something to help you sleep, Reece, a few days-worth."

"Go away."

She turned away, closing her eyes briefly before assessing the mess of her personal items scattered around the house. She bent, picking up a medical journal and a copy of *Les Misérables*. Before she could reach for an empty box, Reece sprung from the chair. He charged her then pinned her against the wall.

"Get your hands off me," Brittany demanded, struggling against his grip. With her back pressed firmly against the wall, he held her tightly by the wrist above her head. Looking to the side, her eyes filled with stinging tears.

"I saw you with Logan Hollinger."

"With who?"

"I saw you."

"Go to hell, Reece." He tightened his hold on her arms. "Get—" breaking loose, she shoved him away "—your hands off me!" She quickly moved out of his reach, wiping her eyes and picked up the few things as she made her way to the door. "I'll come back to get the rest when you're not here."

At the door, she paused, noticing the framed photograph of them together on the end table. A picture that felt like it was taken only yesterday. She reached for it, but Reece beat her to it and flung it across the room. The frame shattered into a thousand irreplaceable pieces.

He watched her go, watched her run to her car and speed away. Sinking to his knees, Reece covered his face with his hands, finally letting go—inconsolable, bereft and shaking.

CHAPTER TWENTY

"Do you feel a connection with Jules?"

"I feel something," Samantha answers. "For her sake, I try really hard, but I worry sometimes it seems forced. It's not, it's just different."

"Like you're hurting her feelings?" I ask. "I doubt its anything you're doing. She wants to know everything and at the same time realizing how much she's missed."

"I'm trying to make more than thirty years up to her. It's impossible. I feel guilty because she lived a nightmare while I had a great life."

"She has no idea who your biological father is? You've asked?"

"I asked once. She said he was a tourist, but I sensed she was uncomfortable discussing it, so I let it drop. It was too soon to press."

"Sam, you need to press. Not only so you'll know but because it might be—"

- - -

"Related to my kidnapping? I know." Sam stirred creamer into her coffee, clanking the spoon against ceramic. We're back at the café, our favorite and frequent go-to after we drop the little people at school.

The roadside café is one of few places place we're able to go without significant concern regarding our whereabouts and safety. I, well both of us really, love the restaurant's slogan: *Keep Your Sunny Side Up!* This morning, and much to my dismay, I'm devouring a veggie omelet instead of my usual. Apparently, today my body requires the good stuff plus sprouts.

Sam nods towards a woman coming through the front door with a younger man, both of which are dressed entirely too professional for our little town. "It's like Darien in a blonde wig invading our sanctuary."

I roll my eyes and ignore them and Sam's dig. "You knew, right? I mean your parents did tell you that you were adopted?"

"Oh, yeah. We were an open family. We talked about everything."

"They're both gone?"

"Yes, they were a lot older. They tried getting pregnant on their own until she reached an age where it was no longer practical. After that, there was years of waiting and one heartbreak after another. Failed adoptions. Finally, they got me."

"She keeps looking over at us," I say, finally allowing the elegant woman sitting several tables away to win my interest. Samantha uses the opportunity to lift her head in their direction and smile. It's one of those 'may I help you' smiles that last only seconds before the woman looks away.

"Do you realize how many people ask me a day if I'm okay?" Sam asks, disregarding the woman and her companion. "Sometimes I think instead of my saying that I am, they'd just for once rather I say something else. Like, 'here I am, in a place I don't belong, with people I don't really know, trying to be someone I'm not.' It's true, I do miss myself...my old self, but this is my life now and where I belong. I was born here for God sake."

"Excuse me," the blonde says, approaching us. Without an invitation, she takes it upon herself to pull out a chair and sits at our table. "Sorry for the intrusion. This should only take a minute." *Hmm*, I think and know Sam is doing the same.

"Black BMW?" Sam asks her, surprising me.

"Correct."

"You're Colby's mother." Samantha turns to me. "I saw her pick Colby up a few times while you were away."

"Sarah Prescott," she offers, extending her hand. Neither Sam nor I budge. Instead, I sit back in my chair and glare. "That's my associate, Ben Lockhart." In sync once again, neither Sam nor I look to the man waiting at the table she's abandoned.

Sarah is dressed to the nines except for the black boots, and even they suggest extravagance. They're cowboy boots with a heel, and the first thing that comes to my mind is, *big deal, rich girl, I have expensive boots too.*

"You must be Ryan. My daughter talks of you incessantly."

"Colby," I correct. Although it's adolescent, I have trouble associating Colby Sterling to this woman. However, now is not the time for thin skin.

235

"As I said, *my* daughter."

"It's not your weekend."

"Buying our breakfast?" Sam proposes more than asks, interrupting the verbal volley.

"I'd be happy to." Sarah smiles at Sam then locks her condescending eyes on me. "I'm here on business but can assure you that I'll be seeing Colby."

It's easy to spot how Dean would have been attracted to her. Sarah's pretty, and while she's professionally so at the moment, I sense an alluring albeit mischievous side. She is precisely the kind of woman who uses her sexuality to get what she wants. The tips of her blonde hair are curling inward, feathering her cheekbones, set in a long and narrow face. Her blue eyes are striking, but that's not saying much, because it's now my absolute favorite color.

"I'm a bit of an oddball but am I the only one who finds this funny?" Sam asks, chewing. "I mean you're sitting here, unsolicited by the way, and why? For a catfight? I advise sticking with him instead." Sam point at Sarah's associate with her spoon. "Because if you're truly here on business, I suggest you mind yours."

"Why are you really here?" I ask.

"The mountains were calling. What better place to pursue fun, food, and fortune?"

"Got it. Planning on offering incentives then?"

"You're catching on. Contributions are effective and something I do hope you'll share. Interested in knowing more?"

"It was a prediction, not an endorsement," Sam explains.

"Presumptuous," I mutter, foolishly baiting her.

236

It seems to intrigue Sarah because she tilts her head and smiles assuredly. Her poise is admirable. "How so?"

"I was under the impression you need to confer with the board of trustees and the buzz around town is you're having trouble with variance and zoning. And come on, let's not pretend you've made any leeway cutting through the red tape up the pass. But I'm only referring to the land along the highway you're bidding for."

"Isn't there a meeting tonight?" Sam asks, jumping back in. "I'm sure I heard something about a meeting with trustees and the people of Buena Vista. I should go."

"You definitely should. You are now official "people" of BV," I add, air quoting.

"I just might. Anyhow, and ultimately, it's in the hands of the city commissioners, but then again many of them are locally born and bred."

"Precisely why I'm here. I intend to persuade." Sarah says, with so much snobbery I feel my stomach churn. She's completely unfazed by us.

"Interesting if not arrogant. If you accomplish that then maybe confident would be a better word. For now, let's agree it's an uphill battle, and I'm not convinced you're prepared for the resistance."

"Quite the contrary, we eat communities like this," Sarah glances at my plate "for breakfast." Sarah stands. "Give Dean my best," she adds, pushing her business card my direction. "And should you ever want to talk, here's my number."

He felt disconnected watching them through the window from the parking lot. Even the podcast on "Tales of Terror" streaming through the radio was boring him. What did he care about two convicted teenagers who broke into homes to kill families? *On second thought, not a bad idea.* He turned the nob, adjusting the volume as the narrator recounted the grisly story, as he watched Samantha and Ryan leave the restaurant.

#

It's December twenty-fifth, and I don't have to dream about it. I am living a white Christmas. It began snowing sometime overnight, and we've woken to the splendor of winter wonderland. There's something glorious about having such a brilliant view through the large bedroom window taking up the majority of the wall. I stare through it as I continue to laze in the comfort of a warm and cozy bed.

I can see the creek. It appears unmoving yet flows enthusiastically beneath a layer of ice, waiting for the sun. It reminds me of white glitter as I stare off to the snow covering the earth that's also anticipating rays of light to poke through the pines. It's as if God is presenting me with His optimism in a world that seems frozen because I worry incessantly for Dean and Jenna.

Fortunately, the house remains quiet. Although he checks on me and my whereabouts often, Bodie sleeps with Colby now, who is finally sleeping in her own room again. Mama stays up late doodling and listening to music—everything from Mozart to Jay-Z—and enjoys sleeping in. I savor these quiet moments before the house wakes. That is, of course, except for my lover who wakes before the crack of dawn every morning.

I do, however, hear running water and one stunning image rapidly replaces another while I forget about the snow and imagine Dean in the shower. Suddenly I muster energy I didn't have seconds ago and crawl out from beneath a mountain of blankets. The floor is cool against my bare feet as I tip-toe into the bathroom clouded with steam. Once I'm able to make him out through the fogging glass, I stop in my tracks.

Dean's hands are planted against the tile wall with his head slumped forward under the spray. I'm transfixed by the sight of him. My breath catches, watching the water cascade down the length of his body like a caress. I strip quickly and step into the shower with him. The hot water immediately beats over my head in hot rivulets. It takes only a second to get used to as I close my eyes while the heat soaks into my skin.

Dean cracks an eyelid and raises a brow, watching me. When he looks at me like this, my thoughts evaporate. Together, in the blissfully warm shower, it feels like we're standing under an everlasting waterfall in a place without worry. Slowly, I raise my hand to his chest and lean forward to kiss him. At the same moment, I feel his hands gliding over my slick body. This foggy illusion is now my reality.

In the aftermath of incredible sex, vivid images race through my mind: Pinned against the tile wall. Legs wrapped around his waist. Meeting and matching his every move. His mouth everywhere, teaching me the difference between intrusion and intimacy. Long, deep and lasting.

"Do I ever scare you?" Dean asks, breaking the spell. I look at him ten, twenty, maybe even thirty heart-pounding seconds before he continues. "You know, because of your past, does this ever frighten you?"

"You *never* scare me, Blue. I don't think of anything but us when we're together."

"If that's true, we can take this to the bed. Or, and this pains me to say, we get dressed and go downstairs before Colby realizes the sun is up and Santa ate all the cookies."

"I'll take curtain number one."

Laughing, Dean kisses my forehead. "Merry Christmas, baby."

I think about that for a moment and realize it's the first time I've ever celebrated or been with people I love on Christmas. "I know what I want!" I say with excitement.

"From Santa?"

"I want you to let me take your picture."

"Not naked."

"No, honey, not naked, *although*…" I joke, reaching for a towel just as I hear little feet and Bodie pad down the hallway.

The morning goes as expected with a lot of chaos and laughter. Santa has been good to Colby, and by mid-morning our small tribe has grown by eight. I insist Sam and Ava spend the day with us and with them comes Jules Jenson and Deacon. In addition to Jenna, Garrett and Nana Sterling, we've also invited Jey and Luke over.

Regrettably, we are missing Reece, who continues to choose isolation. TC, on the other hand, has been gone for close to a week. "Visiting family," Jenna revealed when I

240

asked. He'd left in a hurry, and because she looks unhappy, I speculate something has happened between them.

For a present, Colby made me a rock necklace of fishing line and small colorful pebbles. She gave her dad a garden stone with the words '*Love Lives Here*' painted across. We got Mama a karaoke machine, and Sam and Ava added to Mama's delight by giving her an electric guitar with '*MAMA*' foil stamped on the shoulder strap. I'm not sure if any of them even know her name, everyone calls her Mama. In return, Mama had drawn us all pictures.

When I notice a look pass between Dean and Jey, I wink at Luke. I snatch Ava up by swinging her over my shoulder then tug Colby away by her shirttail and whistle for Rutger, Bodie, and Deacon to follow. We join the others in the kitchen to an abundance of food. It doesn't escape my attention that when Sam goes to refill her coffee, she brushes her hand over Jules' shoulder as she passes.

Instead of returning to the table, Sam leans beside me at the counter. She drapes her arm around my shoulders, and I tilt my head against hers. We've both come so far from where we were only months before. At our best and worst, I believe with all my heart that Sam will always love me, save me, and guard me. Just as I will for her from any person or harm that befalls her. That is our gift to each other.

From where we are, I can hear Dean and Jey talking. "The old people still sustain the betrayal of the treaty," I hear Jey tell him. I have zero knowledge of this but am intrigued. "Approximately one-third of Colorado had been allotted for Utes and a reservation. Ouray was selected as principal chief at the time of the treat in 1868. Years later, and after the Meeker Incident, Congress insisted the Ute Nations be

241

forced north to a reservation here in the Sawatch Range. Otherwise, I imagine we would have settled elsewhere."

"That's how then…how *this* land is mine?"

"The Restoration Act, around 1937, I believe it was, returned over two-hundred thousand acres of land to the Southern Utes. The following year a vast amount more was returned to the Ute Mountain Ute Tribe. Your great grandfather Isaac's father was among six hundred Mouache Utes and Jicarilla Apaches that were attacked on the Arkansas River by Comanches, Cuampes, and Kiowas. Mouache Chief Delgadito was killed. Very few survived, your grandfather was one who did. The council honored him many years later with acreage on Sheep Mountain that was stolen by the government."

"There's so much I don't know," Dean admits.

"Maybe when you expand your family, you'll honor your grandfather by naming your son Isaac, should you have one."

I don't have time to digest what she's just said because the back door opens. Jenna covers her mouth with her hands and Garrett looks up, his eyes rich with emotion. It's Reece. He closes the door behind him as Colby runs and jumps into his arms. "A Christmas miracle," Sam whispers.

Unshaven and with an eye that looks to be infected, Reece carefully sets Colby down. At first glance, it's easy to see he's lost weight and I can smell the stench of last night's liquor on him. But, he's here, and that is *all* that matters. Hesitantly, he walks to Jenna and kneels beside her.

"I love you, boy. You know that, don't you?"

"I know, Jen. I love you, too. Merry Christmas."

I sense Dean behind me and look over my shoulder to smile at him. He's holding a small package. "You forgot one," he tells me. Samantha chuckles and hip checks me forward.

Carefully, I remove a shiny, red bow. Inside the small box is a set of keys. Confused, I look up. I already have keys to the house. "The vacant storefront next to the empty theater downtown? I bought it for you," he says. "Your work is inspiring, Ryan, it's only right you have a gallery to show it off."

I am lost for words. *How did he know?* Thankfully, Colby is pulling on my pant leg, demanding my attention. Her sidekick joins her, and Ava begins giggling. "*H-E-L-L-O?*" Colby draws out each letter of the word.

"Yes?" I ask, finally.

"Do you see it?" Colby asks. I cock my head, baffled. "Well?" she presses. I look to Dean for help, but he only grins. Then, I see it. The world as I know it stops. On the keyring is another ring—a vintage halo diamond set in rose gold. "Will you marry us?" Colby asks.

CHAPTER TWENTY-ONE

"Hi."

Startled, Samantha turned quickly. She eyed Darien in designer everything and choppy, copper hair. It had been a while since she'd last seen her, not that she was counting. "Hey, you're back."

"For a few days," Darien said. "Visiting Ryan."

"That all?"

"No, that's not all. Not that it's any of your business," Darien smiled, picking up the banter right where they'd left off.

"You're not really going to try to put her on assignment somewhere else, are you?"

"No, gatekeeper, I'm not. It's something else entirely."

"Is everything okay?"

"I hope so." Darien inhaled, hesitated. "Her Uncle…I mean her…Jim is looking for her."

"You didn't tell him where she is, did you?" Sam asked, receiving a glare. "Okay, okay, of course, you didn't." Sam turned. "Wait, you could've called, but instead, you came all this way. I hate admitting this, but you're a decent person, Darien Shay."

"The jury's still out on that. Anyway, what exactly are you trying to do?"

"Put up this dumb tent Ava got for Christmas that comes with a trillion parts and no instructions."

"Are you planning to camp in the living room of your spacious accommodations?"

Huffing, Samantha tossed the single aluminum pole aside. "Ava and Colby are having a sleepover at Nana Sterling's. I wanted to surprise them when they get back tomorrow. It's too dang cold to do it outside."

Darien smirked, noticing the silly yet adorably lit Christmas tree—somewhat slumping and unmistakably in its final days—in the corner. "Did you say dang? Really?"

"I cuss." Sam peeked from under the tent's footprint that she'd somehow mistaken for the rainfly. "A lot, actually."

"Sure, you do." Darien took the stakes from Sam and set them on the sofa. "This," Darien points at the heap before her, "is an exoskeleton pole structure. Whatever it is you're doing will never work." Darien chuckled. "And you're right, it's cold. Fucking miserable, if you ask me. "Sit." Darien pointed to the space on the couch beside the stakes. "And watch a true Coloradan show you how it's done."

"Don't you mean Coloradoan?"

Darien rolled her eyes, hand on hip. "I'm going to need wine for this." She peeled her jacket away then faced Sam. "By and large, when a place ends in "o" you add "an." The

245

only exception to the rule is if that place is of Spanish origin, and then you drop the "o" before adding the "an." Colorado is a Spanish word for the color red…you get my drift."

"Sometimes you remind me of Jordan," Sam announced, powerless to take back the words that flew from her mouth. "For the most part, you're nothing alike, but like her, you know something about everything. It's annoying."

"Is recognizing that hard for you?"

"It's just odd when and how things hit me. I was thinking about you earlier, wondering where you'd been. And no, I don't know why, but I was comparing parts of you to Jordan. Just little nonconsequential things. Then you appear out of nowhere, and I say something like I just did. It makes me wonder if that's how God sometimes answers questions. Does he just throw words into your mouth and you have no choice but to spit them out?"

"Interesting."

Sam watched as Darien finished putting the tent together in record time. She continued gawking as Darien pulled a throw from the sofa and an afghan from the chair. After that, several pillows were tossed in before Darien pointed to the inside of the tent. "What are you up to?"

"Get in."

"In there? With you? Shut up!" Adamant, Darien continued to point. "Alright, jeez, because this makes a ton of sense."

Once Sam was securely inside the tent, Darien closed the front door while shaking her head. For reasons unknown, Samantha had left it open which is how Darien had seen her fighting with the tent to begin with. With a quick sweep around the room, she turned off the overhead lights, including two dimly lit lamps, leaving only the Christmas tree on. She glanced around once more and then climbed into the tent, zipping them in.

"Did you remember marshmallows? Sam asked, puzzled by the events shaping rapidly around her.

"Completely forgot them and the wine."

"Good, then you won't last in here too long."

Darien turned to face Samantha, squinting as her eyes adjusted to the dark. "Bet?"

There was no time for Sam to respond before Darien reached for a blanket and tugged it over their heads. "What are you doing now?"

"Making the world go away."

"Why?"

"Because it's Friday night and we deserve a respite."

"Okay," Sam skeptically agreed, drawing out the two syllables. "You alright?"

"Perfectly."

"Did you get dumped?"

Samantha felt Darien's shoulder shake against her own as Darien softly laughed. "Hardly."

"So, it's true? You're in an open relationship with the majority of the population?"

"Not quite. Is Ryan telling you stories?"

"When it comes to you, the only thing Ryan ever says is that you always keep your options open."

"I wouldn't say that. I'm not exclusive to those I date, but that doesn't mean there isn't someone."

"Do you hear yourself?"

247

"I'll rephrase. I'm open to adventure and opportunity until I can have what I want most. I may never get it. I have no other choice but to be okay with that and with waiting."

"Maybe you're spoiled and used to getting what you want. How do you know it's not because you want what you can't have?"

"Because I've never felt this way before."

"You're setting yourself up to get hurt."

"Oh, trust me, it already hurts."

"Then why do it? Why date other people? Are you passing time or trying to salve the sting? And what if you're dating someone you actually like and this other person comes around and decides to go for it?"

"It wouldn't matter. It's awful to admit, not to mention selfish, but it wouldn't matter. I would walk away from anyone or anything else if it meant getting who I really want."

"You? Ms. High Society and Denver's notorious socialite, would settle down? Your lifestyle suggests otherwise."

"I would build the house, Sam. I would buy the ring and paint the fence, although not white. I would quit my job and write the book I've always dreamed of, and then I'd write several more. I'd want kids, snotty noses, noisy meals, and dirty dogs. The whole messy package."

"You would give up everything?"

"I would give up the life I have now to get *everything*."

"And this person knows?"

"Yes."

Sam sighed, ending the phony interrogation. "I'm not ready."

248

"I know."

They were both quiet, thoughtful of the moment and what they finally acknowledged. The kind of moment a feather could fall without drifting one way or the other. The kind where nothing moved until it had to, nothing but their thoughts which twisted and turned.

"I think about you all the time, Samantha. I think about what you're thinking, what you're doing, and who you're doing it with. I wonder about the friends and family you have in Texas and what happened to you. I think about how you are with your daughter, what you eat, the shampoo you use, and the music you listen to. I think about your eyes, your laugh, and wonder how it makes you feel every time you save another animal. I think about…everything."

As the silence grew deeper, Sam heard the steady rhythm of her heart. Darien had crossed the barriers, made the unrehearsed yet grand gesture, delivered the most significant declaration of her life. The quietness that followed was both awkward and comforting. There was no whispering, no rustle of material, only shallow breathing as if there were a conspiracy between the truth and the dark. Sam's mind continued to reel as she lay wrapped in the afghan, using the thick wool as a buffer between them.

"Philosophy," Sam finally said.

"What?"

"The shampoo I use. It's Philosophy." Sam twirled a loose strand of yarn between her fingers. "And joy. When I'm fortunate enough to make a difference and look into that animal's eyes, I feel joy. It's different than being happy. Happiness is easy. It comes and goes. But joy…it's deeper. Everlasting. When you've made a difference, one that counts, it's mutual. You can see it magnified in the eyes looking back at you. That's joy."

"My God, I hope the world never changes you. I know it has knocked you off your feet, scarred and left you with jagged edges, but I pray you never sacrifice your authenticity."

"Jagged. That's a good word to describe me." Samantha swallowed, then dared to look at Darien beside her. "Sometimes it feels like there's someone else out there other than me living *my* dreams."

"You can change that. Small changes, big results."

"Okay, Brené Brown…only because you say so."

"Seriously, start now. Let's make your fucket list."

"Bucket list?"

"You heard me right the first time."

"*Hmm.* I've always wanted to skydive."

"You're insane. What else?"

"Easy. I'd love to spend three weeks every summer off the grid like Ryan and I did last summer. Preferably on better terms and with a better sleeping bag."

"See there, look how good progress looks on you. Next?"

"Skinny dipping in the creek at midnight under a full moon. Wait, I've done that."

"Did you horrify the animals of the San Isabel Forest?" Darien asked, feigning disgust then laughed as Samantha hurled a pillow at her.

"This conversation is beginning to make me hate you."

"Careful who you hate, Sam, it usually ends up being someone you love." That silenced them again. One second. Two. Then, recovering quickly, Darien added, "Besides, this conversation is making my life."

250

"Just so you know, my therapist, the one in Texas, told me healing is an art that takes many years of practice."

"Yeah? Well, we all know someone who speaks fluid shit." That made Sam laugh. "Want to know the sorts of things my therapist says to me?" Darien turned her head, squinting Sam into view. "Reject everything negative in your life, Ms. Shay, except for pregnancy tests."

"Haha! You see a therapist, Ms. I've-Got-My-Shit-Together?"

"I did. Big mistake."

"Mine also says we're bigger than our mistakes," Sam counters, and they both roll with laughter. "See, we don't need your fancy wine. I like you like this. Let's stay right here. Exactly like this. All night." Sam laughed as Darien scoffed. "Did you just scoff at me?"

"Yes, but only at the first thing you said, not the second."

"Relax, Red, you're doing just fine without the liquid courage."

Darien turned on her side, resting her head on her arm, facing Sam. "Tell me something about her, about Jordan."

"There are so many things. I absolutely adored her quick wit and sense of humor. There was this one time, at my nephew Dominic's dinosaur themed birthday party, where he ran up to her. I guess he knew out of all of us, she would be the one to tell him the truth," Sam said, smiling as she remembered. "He asked her what a vagina was, and without blinking, Jordan answered, 'It's the capital of China.'"

"Ava laughs the way you do. Did you carry her?"

"I did after enduring what felt like endless amounts of IVF injections. But, by the grace of God, she's every bit as smart and beautiful as Jordan. Oddly, they really do look

251

alike. Without Ava, I don't know where I'd be right now. Sometimes I wonder if the depression will ever end, but Ava always seems to right me. And still, there's unbalance to it all when I let myself go there."

"Your lives were intricately woven together. You didn't only lose Jordan but all that went with your relationship. Private jokes. References. The dailiness of your routines. It makes sense you continue to whirl from the loss."

"Is that what this is? Whirling?"

"In a way, I think grief resembles depression, which is what? Bereavement? And what are the stages supposed to be? Grief, denial, anger, depression then acceptance? Who's to say what the order or length of them should be? What I'm trying to say, Sam, is how can there be an endpoint to our love and our losses? And more importantly, do you want there to be?"

"No. My memories are all I have, and they're soothing. I want them to stay with me, but I don't want to be miserable forever."

"You won't be. People think they'll never laugh again, but they do. They believe they'll never love again, but they do. They go to the store, watch movies, have sex and overeat on Thanksgiving."

"Then go on a diet in the New Year?"

"Yep. The day-to-day returns. Just because you might hear a song today that breaks your heart doesn't mean you won't hear another tomorrow that makes you dance. Finding pleasure in things you enjoy after she's gone doesn't lessen your love. I bet it probably does the opposite and honors it."

#

In the bedroom upstairs, I was reading while Tayna Donelly's rendition of "Moon River" played softly in the background. I'd just taken a bubble bath and come out to a warm fire blazing in the hearth. He's not in the room, but I know the romantic atmosphere is Dean's doing. Close to midnight, I set the book down and stare through the window, although there's nothing but the dark to see.

Hearing Dean coming up the stairway, I glance down. My ring sparkles from the light cast from the fire. It's beautiful, timeless, and perfect. He walks in and walks to me. He lifts me, taking over my place in the oversized reading chair, and then settles me in his lap.

"You met Sarah?"

"She ambushed my breakfast with Sam."

"I'm sorry you're both getting drug into my mess."

"Stop it."

"You realize Sarah left without seeing Colby? Didn't even bother stopping by to say Merry Christmas or give her a present. Not even a phone call. All Colby got was a card with a check inside."

"I found them in the trash," I tell him. "The card and the check. She's so young, Dean, and already knows she doesn't want Sarah's money."

"Money," Dean repeats with a sigh. "I won't lose our house, Ry, but we might lose the mountain." Dean reaches for my hand, bringing it to his face, and kisses my palm. "Before, I would never concede because the land means everything. Now...I don't know. There's nothing more

253

important to me than Colby. Than you. You showed up, and everything changed. I start every morning knowing I can't get through a single day anymore without you. Nothing is worth risking my family for."

"Please don't give up. I'll do whatever you need me to do for you to feel safe."

"We can't sit around hoping nothing more happens. There's no reason to believe it will stop now. If anything, it's going to get worse. All I can think about is Drew and the maniac that broke in here, who almost hurt you. I can't see past that, Ryan. I'd never come back from it."

I turn to face Dean, straddling him with my hands holding his head before planting small kisses all over his beautiful face. "I love you. I love you today, tomorrow, and the days that follow after that."

I close my eyes when I feel his hands glide up my back beneath my thin shirt. In his arms, wrapped in warmth and desire, everything else begins to slip away. All that's between us now is the heat of his body against mine and the comfort of his touch.

Against my ear, he says, "We should talk about it."

"I don't want to. It will never happen again."

"Ryan—" but it's too late, I'm already pulling back. He tightens his hold around my waist. "Stop," he demands, and bows his head to mine, calming me.

Instead of fighting it, I decide to recommence the seduction. I'll do anything to avoid this conversation. "All I want to talk about right now is how much longer it's going to take you to get my clothes off and make love to me."

"I will."

I pull away only enough to look into his eyes. "You haven't touched me since Christmas. That was three days ago."

"You know why. When I climbed into bed, I didn't know you were dreaming before I put my arms around you. You jumped up, were terrified, and wouldn't let me near you, screaming that you hated me. You told me never to touch you again, and then you called me Jim."

"Dean," I start, unable to run from this. "I have no idea how this will make sense or where to start. I need you to know that I'm better now. I'm like…like a house."

"A what?"

"A house, honey. I'm that house we've all heard about. The one that over a long period gets destroyed then falls apart. Violence cracked the foundation, neglect tore apart the walls, and eventually, the roof caved from the weight of all the pain."

"Ryan, I don't want you to relive—"

"Ever since I came here, since I met you, all of that feels like a lifetime ago. I'm not saying that suddenly it's easy. It's my biggest life challenge, but I'm doing it, Dean. I'm rebuilding my house one brick at a time. There will always be times, like the other night. Times where I'll find a crack here and there, but I'm stronger now and can patch them as I find them."

"All I'm asking is that you trust me enough to talk to me."

I think about this. "I know, which is why I should also tell you Darien is here. Jenna put her in my old cabin. She came by earlier with Sam to tell me that Jim is looking for

255

me. He wants to talk. I'm not hard to find, Blue. It's time for me to face him."

CHAPTER TWENTY-TWO

"Dr. Saben, you have someone waiting to see you."

Brittany looked up from her desk in the cramped office she shared with her PA. She was knee-deep in the biggest problem plaguing primary care which was the burden of paperwork. "Can Jackie take it?" Brittany all but begged.

"It's Reece." For a slow-ticking moment, Brittany thought to have him turned away. "He doesn't look well."

"Okay, put him in room three. I'll be there in a minute." Brittany sat back, setting the pen on the desk. The last time she'd seen him, she'd fled his house in a hurry, brokenhearted. She'd gone home, cried, and then cried some more before finally waking Christmas morning insisting no more. She was done.

Inside the examination room, she found Reece pacing. When he turned to see her, she saw his eye. She turned back, poking her head out the door with her hand resting on the doorjamb. "Jackie, can you wash his eye out, please?"

Brittany then turned back to Reece. "Sit down, behave, and I'll be back in a few minutes."

She left the room, entered a private restroom and leaned against the locked door, squeezing her eyes shut. It was hard enough to see him, worse to see the condition he was in. Returning almost ten minutes later, she leaned into him, looking into his grossly infected eye, pressing gently on the eyelid. "Jackie tells me you wouldn't let her clean it. Be rude to anyone here again, and you can leave."

"I'm not here for that. My eye is fine."

"Really? Have you looked in the mirror lately?"

Reece stood. "I'll go." She noticed how thin he was, and then met his gaze. She blinked, and he was sidestepping her toward the exit. "I'm sorry, I just…I'm sorry," he repeated, closing the door behind him.

When her shift ended an hour later, she left the medical center thinking she'd been too indifferent and cool with Reece. She unlocked her car, turned the engine on, cranked the heat, then thumped her head back against the headrest and closed her eyes. She dreaded going to the small basement apartment she was renting several blocks away. Perhaps it was time to put in for a transfer, time to move on.

She jumped nearly out of her skin when she heard tapping against her passenger window. Reece. She would kill him for scaring her like that. Inhaling deeply, she pressed the lever to lower the window. He bent to eye-level. "Reece, I'm tired. If there's something you need to say to me, you can follow me to my place and say it there."

Descending the steps to her small apartment, he asked, "This is where you live?" When she didn't answer, he stepped inside, glancing around the small space. There were

258

exposed pipes, concrete floors, and no windows. He spun slowly. "What are you doing in a place like this?"

She wanted to scream all the reasons why but inhaled deeply instead. "I had to act fast," she said, leaving out the insinuation that it was his fault. "Staying with my parents wasn't an option any longer. Want a drink?"

"I haven't had a drink in several days."

"I meant water, coffee, tea," Brittany responded, pointing at the stool.

Across from her, on the other side of the counter, Reece sat. "Coffee's fine. Black, please." She handed him a glass of milk instead.

"Drink it. All of it." She reached for her purse then tossed a small box at him. "Collyrium. It's eyewash. Use it every day for five days. It will help alleviate the irritation. The twitching is a muscle spasm. That, I'm guessing is from fatigue and stress on top of injury. From what little I saw, you appear to have a subconjunctival hemorrhage. Other than that, you're just an asshole."

"What are you doing?" Reece asked.

"Making you something to eat. How much weight have you lost? Never mind, it doesn't matter."

"Britt, please sit down. I'm not hungry."

"I am." She pulled out items for omelets one ingredient at a time. When she looked up, noticing his eye was red, swollen and watering, she pushed the ingredients aside. With her hands on top of the countertop, she gave in. "You pushed me away."

"I'm sorry."

"I'm already tired of hearing that."

"I wish I could explain."

259

"I'm not asking you to. I understand why, Reece. But how you treated me is not okay."

"I hate that you live here. You're a doctor for God sake, why live here?"

"I'm hardly ever home. Did you hear what I said?"

"I wouldn't blame you if you never wanted to see me again." He stood and began pacing the short length of the room. "I put your things back together and tried fixing the picture frame I broke."

"Not everything can be fixed." With her appetite gone, she gathered the eggs and vegetables and put them back into the fridge. Closing the refrigerator door, she locked eyes with Reece. "I'm thinking of transferring."

"Please don't."

"Reece, I can't do this tonight. I need to sleep and seeing you…it's too much. I'm just too tired."

"Move back into the house. I can go stay with Garrett. I'll do whatever you ask me to, whatever it takes."

"Reece, no."

"Please," he begged, his irritated eye red and watering. "I can't lose you too."

He clasped the back of the stool for support, attempting to hide his grief before it overwhelmed him once again. He couldn't afford to break down in front of her, not anymore. He had to prove he could move on from his devastation. And then it hit him, what she needed most was for him to trust her with his vulnerability, to share his pain.

"I'll never be who I was before my brother died." Reece paused, blinking tears, carefully wiping his infected eye. "But I do love you. I'll do everything I can to make up for what I've done to you."

Wiping at her eyes, Brittany moved closer to him, but careful not to touch him. "I can't stay in your house without you there, Reece. I can't. We need time, time to take a step back to figure ourselves out before we try to fix each other over what's happened."

"But you'll stay? You won't leave?"

"How can I?" When Reece stepped forward, ready to wrap himself around her, she lifted her hand, keeping him at a distance. "Easy," she whispered. "You need to know that what you're saying matters. You're not alone, Reece, I'm here, but slow down."

"Can I stay here tonight?"

"That's *not* slow. You can sleep on the couch."

A feeble grin played at the corner of his lips. There was hope, she realized, and couldn't help but smile. They'd taken a small yet very real step toward recovery.

The optimistic glint in his battered eye was enough. There was no choice but to trust him, to draw from him the love he was meant to share with others. If only he could see the truth of himself. Only then would he find peace. She remembered it then, remembered months before when Drew had joined them for dinner. He'd been so animated in the longwinded monologue that he'd learned at AA that afternoon. He'd smiled brightly sharing that "truth is peace."

\#

"Grandpa!" we hear Colby screech with excitement. Dean's quick to leave me in the kitchen to go to Colby in the family room. Following closely behind, I stop short when I

261

see Dean's father coming through the front door that Colby has opened. It's the first time I've seen Ray Sterling and Dean together, the first time I've seen Ray at all.

There are minor resemblances, though nothing in comparison to Jey. Nonetheless, I see it. The height, the frame, the pride. My eyes fall to Ray's hand as he lifts Colby into a hug, and I notice Dean's hands are the same. They stand alike, sound alike, brood alike. There's no denying that passing likeness, but the more I watch them, the more I see particular distinctions.

"You must be Ryan McCray?" Ray asks me, though he's beaming at Colby. "This little one believes you've hung the moon." Ray quickly glances at his son before returning his attention to Colby. "She doesn't appear to be the only one."

"It's nice to put a face to the voice," I say, letting Ray take my hand. His grip is friendly but firm. I lift my eyes to Dean and see the question in his. There are so many things we still have not discussed about my time away. Primarily the removal of my mother from the mental institution. "Thank you for your help, for everything you did for my mother and me."

"You should have called," Dean diverts, prickly that his father and I have talked without him.

"And miss getting to see my princess," Ray kisses Colby's cheek, "not a chance."

"We're married!" Colby shakes her hand in front of Ray, showing off the small birthstone set into a thin silver band. It had been an impromptu gift I found a few days after Christmas to solidify our commitment to be a family.

I laugh, snatching Colby from Ray. "Not yet, but soon," I tell Ray, and cart Colby into the kitchen, hoping the men will follow. "Coffee?"

In the kitchen, both men reluctantly sit across from one another. "I didn't expect you until next week," Dean says, at last.

Ray doesn't respond but instead gives Dean a stern look, and I have a feeling they should talk privately. "Let's go see what Sam and Ava are up to," I suggest to Colby.

"Actually, Ryan, if you wouldn't mind, let's chat for a minute before you go." Ray chuckles as Colby shrugs before going to hunt for Mama.

I sit beside Dean, automatically leaning into him, and smile at Ray. It almost feels like I'm the rope in their game of tug-of-war. Of course, Dean wins by reaching for my hand to hold in his. Still, I'm grateful for everything Ray has done for me, so I willingly stay. And, if I'm honest, I'm curious what this unannounced visit is all about. *Crap!* Please don't let this be about my mother.

"Nothing too much to worry about. Without going into futile detail, there's an issue that may arise. As your attorney—"

"Her *what*?"

"Blue, I've got this." As soon as I say the words, I realize it doesn't work that way anymore. I turn in my seat, facing Dean. Ray can wait. "I was over my head in legalities with no understanding when it came to policy for her emancipation from psychiatric hospitalization."

"Involuntary treatment and involuntary commitment laws," Ray explains. "Parens patriae powers are used to help those who can't help themselves, and in her mother's case, to justify taking away her rights."

"Right. While I was away, I called your dad because of what you and I argued about the night I left. The things you told me, and the truth about my unc…about Jim."

"By representing your mother, essentially you for that matter, crosschecking occurred."

"You did a background check on my wife?" *Wife*. The word stuns me even though we've yet to tie the knot. I tighten my fingers around Dean's.

"Provisions, Dean. When filing for guardianship, there are requirements. As I was saying, Ryan, as your attorney, I need your permission—"

"Not a good idea. I don't think—"

"Yes." I agree, not intending to cut Dean off. "You have my consent to do whatever you need to do, Ray." I get to my feet and bend to kiss Dean's temple. "I love you, so trust me," I whisper. "Ray, it's nice to meet you finally. I need to run next door, but again, thank you."

Colby is on the floor in the living room playing with her Smithsonian Magic Rocks Kit Jenna gave her for Christmas. I almost interrupt Colby telling Mama that Rutger has run away before stopping in my tracks. *Rutger's gone?* But it's not only Colby who I can hear.

"For once, can you not lie and tell me the truth?" Dean says.

"Relax, Dean. I got it. I wore the wire."

\#

Amid our short stroll next door, Colby stops walking then slumps to a heap in a pile of snow. I have a feeling we are about to have a heart-to-heart. I look around and sigh. It's unavoidable, I'm going to have to plant my butt in the slush and pretend I'm not freezing to death.

Before giving in entirely, I see Darien through the window working away. Such a creature of habit. The grip Colby has on my hand is tugging me down. My plan to park her with Ava to sort through many slides with Darien will have to wait.

I'm not up for frostbite, so I kneel. Colby is well into her first round of crocodile-sized tears. This is going to be a doozy. She's sniffling and sobbing, amplifying her dilemma. I run my hand over her dark hair when she clutches my arm and wipes her face, snot and all, onto my sleeve. "I can't fix it unless you tell me what's wrong."

"Daddy's gonna kill me." I bite my lip to keep from smiling. "Stanna Truitt called me a tomboy, so I called her a shitface." More sniffles. "My teacher heard me say it. I got sent home with a note for Daddy to read and sign. When I go back to school after break, I have to give it to her, or else."

I watch as Colby unzips the right pocket of her bright blue jacket and pulls out a crumpled piece of paper. With dramatic effort, she begins to unfold it. I see a lot of ink and scribbled out words. "What's that, Colbs?"

"It's my will. I'm leavin' you my rocks. When big days come like Daddy's birthday, you can give him one rock at a time. Tell him it's from Colby Sterling before you went and killed her."

"I'll make you a deal. If you promise to stay away from Stanna Truitt, I'll handle your dad. Can you do that? If Stanna says anything, you have to ignore her no matter what?"

"You'll talk to Daddy?"

"Only if you promise."

Colby sticks a fat finger into her mouth biting on the tip of her glove, yanking her hand free than offers me her pinkie. I do the same and seal our pinkie promise. "There's something else. Rutger ran away, so Bodie's gonna be lonely. Bodie needs a friend at night 'cuz Deacon doesn't sleep over at our house."

"You want another dog?"

"A puppy for Bodie."

"*Hmm*. We have to talk to your dad about that one."

"Ryan, if you talk Daddy into it, I promise not to give a single damn about Stanna Truitt."

Okay, even I can't let this go on.

CHAPTER TWENTY-THREE

"Lost?"

"Garrett! Jeez, you scared me!" On horseback, Samantha halted with her hips in a neutral position, her spine straight and back flat. "Hey."

"Sorry, didn't mean to." With his boot, Garrett shoved a broken limb away obstructing the path. "Nice ride."

"He's getting there, has good ground manners."

"He's big."

"This is Dante, and yes, he is. He's sure-footed and confident, so he'll be great for navigating our rugged trails. Doesn't hurt that he's quiet-minded and gentle."

"He's that chestnut paint stallion you moved over from Texas? Jenna said he was a looker."

"Tobiano paint. Handsome, isn't he?"

"If I knew what you meant, sure." Garrett smiled, reaching out to run his hand along the horse's smooth neck.

"Tobianos, dark with white spots. Overos, white with dark spots. Chopping wood?" Sam asked, seeing the ax in Garrett's other hand.

"Was. Heard you before I saw you. Not a fan of how jumpy we all are these days."

"My fault. I didn't plan on riding this way, or I would have given you a heads-up." Sam looked up, noticing the A-Frame house in short view. "How is it possible I was all over these parts last summer and fall, and this is the first time I've been by your place?"

"You haven't seen it? Hop down, and I'll show you around then bless you with the best coffee this side of the Continental Divide."

"Yeah?"

"Small shop over Poncha Springs Jenna and I stumbled on several years ago. Small town vibes, big-time brew. Been hooked ever since, so Jen sees to it I get a delivery every month to feed my addiction. Even still, she prefers the coffee shop here in town." Out of habit, Garrett glanced around. "Dean know you're out riding around alone?"

"Nope. I was wrapping things up at the stables when this beautiful creature here pestered me into some one-on-one. We stayed close to the road and were about to turn around before you shaved a year or so off our lives."

Garrett laughed. "Hard to be sorry, considering. Come on, have a look around, enjoy some java, and then I'll follow you back. And quit looking at me that way. Until we get some answers, none of you need to be out wandering on your own."

Secluded and sitting on a knoll, Garrett's house was built to capture the southern exposure with panoramic views of the mountains. Entranced, Sam admired the rock-framed home with a wood burning stove, steep vaulted ceilings, and metal roofing. Aside from the attractive features, it was the landscaping Sam liked best. She gaped at the wrap-around patio overlooking a meadow beaming with cottonwood trees, a trinity well, and brook fed pond with a small redwood gazebo.

"Like it?" Garrett asked after disappearing in the back of the house for several minutes. He returned with what looked to be a folded newspaper under his arm.

"I love it. It's what I picture for Ava and me."

"You looking to buy?"

"Possibly next summer. I decided to get a feel for the place before we dug in too deep."

"We should talk, you may be in luck."

"You're selling?"

"Been tossing the idea around. Got my eye on some raw land up the way several miles I'm considering. Here, you'd be close to the stables, and walking distance for Ava and Colby to play together."

"Who do I make the check out to," Sam joked, turning to appreciate the view once again. "Garrett?" she called, her voice clipped. "Did you see that?" She asked following the shape of a man in a dark green hoodie scale the boulder wall along the riverbank in the distance.

"Yeah. It's TC. Strange guy, that one. Don't worry, he's fine. He's always out, hiking all over these parts."

"Strange guy?"

"Maybe not so much strange as a recluse. Prefers to be alone. I've interrupted him often enough now to leave him be. Another thrill seeker who idolizes Dean. Has his eyes on the same special operations unit Dean coordinates with SAR. I'd bet TC spends ninety percent of daylight out there training.

"Have you told Dean?"

"Dean and Jenna both. They've got a soft spot for the guy, so I leave it alone. Supposedly, he's a hero before coming here."

"TC? A hero? I guess I can see that."

"Medal of Honor. Those medals are exceptionally rare. No doubt he saw some things no one likes to speak of, which probably explains why he is the way he is. Word is he was a courageous, resilient, selfless captain who saved a handful of lives in combat. He's never told any of us other than Jenna, and all he's ever told her was the situation and conditions were unimaginable."

"What's that?" Sam asked, pointing at the aging newspaper under Garrett's arm.

"Chaffee County Times." Garrett handed Sam the paper focusing on Buena Vista community news. "Dean and I were seven when you disappeared. Jules wasn't the only one who lost you, we all suffered. It rocked the entire town to the core. There were search parties, Sam. Everyone looked for you." Samantha looked closer at the paper with a little girl on the front-page staring back at her.

"Here, take it. It's yours."

With shaky hands, Sam accepted the yellowing newspaper, unable to read any of it yet. "I don't know what to say. All of it…it's surreal, Garrett. How did this happen to me? How am I not so messed up over it? Or am I?" Sam asked, with tears brimming. Garrett stepped forward, wrapping her in his arms.

"You're no more messed up than any of us. The only thing that matters is you're home now. The rest is just noise. Block it out. Let us help you do it."

#

I'm the one, the nemophilist. The haunter of woods, the one who loves the forest, it's beauty and solitude. My home—the forest I know so well, the one I've grown up in, now worries me.

It used to be, when things got to be too much, I would hike into the thicket to listen to the silence that was never really silent at all. Now, I can't hear anything. My refuge, the effervescent hideaway of ancient souls, chords of running water, whispering limbs, and birdsong are jarringly quiet. The forest never weeps over one tree, and still, the subtraction of Drew remains raw and deep.

There has to be a way to end the madness, to stop the progression. I can't let them destroy these woods that are dark and deep, thick and old. Not only for me but for the many times it has been said before: "the human spirit in us all need places like these, where nature should never be rearranged by the hand of man."

"Planning?" Jenna asked, interrupting his digital entry. Dean glanced up, noting the time. It was after eight and time to turn away from the screen of the laptop on his desk. Time to close out the document intended to be for upcoming projections but had instead become a personal essay.

"Procrastinating," he corrected, as Samantha opened the door then stomped her feet before coming through, knocking off clumps of ice from her snow boots. It was also time for their weekly morning meeting that had turned into a daily one more often than not.

"Morning." Sam plopped down in a chair beside Jenna. "I practically got run over by Garrett. He stopped long enough to razz me about property value. Then babbled on about the deal of a century he's offering before asking me to tell you he'll be late to dinner. Something about pruning."

"That guy, such a believer that cutting deciduous trees in winter promotes faster regrowth in the spring. Think you're going to do it?"

"Buy his place? I *really* love it, but we'll see."

"Yeah, I hear Darien has a nice piece on Princeton," Dean joked.

"Very funny."

"Dean, is TC on a call?" Jenna asked.

"Not that I know of."

"He's not here. He's always here." Jenna's reaction confirmed Samantha's suspicions but before she had the opportunity to pry the door was swinging opening again.

"Jules!" Sam stood. "Is everything okay?"

"Sit, sit. I'm fine, honey. Well, mostly. I was hoping to catch the three of you together before my hair appointment, so I'm in a bit of a hurry."

"Morning, Ms. Jenson. You look as gorgeous as ever."

"Careful, Dean Sterling, or I'll give that pretty girl Ryan a run for her money.

"My mother flirting with my boss might get me that raise after all."

"Your boss," Jules stated matter-of-factly, considering the statement more than it warranted. "Forgive my brash behavior. It's not so much that I'm in a hurry, but more of needing to get this out once and for all." She tapped Dean's hand. "It's no secret what's happening around here. Dean and Jenna, it takes a great deal of bravery to stand up to your adversaries. And Sam, my sweet girl, it takes every bit as much to take a stand for your friends. Loving people and places so deeply give us the courage we wouldn't normally have otherwise."

"Are you okay?" Sam asked again, confused by these announcements and more so by the impromptu visit.

"I'm fine, Samantha, and as I said, I need to do this while I dare to do so. There are three things I came to say. The first is that I had no greater hope other than to find you. The second, I wished never to divulge because I was ashamed. Never of you, but of what I'd done. The third which will explain the second—"

"I already know," Sam interrupted.

"I think I do, too," Jenna said.

"So, I'm not just the only guy in the room. I'm also the only one who doesn't have a clue what any of you are talking about."

"Let me," Jenna pleaded with both Sam and Jules. She turned to face Dean. "We're cousins, we know that. Everyone knows that. But I've spent my entire life thinking and loving you as my big brother. We think alike and have built a business together. We share interests and live and breathe these mountains and the relationships we've

273

developed because of this mystical place we both love so much. You are my family, Dean, but you're not mine alone."

"*Okay?*" Dean tilted his head, failing to understand.

"Your hair is dark whereas hers is light."

"Whose hair?"

"Dean," Jenna chuckled. "Listen carefully to what I'm saying." She stood, hitching her hip to the corner of his desk. "Both of you have this skin like it's sun-kissed year-round. Your eyes are reddish brown rimmed in gold and green. Hers are greenish gold outlined in brown. The shape of your noses and even your hands. Hers are much smaller but much the same. You laugh alike and so do both your daughters. You're equally passionate about what you each love most. From the outside looking in, and once you're around it enough, its crystal clear. Your personalities, the similarities. So many of them. You're exactly alike."

"When you were just a boy," Jules began, taking over. "You had a keen sense to you even then. You watched over these two girls so protectively, so nobly. The connection, though unknown to you, was undeniable. No one lost more than I did when she was taken except for you. You were so very young yet so haunted and hurt by her abduction."

"Dean, Jules is not your link to Sam. Ray is," Jenna finally blurted.

"He was handsome and so charismatic. All the girls in town grew up having crushes on Ray Sterling at one time or another. One weekend while he was home visiting, we were at the same party when I finally caught his eye. He never spoke to me again after that night, and I never told anyone."

"You're my sister?" Dean asked. "How long have you known?"

"Not long, a few days."

"And you?" he asked, looking to Jenna.

"For a while, I think. It wasn't until this morning, seeing the way Ms. Jenson looks at you both that I was certain." Jenna leaned forward, resting her hand on Dean's shoulder. "Are you okay with this?"

Dean stood then walked to the window. With his hand against the wall, he looked out, watching the creek's steady current. "That river didn't cut through this mountain because of its strength. It's there because of persistence. Persistence is the only way for dreams to come true. You're persistent, Sam. You don't give up. I don't know how it's possible, but you found your way back to us. What more could I possibly say besides how lucky I feel, or how proud I am of you?"

"Dean? Check your phone!" Jenna interjected, quickly scrolling the text messages on her phone. "Garrett's trying to reach you. Wait! Here's another from Reece—"

"I just got a message from Ryan," Sam added. "She's dropped the girls by school and is saying something about Garrett flagging her down."

"Reece can't reach you. He was on his way up to find you when he ran into Garrett."

"Sam, what's Ryan telling you?" Dean asked, rounding his desk toward his phone. "Read it to me."

"She's asking me to find you. That Brittany called Reece and then Reece ran into Garrett who ran into Ryan. She needs you to hurry, and to bring Jenna because…Oh, God…"

"What Sam?"

"It's TC. Something has happened to TC."

CHAPTER TWENTY-FOUR

Jenna stared at her phone, unable to sleep, and refusing to leave. Brain injury. The words clung, stinging like salt water to razor burn. They'd all gone, driven to Denver and stayed together overnight in a small waiting room.

TC had been airlifted to Denver Health's Level 1 Trauma Center. It should have mattered that it was one of the world's leading trauma centers with the highest survival rates in the country. It didn't. All she could comprehend were the surgeon's parting words: "critical condition."

By midafternoon the following day, they began ventilator weaning trials to see if TC could initiate spontaneous respirations on his own. Jenna insisted on staying when it was advised they return home to rest. Dean had argued to stay, as did Garrett, but she encouraged them to go, promising to update via text messages as often as possible.

From: Jenna
To: Dean, G, Ryan, Sam, Reece
7pm. No major change. His pupils did react to light. Is that good? They don't say. He's not following commands. Dr. Maric (orthopedic surgeon) is taking him to OR tomorrow morning to repair his wrist fracture. How did this happen? TC never falls!!

From: Dean
To: Jenna, Garrett, Beautiful, Samantha, Reece
Try to sleep. I'll drive back up in the morning to be with you. Love you, cousin.

From: Ryan
To: Blue, Jenna, Garrett, Sam, Reece
I'm sending Dean w/ food & clothes for you. PS. I called Darien...she's got a place for you to crash and shower when you're ready. Xx

From: Samantha
To: Ryan, Deano, Jen, Garrett D, Reece
Broken crayons still color. Stay positive and call if you need anything.

From: Reece
To: Bear Mama, Picture Lady, Bossman, Sister J, Brother G
Love you Jen

From: Garrett
To: Bro1, Samantha, Ryan, Sterling, Jen

Been up and down the ridge looking no less than 10x since we've been back. Nothing but a few patches of ice here and there. Who found him? Nvm, don't worry about that right now, Reece and I will go and find out tomorrow. Remember this…TC's a hero, right? Heroes step up when others back down.

#

Through Darien, I've agreed to meet with Jim. Not to say that Darien didn't vehemently advise against it. Now that I have, Jim is insistent on it being today. Dean doesn't know. His plate is already overflowing. I can't fathom how he's able to keep rolling with the punches. And because I'm worried about him, I haven't said anything about Jim. Besides, Dean's on his way to be with Jenna and check on TC. He doesn't need the added weight of the trash of my past.

Darien refuses to let Jim set the tone, pace, or scene. She's already consorted with Sam, and they are both adamant about coming along. My guardians by nature are the epitome of true friendship, even now. They're leery and don't want me to go, but with them, I can do this. If Jim doesn't like it, it's a no-go.

It's also by design, we're meeting in Leadville, a small Victorian-era mining town thirty-five miles north. Months earlier, Garrett had shared that in its heyday, the town was famous for its saloons, dance halls, and brothels, thanks to

278

gold and silver mines. Therefore, just in case seeing Jim is a bust, which I'm sure it will be, I'll at least have my camera.

I would have preferred to meet him at the café and lounge with a neon burro on the sign, or not at all. However, I've let Darien navigate these waters, and as the captain at the helm, she's selected a quiet restaurant inside a hotel. Upon our arrival, I could care less it's now permanently closed. *Thank God!* Now, we can forget this entire ordeal and go home. Or, maybe I can talk them into walking around Twin Lakes.

I tried persuading them to no avail. Such things as a crick to the plan don't happen to Darien Shay, and she's in full-blown dismay when I get a glimpse of Jim from the corner of my eye. The monster of my past. I scream, but no one can hear it. It's silent, something I learned to do when I was very young.

He's disguised in nice clothing, a clean-shaven face, a fresh haircut, and a cane. Only I can see the Devil's spawn. Sam clasps on to my hand. While not apparent to anyone else, Sam takes the brunt of my weight against her. Until I get my bearings, she's here. That liaison alone is the first swipe at the evil man limping our way.

"There's a teashop on Harrison," Darien redirects to somewhere else she's located on her phone.

"We're on Harrison," Sam states the obvious.

We walk the short distance with Jim hobbling behind. We are yet to acknowledge him but know he's here, lurking, and all I want to do is leave. Inside the café, we're seated at a table for four beside a blue wall. I find comfort in that. No one plans to sit beside Jim. Darien pulls a chair to our side of the table, and they plant me snuggly in the middle of their protective wall.

"Coffee, none of that fancy stuff." It's the first thing Jim says when the waitress approaches our tables. I feel sick.

"I'm out," I say, standing, looking for the quickest escape. Together, Sam and Darien stand and are prepared to follow my lead, whatever that may be.

"Runnin' is whatcha do," Jim says, with the nerve to look me in the eye. I sit. No part of me wants to continue letting this man have control over me.

"He's weak, you're not," Sam whispers. At the same time, I feel Darien grip my hand under the table. *I can do this*.

"I'm here. What do you want?"

"You got somethin' I need."

I can't help it. I laugh. "I can assure you, I left that place with nothing but the shirt on my back and a bus ticket in my hand."

"Your aunt, she's dead."

"Old news. I came, remember? Paid for the service then left. Are we done?" Part of that declaration surprises my friends. It's not common knowledge, nor am I proud that I paid for my aunt's funeral. In fact, I wish I hadn't, but for Mama's sake I did. And in some twisted way, the closure presented me with a sense of liberation.

Jim's balding with deeply pronounced crow's feet at the edges of his beady eyes. His nose is bigger and veiny, the evidence is sure to be from years of drunkenness. The tattoo on his right arm is exactly as I remember—a naked woman coiled by a cobra ready to strike.

"When we married, things was put in your aunt's name from mistakes they made with my credit 'n all."

"Here we go."

"That right there," Jim says, pointing the fat side of the spoon at me. "Is sass. I worked at that goddamned correctional facility to keep your butt in britches 'n fed. 'Bes watch your tone."

"I suggest you put the utensil down and get to the point," Darien says. "As I'm certain everyone here is aware you received compensation from the government for years after a short stint with the Eden Detention Center. Where you were promptly fired from, by the way." It doesn't surprise me to learn Darien has uncovered all there is to know about this vile man.

"Why 'ya need them here for anyhow?" Jim asks me, shifting the spoon between my two saviors. "This is family business, ain't no one else needin' to bud in."

"Jim, all I have to do is say the word, do you understand that? I can have sexual assault of a minor charges slapped on you quicker than you're able to hobble out that door. The truth is, I'd rather not do that. It would be messy, drawn out, and a long shot. I know that. But what I'm really getting at is you'll have to hire an attorney to fight it. That will be expensive."

"Been too long, girl. Besides, I never did nuthin' to 'ya."

"Every state is different about the statute of limitations to charge an alleged perpetrator. Even if proven true, it's unlikely you'd be convicted. Sadly, the legal system would probably take into account the amount of time that's passed since you put your hands on me."

I give him a second to digest what I'm saying. I look around then back to him. "You're wondering why it even matters then? Here's why. Texas. Sex crimes in Texas can be brought before a judge as much as twenty years later. Or, better yet, depending on the sex crime, length of the abuse, and age of the victim, there are often no limitations at all to prosecution."

"Calm down, we're 'jus talkin' here."

"The fact that I am calm should worry you."

"Your aunt, she died leavin' things to you."

"Really?" This shocks me. My aunt left me a single-wide trailer in the middle of nowhere. *Amazing*. "It's not a problem, Jim, I want no part of it. Send whatever you need me to sign with two conditions. You never contact me again and never do anything to obstruct my mother's freedom."

"I gotta have me a place to live, Ryan."

"She's agreed…with terms," Darien interjected, placing her business card on the table. "You can forward any documentation to that address. I'll see she gets it. That's as good as it gets, so we're done here."

"Fine, fine. This is good of you, kid, you always done right by me."

We stand—Darien, Samantha and me. I was ready to leave this man behind once and for all, but his parting words were like claws searing into my skin, holding me in place. I look into his eyes one final time. "I've changed my mind. Go straight to hell, Jim. Live in a gutter for all I care."

#

From: Dean
To: Ryan, Samantha
1/3
Leadville, huh? You can blame Nana Sterling for telling me. She's called 100x (at least) to check on everyone. Sam, she's yours now too, you know? Might as well up your data plan to unlimited if you haven't already.

From: Dean
To: Ryan, Samantha
2/3
TC's awake. Kind of. He squeezed Jen's hand. Doing most of his own breathing w/ good 02 Saturation on CPAP. Getting food via tube. OR went well. Something about open reduction and internal fixation. Vitals stable. If all goes well, he might be extubated tomorrow. That's all I got, love you both.

From: Dean
To: Ryan, Samantha
3/3
PS. Ry, I'm back but stopping for a quick beer w/ G.

#

"Wind's got a bite to it," Garrett said, occupying the barstool beside an empty one he'd been saving for Dean. "Any improvement?"

"Hard to say." Dean shrugged out of his coat then blew on his hands to warm them. "Still hooked up to all those breathing tubes, but his eyes were open, and it seemed like he could hear us. Not sure if he understood, though. He tried sitting up a couple of times."

"Jen's taking it hard."

"Yeah, about that—"

Garrett lifted his hand. "I got it. I think I've known for a while. Not proud to admit it, especially now. It bugged me, you know, and I haven't been too fond of TC because of it. That's on me." Garrett spun the glass of locally brewed beer in his hands. "I've loved that cousin of yours my whole life, but it's time. I've got to let her go. Should have done it a long time ago."

"You're her best friend." Dean looked his lifelong companion of over thirty years in the eye. "She's put her life on hold to spare you."

"I want her to be happy, I'll make it right." And the subject was closed. "Still nothing. I've gone back to everyone you've already talked to. There isn't a medical center within a hundred-mile radius that's admitted or heard of anyone with a gunshot wound to the leg."

"Darien shot that guy, Garrett. He's out there, and he's hurt."

"Whoever it is, he didn't get help. And I know you don't want to hear it, but Jen's right. TC doesn't fall."

"You think someone else was up there with him?"

"Don't you?" Neither said anything for several passing seconds, then, "That's not all of it. Reece and I asked around. The call in, whoever reported TC's accident to the

284

authorities? It was an anonymous caller using a public landline."

"It's not safe here anymore. It's like a nightmare except my eyes are wide open."

"First thing we've got to do is stop letting fear be the enemy. As long as we're doing that, we're failing to understand who we're dealing with. So far, I'm betting all of our reactions are expected, so let's shake it up. We get to choose how to respond and we need to fight back. We know this land better than anyone and know Prescott's hand is in this but this stuff…this feels different. You agree that Ryan and Sam need to take the girls and go? Jenna stays put in Denver?"

"Yeah, those aren't conversations I'm looking forward to. I'll handle it, then do whatever I've got to do to lure this sick fuck out. You're with me?"

"We're playing with fire, Sterling, but if you're asking if I want to avenge my brother's death? Hell, yes I do." Looking through the glass of dark lager, Garrett added. "Let's do this for Drew."

They clinked mugs, the lingering stray thought sealing their fate. "For Drew."

Meanwhile, and within close proximity, he tugged at the brim of his ballcap, keeping his eyes low and ears open. *Keep talking. No one even knows I'm sitting so close, hanging on to every word.* He smiled, wondering how they can be so stupid. So blind. All of them. He rubbed his leg, careful to avoid the wound beneath loose khakis, careful not to limp when he stood to use the restroom.

"Got a reply from Jen." Garrett handed Dean his phone several minutes later.

From: Jenna
To: G
I'm okay, thanks. Sorry I couldn't talk earlier, Dr. Evans came by. They're ahead of schedule, so that's good news. TC's breathing on his own and speaking very little. His voice is hoarse from being intubated. He thinks it's 2014. Thx for checking on me, talk tomorrow!

Dean handed Garrett's phone back as a passerby bumped into his shoulder, skirting other patrons, and then sat two stools down. Ignoring the intrusion, Dean studied the deep amber of his beer. The need for revenge was like a relentless rat gnawing at his soul. It was time to set the trap. "I've got an idea."

CHAPTER TWENTY-FIVE

There isn't a cloud in the sky except for the steep stream from smoke pods of a single pilot airplane flying patterns near Cottonwood Lake. The mountain is gorgeous, dark at the base and topped in white, the avalanche shoots looking like ski slopes. It's the warmest it's been in days, a balmy forty-two degrees. I've noticed the temperature here in comparison to the cold days in Texas differ drastically. Perhaps it's the humidity that makes low temps in Texas downright painful at times. But here in Colorado, with the sun shining brightly over the mountain sitting proudly, it feels quite comfortable.

I rinse my mug after only a half cup of the addictive liquid I usually can't live without. I can't wait another minute to get outside and get to work. My goal is to capture the ice breaking apart and floating easily away and down the creek. There's also a massive mule deer making beautiful tracks in the fresh powder as she carries her noticeable pregnant belly from under one tree to another. *Oh, and squirrels!* They're playing chase with a side game of hide-and-seek on a large pile of freshly stacked firewood.

The blinding reflection from the snow is so bright it's impossible with light-sensitive eyes to be out without sunglasses. But it's the sound that captivates me now, the crunch of packed snow and ice beneath every step I take. In other areas, the powder is so thick my boot disappears beneath. I inhale long and deep, the smell is crisp and clean, the cold air pushing through my lungs. It's invigorating, as if I'm granted a new life with my new start in my new home.

In another track, most likely from deer, I can't help but think of my bear. I'm both delusional and hopeful enough to believe that my bear is nearby at all times and will always protect me, even if I never see him again. These tracks, however, are just more signs in a laundry list of signs. I'm where I need to be, becoming who I've always longed to be.

My eyes shift back to the creek. Cottonwood Creek, the small yet fluid body of water that has stolen my heart and soul as it flows in that understated way, smoothly onward without much fuss. As beautiful as the winter has been, I cannot wait for warmer weather. I was not meant to stand on the banks. I'm counting the days to wade these waters again, to be part of this creek that lays before me like a broad belt of copper and gold.

Cottonwood Creek— these two defining words stir such meaning that I want to utilize them in the most honorable way I know how and also to thank Dean. This creek is essential to this place, integral to its life. It hits me then, the shock and awe of what I've probably known all along. The gallery, my gift from Dean, will never lack local imagery and substance and will be branded as Cottonwood Creek Impressions, Art in Motion.

Glancing up, away from the ducks swimming in-between patches of ice, I see Dean making his way to me. It's possible I'm in trouble. We had already disagreed last night and again this morning about whether or not Sam and I should take Ava and Colby and go stay with Darien in Denver. Neither Sam nor I are thrilled by the idea. In fact, we've both pushed hard against it, although we do concede that Ava and Colby should stay with Nana Sterling throughout the week.

With a stroke of luck, I've discovered Jules Jenson has all the credentials necessary to be a home care provider. It was Jules' idea, and I jumped at the prospect of obtaining assistance with Mama. It eases my conscious knowing Jules is Mama's age and is becoming more of a companion than a nurse. Mama is staying with Jules temporarily, which I don't like, but have also agreed to while things here remain dangerous.

When I hear Dean coming closer, I focus again on the creek. It possesses strength, flowing with confidence and perfect consistency, an artery of resilient water I need to mimic. If I'm capable of mirroring the behavior of the stream, I will be able to help Dean. It's more than a matter of rationality that I stay with Dean, it's a necessity.

My back is to him. I can't see his eyes but feel them on me. I sigh, forcing my lungs to suck in another sharp breath of cold air and swallow my heart back down my throat. Dean and I are complicated. The intensity between us swings like a pendulum, moving from a drug store romance to the other end, an end which holds a harsh reality. A truth that keeps us from what we want and what we think we can have. The fact that a mad man is lurking, and one of us could be hurt at any moment or worse.

"I'm not leaving," I huff.

"So, you keep saying." Dean steps closer, turning me to face him. "Baby, you can't keep coming out here alone."

I scoff a pained laugh, not that any of this is funny, and then bridge the gap between us and tug Dean into a hug. "I broke my promise, I'm sorry," I whisper. "I get out here, and my mind drifts to all the things I love most about it. Before I know it, I'm thinking of ways to replicate those feelings through a lens for the gallery to share with the world."

"Ryan, you're only driving my point further home. If you're that easily distracted, then you're a perfect target. Can't you see this from my point of view? Can you at least try?" I respond by covering his hand on my arm with mine which makes him remember us and soften. "I don't want to be apart from you either. I don't, but I'll do whatever it takes to guarantee your safety. Even if it means you're going to be royally pissed at me."

"I'm not going to be mad at you because I'm not going anywhere. We can sit down and make a plan. You can give me a list a mile long of what I can and cannot do, but I'm staying. It's non-negotiable. If you think I'd leave when things are the worst for you, you've lost your mind."

"I thought we agreed this morning."

"No, that was us having sex between disagreements."

"Well, to be fair, all I kept hearing was you saying "yes.""

I smile. "Nice try. And for the record, in that regard, I'll never say no."

"Good to know, but if I remember correctly, it was you who initiated it."

"That's because I've finally figured out the appeal of sex. All those sonnets actually have a point. And not to gloat but look how easily I've just distracted you. It happens."

"That's just it, though. It absolutely cannot happen, Ryan. If I let you stay here with me, you can't slip up again. If you do, even once, I'll haul you over my shoulder and carry you to Denver myself. Are we clear?"

"We're clear."

"What about Sam? She can't stay in that cabin alone. She either comes over with us, or you need to talk her into going to Denver."

"Samantha isn't going to go stay in Denver with Darien, Dean. She can barely wrap her head around the fact she even likes the woman. It's as if she has a deal with the devil to punish herself by warding off anything that could make her potentially happy."

"Then she stays here. I'm her brother. If I can't protect her, who will?"

"I'll talk to her."

"If she doesn't want to," Dean begins, dispirited, "she can stay with Nana Sterling or Ms. Jenson. Still, I'd feel better if you both went to Denver and took the girls." I squint. "Okay, whatever. It's her choice where, but it's my choice to make sure she isn't alone."

"She's pretty fearless, she might refuse."

"I could care less about her mammoth-sized ovaries. Convince her or I will."

Hmm. I'm not exactly sure how to navigate the rest, so I dive right in. "Actually, she's not alone. Darien is still here."

"Then Darien needs to stay with us too."

"Well…" There's only one way to find out how Dean feels about all this, and that's just to toss it out there. "That's not what I meant. Darien has been kind of staying with Sam."

"With Sam? Why?" I inhale, giving him a look. "Wait, what?"

"Nothing is going on. At least, I don't think there is. Yet. They've got this weird thing going on between them. They sleep together in a tent inside that tiny cabin but not like sleeping, sleeping together, if you know what I mean? They talk all night and keep each other company. It seems like it's been good for Sam, so I haven't meddled much."

"Sam likes her?"

"Honey, where have you been? Have you not noticed how hard Sam tries to avoid Darien? How she watches every move Darien makes, but also pretends to be irritated by everything Darien says and does? It's the same for Darien. I think Sam had her at "go away!""

"But Sam's still so…so sad." Dean looked over my head into the distance. "Just the other day I walked in on her when she was with the horses. I didn't say anything but could tell she'd been crying."

"I know you don't want to hear this, but I don't think Sam will ever not be sad. Sometimes she tells me things about Jordan, and when she does my heart breaks, Dean. She'll *always* love and miss Jordan. I believe Darien knows and understands that. I don't know what will happen, but I do know I've never seen Darien look at anyone the way she looks at Samantha."

"So, you're asking me to leave them alone as long as Darien is here?"

"I think we're safe in numbers. I think Darien has proven to us all that she's not going to let anyone come after Sam or me. Are you okay with that?"

"I'm okay with Darien helping her, but she better not hurt her."

"Oh, Blue...Darien might be the one we should be worried about on that front."

"Sam's been through enough."

"I agree. You know how I feel about Sam. If I have anything to say about it, she'll never suffer again." The sun has shifted, and ominous clouds have begun looming over the mountain. *So much for my bright, sunshiny day.* Within minutes the temperature has decreased. The "real feel" feels like it's quickly dropped into the teens, and I've started shivering.

"You're adorable when your nose gets all red, and your eyes are glossy. Am I that cute when I'm freezing?" Dean asks, grinning.

"Yes, and delusional," I tease. "It *is* freezing, and the cold is no place for lingering." Walking back to the house while holding Dean's hand, I ask, "Any news from Jenna?"

Dean sighed, distracted. "Yeah, she called right before I came looking for you. TC's talking better but only able to get about three words out before he gets confused. Doctors seem to be pleased with his progress and are trying to get him to sit up and move to a chair. They weren't able to finish a swallow test because he keeps falling asleep."

"It's good news, honey. You're killing yourself with worry."

"How much longer before you tell me about the other thing we're probably going to disagree on?"

"Sometimes you scare me," I say, squinting at Dean. How can he possibly know? We've all done so well at hiding it. "I can explain." Dean looks at me skeptically. "We made a deal. We made a pinkie promise. That's a big deal, you know? Think of it as a female version of a code of honor."

"Colby made you do this?" Dean asked, doubtfully.

"Not exactly. She promised to make a valid effort to stop cussing if I'd talk to you about letting her get a puppy. Every girl needs a puppy, honey. It's like a rite of passage." I finish with reaching up, balancing on the toes of my snow boots to bite on Dean's lower lip before kissing him.

"This is sexual manipulation at its finest."

"We've been hiding it in Sam's cabin, and they're about to kill me because I haven't told you yet. I was about to this morning but then, well… you know how easily sidetracked we get in bed together. Anyway, when we were in Leadville, there was this litter of puppies for sale right there in town as we walked by. Golden Retrievers just like Bodie! How could I not? One of them latched onto me, and I had to have her for Colby."

"I was actually talking about you piercing her ears. You got Colby a dog?!"

Oh boy! "In my defense, it was girl's night. We did Ava and Colby's ears together. Blue, these are the things girls do together and some of these things you will never understand."

"She's a little young for that."

"She's not, but I should have asked you first."

"About which?"

294

"Both, the puppy and the pierced ears. Exactly how much trouble am I in?" I ask, leaning forward to brush my lips along his neck just under his chin.

"See, you're doing it again. That's cheating. And don't bat your eyelashes at me. You're totally trying to take advantage of me, aren't you?" Dean stepped out of reach. "We need to talk about these things."

"You're right, we do," I agree, invading his space once again then whispering near his ear as if it were a sweet secret just between the two of us. "Can you forgive me?"

"Do I have a choice?"

"Not really."

"Then I guess I'm looking the other direction."

"Then I guess I am taking advantage of you. I also happen to think you're a very wise man. It's no wonder your spirit animal is an owl."

Our idea to fall back into bed dies flat upon our arrival back to the house. Jey is at the door knocking as we round the corner. It's no hardship to invite her in, I enjoy watching Dean interact with his mother and the stories she shares with him.

"Where's Luke? Dean asks."

"On a mission in Montrose. He, along with several others who were elected to the Southern Ute Tribal Council have been feeling the heat about Buckskin Charley."

"Buck who?"

Jey smiles, taking in all of her son in one adoring sweep. "Many tribal elders have been riding Luke about Buckskin Charley's headdress. The eagle-feathered headdress has been hanging in the state history museum in Montrose for over fifty years now. The tribe is demanding it to be returned, but

Colorado officials denied the request. The elders want to go to court under a new federal law pressing artifacts of religious worth to be returned to the tribes."

"Then what's the problem?" I ask, interested. I've stood to refill our mugs with coffee only to lean over Dean's shoulder, running my fingers through his hair.

"The problem is Buckskin Charley apparently gave the headdress to a Durango lawyer, Barry Sullivan. It's said they were close friends. Years after Barry died, a friend of his daughter's found the headdress and took it to the state museum."

"How does Luke feel about it?"

"He wants to respect the wishes of the elders but stands dead center in the middle of a misunderstanding. The Native American Graves Protection and Repatriation Act was developed to unite museum curators and American Indians in a partnership. To date, Luke has had little luck in joining efforts. My Luke, he's a tribal man, so he thinks the headdress should be returned to the tribe, and so do I. Buckskin Charley was the last official hereditary chief of the Southern Utes. The children of the tribe need such things to identify our culture with."

Dean's cell buzzes, interrupting. "I need to take this call." Before Dean is able to answer Jenna's call, we receive a text message.

From: TC
To: Jen, Dean, Garrett, Reece, Sam, Ryan
I didn't fall. I was pushed.

CHAPTER TWENTY-SIX

"Darien," Sam whispered, attempting to wake her tentmate a little after 3 a.m.

"Shh," Darien muttered barely audible. "Stay behind me and slowly scoot over as close to me as you can."

Deacon's head shot up, tilting it from left to right and back to the left. One second then two before he was up, leaping into the kitchen, barking fervently. On her knees and with one arm behind her back to confirm Sam was behind her, Darien closed her eyes then slowly opened them, focused. With her arm fully extended, she aimed a handgun toward the opening of the tent.

In the kitchen, there was a deep and ominous growl, a brief struggle before a sharp whimpering cry, and then silence. Sam jerked from Darien's grasp, ready to confront the intruder, and prepared to fight for her life if necessary, to get to Deacon. Deacon was lying motionless, heavily sedated, and blinking his eyes open then closed, trying unsuccessfully to paw his way toward his attacker to defend his keeper.

Searching, unaware Samantha and Darien were inside the small tent, the prowler passed. They heard the bedroom door splinter open as it was kicked in. Another brief silence. Then swift and thunderous footsteps moved upstairs toward the loft. Darien reached for Sam, halting her only long enough to look into her eyes and relay the message. *Run, Sam!*

Samantha wriggled free of the tent and raced to Deacon, hoisting him before using her sock-clad foot to widen the burglarized door that had been pried open. She paused a fraction of a second to look over her shoulder, to be certain Darien was behind her. She wasn't. In lieu, Samantha regarded the towering figure in a ski mask clomping down the stairway. When Darien made a move for the door, he jumped, virtually flying to land heavily on Darien, knocking her to the ground and the gun from her hand.

Samantha set Deacon's comatose body on a patch of snow. "Be strong, my boy. Stay with me a little longer." She knew Deacon was close to passing out, knew the strength of Ketamine—a horse tranquilizer that had gone missing weeks before. It was strong, too strong. Deacon would die after passing out if she didn't get him to the barn quickly and administer an antidote to reverse the overdose.

Running to Darien, Sam skidded to an abrupt stop at the base of the steps to her cabin. She was met by the masked man coming out with Darien in a choke-hold, holding Darien's gun to her head.

"Sam?! What the hell?" Samantha doesn't turn to register Dean barefoot and hollering. As he runs toward her, slipping on ice and yanking on jeans, I'm chasing him in little more than a t-shirt and unlaced snow boots.

Pop! Pop!

The shots echo through the canyon like silver-tail bottle rockets but closer, louder. Dean dives to the ground taking both Sam and me with him, shielding our bodies from stray bullets. He inclines his head, no more than an inch, unable to see past the ringing in his ears. He squeezes his eyes shut then opens them to see two blurry figures gradually descending the steps.

I try shaking the drumming in my ears, try to make out the sounds. I struggle to make sense of the demands being whispered to Darien, struggle to see her clearly through the dark. Shaking my head once more, I'm able to make her out. Barely. I shriek her name, registering the terror she wears. She's terrified yet tenacious to protect.

"Are you hit?" Dean asks her, and I can feel his weight shift. I have a sick feeling he's about to lunge toward a man holding a gun.

"No, it w-wwas a warning." There's a second more of whispering, and then Darien swallows, summoning her strength. "Dean, please," Darien begs, her voice less shaken. "If you let him take me, he won't shoot Sam. He won't kill her or Ryan if you get out of the way."

I jump to my feet. "No! Take me!" There was sinister laughter—evil and entertained and oddly disguised. "Come on, you chickenshit! Take me, not her! Let's finish our conversation in person, not letters! Let her go!"

299

Dean tugs my arm, pulling me hard against him to the ground. "Stop it, Ryan!" His actions are echoed by Samantha, who latches onto me and doesn't let go.

Slowly, one knee at a time with his hands pinning us down, Dean begins to rise. I can see the intent in his eyes just as another shot is fired, ricocheting off the ground inches from Dean.

"Dean," Darien tries. "He...he wants..." She breaks off, listens, then tries again. "You can stand very slowly with your hands up, and then back away. Please. All of you, together."

Cautiously, with one step and then another, Dean steps with a death grip on both Sam and me to do the same. We have no choice but to follow. Darien's eyes bounce from mine to Samantha's. "I won't let him hurt you," she murmurs, her eyes flashing panic through a veil of tears. Her promise ends when the chokehold around her neck tightens, and we can hear her gasp for air.

I dare to look at Sam. She's glaring at the man dragging Darien away. We're both shaken, forced to ignore the horror we should feel, the fear that will haunt our days and nights to come. I drag my eyes from Sam to the shadows moving away. It's no longer my shortly-lived bravado Dean should worry about. I won't do anything to jeopardize Darien's safety, but Sam will. She is quaking with fury.

Carefully, I reach for her, but it's too late. Samantha steps away, risking her life to move closer to Deacon. Nearing her dog, she closes her eyes, powerless to anything as this man takes Darien away.

It feels like an eternity, not only minutes when we hear an engine roar to life in the distance. It's quickly followed by

300

sounds of tires slicing and sliding through slush speeding away. I blink, and Dean is already in motion, running to catch a glimpse of the vehicle. There's nothing to see, nothing but a hint of red taillights fading into the black of the night.

Samantha, with a pain-stricken emotion, bends to Deacon. I kick, flinging my snow boots off. "Sam, put those on." Forcefully, she tugs the boots on, not bothering to tie them, then lifts Deacon, embracing the deadweight tightly in her arms.

I run into the house to collect a jacket and boots for Dean and throw them at him. Without a shirt, he hops from one foot to another, pulling his shoes and jacket on then runs. Over his shoulder, he yells, "Get inside! Lock the doors! And get help!" His voice is fading as he sprints away. "Call the police! Call everyone!" It's the last I hear him say.

Quickly after, I hear a snowmobile. The engine balks at first then cranks over, the sound is thunderous as Dean darts by at a startling speed. I deadbolt the door and rush to my phone.

Darien has been captured and taken by the same man who killed Drew Young. I'm sure of it. Samantha is running through the woods through the pitch-black of night. She's practically skating over the thin sheet of ice blanketing the dirt road, trying not to slip or stumble with her dog dying in her arms. And Dean, the absolute love of my life, is chasing after the killer on a snowmobile in negative eight degrees. The time that follows is a blur.

#

Blindfolded and bound by something tight around her wrists, she shivered. Her teeth were chattering, and her body was tense from the severe chill. There was a sputtering sound, she didn't recognize, perhaps an older generator, but nothing more. Nevertheless, it was cold, harsher than she'd be able to bear much longer inside the small, unlit room. It smelled musty and old, like a discarded antique store that hadn't been opened in years.

She listened for more sounds, detecting none. She could be anywhere. She wondered if he was sitting close by and observing her, or had he gone? If he'd left, would he be back? She didn't know what she wanted more, him be gone or return, not confident she'd survive either way. When she rocked against what felt like a damp floor, she heard the creak of aged wood.

Her limbs were throbbing from being constrained too tightly. Power cords, not rope, were used to bind her wrists and ankles together, making it impossible to continue her fight. Scattered around her feet were unused zip-ties, rolls of plastic, and the evidence of mildew.

"Are you here?" she panted, shivering. "You are, aren't you?

Kneeling closely by, he answered by reaching out, running a finger over her thigh then moved slowly up to her chest. She flinched, unable to move beyond the tremor. Repulsion stuck thickly in her throat, bile that had no place to go but to be swallowed down.

"You're warm enough, for now. You won't die just yet. Who's to say, though. A storm is coming. It's a big one, so no promises."

"Who are you?"

"Your friend, she calls me Killer."

"Stay away from her."

"Or what?" He laughed. "Easy, now. Settle down, or you'll cut up those pretty arms even more. "Tell me, why would I bother her when you're the one who shot me?"

"I should have aimed for your head."

"Where's the fun in that? We are having fun, aren't we?"

"This isn't a game. You're trying too hard to mask your voice. Show me who you are. Be a real man, not a coward."

"Coward? You don't mean that. Now, come on and tell me. Who should I kill first? Your friend or the blonde?"

"Fuck you."

"Would you like to? We have time," he added, his voice not nearly as masked.

\#

"Is he back?" Garrett asks, rushing in, glancing around for Dean.

"No!" He's still out there," I flail my arm, gesturing outdoors. "I called the police then called you. You're the first one here."

"What happened? Are you okay?"

"Just what I already told you. Garrett, I'm scared, I don't know what to do. He has her...the Killer has Darien." I lean

303

forward, burying my face against Garrett's chest and cry. "Where is everyone? Why is it taking so long?"

"They've probably already caught up with Dean. Ryan, where's Sam?"

"She's with Deacon. I have to go to her. I need to help her."

"Forget it, you're staying here. On the way over, I called Reece. He's on his way. We'll find Dean, and then we'll find Darien, but you have to promise to stay put." Garrett runs down the porch steps then turns, nearly slipping to a stop at the bottom. "I mean it. Get inside and stay away from windows. Don't unlock the door until we're back, not even for the cops."

"Should I call them again? Make sure they're on their way or with Dean?"

"Yes. Reece and I will catch them on the road one way or another. Ask for a car to patrol the house, but I'm serious, Ryan...*stay* inside!"

The instant I see a second snowmobile shoot by, knowing Garrett is trailing Dean, I don't hesitate. I run to the closet beside the door and pull on another pair of boots then fly out the front door. They'd have to put a bullet in me before I'd ever stand by and do nothing while my best friends are in danger.

Running toward the stable, I can feel flakes hitting my skin, melting as quickly as they land. It won't be long before the soft flakes feel like pellets of ice. Narrowing the distance, I see the light inside the barn and a shadow quickly moving from side to side. I kick the door wide open in haste and bend at the waist. I glance up, breathing heavily with puffs of white cloudy air escaping my lungs. Startled, Sam jumps then moves like lightning from the table where Deacon is covered in a horse blanket to me.

"Deacon," I pant. "Is he okay?" Adrenaline has gotten me here, but I'm so cold and frightened that I struggle to form the words coming through the chattering of my teeth.

"He will be," Sam says, pulling me into a frantic hug. "That sonofabitch tried to kill my dog, and he has—" She's unable to finish as I feel her shudder against me.

"I have to tell you something." I grimace. With a firm grip on my upper arms, Sam pushes me back enough to look me in the eye. She's scowling, her eyes beaming into mine. "I think I know where he's taken her. I…I could be wrong."

"Where?"

"I leave him letters."

"Who?"

"The Killer."

"Ryan!"

"I provoke him. I keep thinking he'll mess up and say something…anything to give me a clue, so they can catch him."

"Who is the killer, Ryan?"

"I don't know." I blink. "I wrote about a place in my last letter, challenging him to meet me there. I was going to tell Dean but then things with Jim and then TC…and I…I forgot. The Killer is smart, Sam, but he finds me amusing and crazy enough to endanger myself to prove a point. I wanted to trap him. I was going to tell you."

"You're still writing this person?" Sam yells, something I've never heard her do. It's all there and all at once, everything in her tone: the scold, the worry, the alarm.

"He's going to slip. One of these times, he's going to make a mistake."

"In exchange for what? For you? Is that what you're telling me?!" Samantha is furious, uncompromising with her anger. "That's insane! *You're* insane! Only you would dangle your life in front of a murderer so carelessly! Did you ever stop to think what would happen to Dean or me if anything happened to you?! You think you're invincible, Ryan, well newsflash, you're not! Far fucking from it!"

"Please stop screaming at me," I manage. I can't bear her anger, especially now. Images of Darien are burning holes in the backs of my eyelids. "This is all my fault."

Samantha inhales sharply then slowly exhales. "You're an idiot," she declares, more calmly now. "But this isn't your fault." Sam blinks. "He's got her...he's got Darien." She turns, glancing at Deacon. We witness the rise and fall of his chest as he sleeps the toxins away. "Where is she?"

"I don't know how to get there in this, Sam. It's snowing, and there's no road. It's...up there." I point up the mountain.

"Can we do it horseback?"

"Maybe." I think about it. "Yes," I say, eager to try.

"On the trail?"

"No. We stumbled on it by accident. It's at least a mile from the second radio tower. Drew was tagging along one afternoon in July when I was working. He said he'd never seen it before, said we were probably the first to come across it in years. It's secluded, tough to see."

"What is?"

"A cabin, a very old and small, deserted cabin."

"The creepy shack you told me about? Past the waterfall?"

"The one with a missing door, broken windows, decomposing floor and a rotting roof. Yes, that one."

Sam is a flash of motion, working swiftly around me to secure the barn. She slows only to check Deacon's vitals then looks up to me. I grasp the magnitude of what we are about to do. Sam kisses Deacon on the forehead then moves to the door. I look her in the eye before stepping out, both of us dragging in one final, deep breath before running back to the house.

The wind is gale-force and howling. As I dress in layers, I hear windchimes and Samantha rambling to herself. "Your home, the place you live, it's where you're supposed to feel safe. The one place to let your guard down and perform your most personal routines. The space in which you are your most vulnerable," Sam scoffs, lost in her thoughts. "Think again if you think you're going to break into my home, take *my* things, and get away with it."

CHAPTER TWENTY-SEVEN

"Ryan!" Dean shouted, searching every room feverishly then took the stairs three at a time to their bedroom. "Ryan!"

"If she's scared, she could be hiding," Reece suggested. To be sure, Garrett and Reece began looking in closets, behind doors, and in the utility room. Inside the kitchen, Garrett found Bodie, anxious and pacing in circles by the back door. Peering through the window panes of the door, Garrett caught the first glimpse of faint footprints in the fresh sheet of snow on the deck.

"They're small," Dean said, kneeling beside the tracks. "She's with Sam." Dean jumped to his feet, racing toward Sam's cabin, sliding but catching himself before a fall.

With his arm raised, ready to pound on Samantha's cabin door, he froze. Bodie was barking, running a circle up the road then back, beseeching Dean's attention. "What boy?" He followed Bodie with his eyes toward the stables just as headlights blinded him.

Jenna braked, jumping out. "Dean! What is going on? I was driving home when I got a message from Garrett." Before Dean could answer, he saw TC climbing slowly from the passenger seat.

"What the hell, Jenna?! What's he doing out of the hospital? Reece!" Dean yelled. "Get him inside!" He pointed to TC then the house before turning back to Jenna. "It's slick out here and dangerous, what if he fell? Forget it! I don't have time for this, I have to find my wife!"

"Look at him!" Jenna pointed at TC. "You think I could stop him?" She slammed her car door shut. "It was after midnight when he just up and decides he's leaving. You think I didn't try to keep him there? Now stop glaring at me and tell me what's going on? Why are you maniacs all here at this time of morning? It's not even light out!" Jenna kept on after Dean had stopped listening and ran inside.

"Is he well enough to be out? Should I call Brittany?" Reece asked, already dialing Brittany as he approached a pale and frail TC.

"No. But like each of you, he's a stubborn ass. And did Dean say wife?"

"He does that now," Garrett answered, moving to help Reece get TC safely indoors. "Don't worry, he'll never get married without you here. You got past the barricade?"

"I had to bite the sheriff's head off to get past it. What is going on?!"

"Someone broke in Sam's place." Garrett swallowed, hesitant to share the rest. "He took Darien. We couldn't track it. The wind… the snow…there's nothing. We've gone up and down the pass and into every outlet before the road closure. She's gone."

"Reece, fill the tanks!" Dean ordered, descending the slippery steps and tossing Reece a pair of goggles.

"What tanks?" Reece asked, dumbfounded with an arm around TC's waist.

"The snowmobiles! Fuel up the Firecat for me. Jenna, hurry, I'll help you two up. You stay with TC and do not leave. Garrett, take my sled. It's mostly full. Go to your house and get every gun you've got. Meet Reece and me at the hollow in five. Dress for it. We're going up."

"Dean!" Jenna yelled.

"What?!"

"The sun will be up soon. Please wait."

"No."

"Do you remember when Nana Sterling told us about Chipeta? The wife of Ouray?"

"Jen, I don't have time for a history lesson! I've got to find them before it's too late."

"Sam and Ryan…they're both like Chipeta, always trying to save the hostage. Respect their bravery. But you *are* the bear. The symbol of strength and leadership, so slow the hell down, and be smart."

"Fine, but I'm not waiting," he said, forcing them inside and closing the door. He waited until he heard the click of the lock then skidded down the steps once again, catching up with Reece.

Through the window, Jenna watched the mystical dance of zig-zagging red lights vanish into the woods as another row of flashing blue and red lights came into view. "Oh, my God."

Darien Shay

I am freezing to death. Literally.

I have to keep thinking, keep doing this, doing everything I can to stay awake. What's today? It's January 5th. Is the sun up yet? It doesn't feel like it. It was barely three when I was taken by gunpoint. How did I get here? I was shoved into a single cab truck and driven a short distance before being blindfolded and moved to a motorized sled. It felt more powerful than a regular snowmobile.

Did we stop after that? Yes. Idling only long enough for him to cover my windburned face with a plastic garbage bag. I can breathe, I'm not being suffocated. Still, he's going to kill me.

Inside the damp plastic and beneath the blindfold I have to fight to keep my eyes open. I am desperate not to get tired. What I think was a generator has stopped working. How weak. It gave up before me, leaving me to die alone.

He's taken everything from me, even my clothing. I am naked, stripped of warmth, dignity, and perseverance.

Think of something, of anything, but not this. Except for that. Stop thinking of how roughly he tore your clothes away. Don't go there, not again. Forget his gloved hand spreading your legs before he stopped. Forget that two heartbeats later, his hand was back. That time without a glove. It doesn't matter that his hands were calloused and probing.

Wait. Am I alone? I am. I can't be sure. It's possible he's close, I never heard him go. I don't remember. Why don't I

311

remember? I passed out, didn't I? I feel...what? Cold but not defiled.

Don't fall apart, just rest. No, never mind, do not rest. Think of something good. Samantha. Yes. Think of her. Why? We aren't even a couple. We aren't anything. I'm admitting it now, declaring defeat. Keep it together, you can't die on her, too.

Please, Lord, show mercy with that ever so slight yet significant wish. I will cuss less and pray more. I won't fire anyone for an entire year, unless...well, okay, I won't. I'll abide by traffic laws set by the foolish elected officials who think driving at a speed of sixty is acceptable. I'll admit it's unlikely that I'll bestow my natural born gift for good taste. Let's be real, we both enjoy a glass of fine wine.

I've never been so tired. Why is it so cold? Close your eyes, don't think about it. Okay, only for a minute, just until...

#

"You good?" Sam asks, peering over her shoulder. We're both in beanies with headlamps attached. The LED lighting is bright, but I'm relieved for the sun beginning to rise, albeit slowly.

My horse and I have already bit the dust more than once. Three times, to be exact. Sam, however, remains saddled and spry. She's determined. I've seen her driven before for the greater good of an animal lost and traumatized, but this is different. Now she is single-minded, untiring, and trudging our way off trails and up.

My first fall was underestimating the depth of the snowbank when jumping the gulley. The result was landing in snow over our heads, horse and human. The second was when a tree limb caught my jacket and promptly yanked me off. It tore my coat and hurt. I'll have a bruise on my butt and probably a broken finger, but I refuse to remove my glove to see. It's *that* cold. The third, the one I'm most upset about, is because it's clearly the one Samantha is most upset about.

My horse continues to slip. Sam has said the word "snowballing" no less than five times. We're riding two of the most physically fit horses on the property, two without previous ailment or injury to spark joint pain from the harsh temperature. Sam's paying close attention, looking for signs. "Winter riding can pose challenges," she'd said. "The horses don't move around nearly as much during turn-out as they do when it's warmer. In bad weather, they need breaks." Something we don't have time for.

Snowballing is the accumulation of ice and snow at the bottom of the horse's foot. "It's a major problem," Sam said, just before Rocket, the quarter horse I'm riding, slipped on an incline, sending us both over backward. Apparently, the snow melts some on contact with the hoof then refreezes quickly, and that creates a mound of snow and ice that is difficult to remove. Rocket is longer-toed and flat-footed and is unable to pop the snow out.

I suggested we leave Rocket, only temporarily, by securing him to the trunk of an Aspen and I ride with Sam the remainder of the way. Honestly, the only thing on my mind is getting to Darien, praying she's where I think she is. I can't let my mind wander anywhere else. If she's not there, we may never find her. But Sam is quick to refuse. "We need him to bring Darien home." I say nothing, curious if this could be the one and only time Samantha has ever willingly put a human before an animal. Then, "Besides, we don't want him to think we've abandoned him."

Our locale is insanely dangerous—we are now in whiteout conditions. I'm a novice rider at best, and the snowpack, unlike previous years is troublesome with recent and current weather. I'm concerned we are going to misstep and be in for an unintended avalanche ride down a steep ravine. I frown, understanding the only speed over the first switchback is fast. It's ill-advised, but we are racing the clock on too many fronts to care.

Because we are on horseback, we don't have to bother with deep post-holing. It doesn't prevent us from reminding one another to be alert. The last thing we want is to traverse the slide gulley. Not to be redundant, but it's just that important.

We cross a line veering more southerly than anticipated but head up the hill near tree-line in the nick of time. Nearing the eleven-thousand-foot knoll, we barely see it nestled snugly between pines. The cabin. Approaching slowly, we come across a pair of snowshoes partially covered in fresh powder. It's spine-chilling: the elements and the cabin. Sam and I are both petrified of what we will encounter inside the deteriorating structure. We are terrified of finding Darien, terrified of not.

The cabin stands alone, barely visible among the woods preserving its secrets. The front door is nowhere to be seen, and the windows are missing glass. I'm remembering most of this vaguely, as the weather conditions make it hard to detect detail. What's worse, is it's similar to what I would expect in a Stephen King novel. Except this is real, and it's possible that my friend's remains are inside of it.

Sam and I are quiet with our dismount behind thick rows of Pinyon pines. My heart sinks. We're close enough to see there is no smoke piling from the lone pipe exposed from a half caved in roof, which means there is no heat. I remember a rusting metal stove in the corner. Suddenly, I find myself praying that I'm wrong and Darien's not here.

The horse blanket Sam's strapped between the saddle and her horse's croup is now draped over her shoulders. She's crouched behind a sturdy tree trunk inhaling slowly, in and out. Her eyes are closed. I realize she's pumping herself up and about to go for it. "You should stay here," she suggests, her eyes still closed.

"Forget it. But, Sam...you have Ava to think about. You've gotten us this far, let me do the rest. Please."

Sam cracks one eye open. "Do you like trains?"

"Trains?" *What the hell? Not again!* "Sam, you did this bizarre chatter with our bear too! We don't have time to do that again. Not now. Stay here, keep an eye on the horses, and wait for me. I'll bring her out, and we'll go home. All of us. Together."

"Ryan?" I look at her. "Have I told you about my friend? My brother-in-law, Mike?"

I sigh. "Yes, Sam, you have."

"He loves trains."

"Great. But later, okay?" I'm worried the cold has reached Sam's mind.

"He told me once that he hopped a train from one side of the country to another. He said the ride felt like the loneliest place on earth. Everyone else on board got off at some point. They had purposes and places to get to. His point was that it's easy to be a passenger, but that's not real life. Life is about purpose, about going places. So, he got off that train." Sam gets to her feet. "And I'm not one to stand still either." And with that, Samantha took off.

I frequently run, so I'm marginally faster and manage to gain the lead. The adrenaline and determination to defend my friends also helps to drive me forward. I shift my eyes and see the foundation is a mixture of corroding cement and river rock with many stones missing, creating an uneven entry. Not that I stand a chance against a man with a gun, but I unsheathe the knife I've taken from Dean's nightstand and release the blade anyway.

It's dark inside. I squint and make out a small table with a knocked over salt shaker. There's a teacup in perfect condition, and beside it, a plate that's eroded into a black, crusty mess. There's nothing else to see, nothing at eye-level. I lower my eyes to the sodden floor. I'm nudged aside as Sam rushes to the bundle in the fetal position in the corner of the odorous room.

Darien is naked, her clothes nowhere to be found. She's unresponsive. My eyes drown in tears as I collapse to my knees. My only thought: *Darien is dead.*

I'm struck by something, knocking me from my stupor. Sam has thrown the horse blanket at me. "Shake it. Keep shaking it until I tell you to stop," Sam demands, tossing her jacket aside then yanking her sweatshirt over her head.

"What are you doing?"

316

"Body heat. I'm going to cover her, and then I want you to cover us in the blanket and then my clothes on top of that." Sam pauses long enough to look at me, then, "Ryan, I need you to listen to me." I know what's coming, and I don't want to hear it but know it's our only chance. "You have to go for help. Ride down, follow the trail we made coming up. Take Dante, not Rocket, his footing is better. Cover us, then go!"

I run as fast as the deep powder will allow only to find the horses gone. I run nearly fifty feet more, but Rocket and Dante are nowhere to be seen. I turn in circles. Evidently, I've run in the wrong direction. Already, I'm turned around. Except, I'm not. The horses are gone.

I run back inside to hear Samantha whispering longwinded yet incoherent words to Darien. I stop moving, rooted to where I'm standing. I look at Sam in disbelief. They aren't incoherent words at all. They are the kind of words, aesthetic ones, that anyone with a soul would want to hear if they were slipping between lives.

"Sam, they're gone."

Sam responds eerily calm, an attribute only she can pull off in crisis. *Crisis*, I think, sinking back to my knees. I'm failing them. I'm having a crisis in confidence, and it's consuming me. "Screw it, Drew and I made it here on foot, I'll make it down the same way."

"Come here, Ryan." I move closer. I don't have the strength to look at Darien's face. I can't do it. My hands are shaking, my entire body is shaking. I want to scream but don't. "Hold my hand." I reach for Sam's bare hand with my glove covered one. "We're going to be okay. She has a pulse, I can feel it. She's alive. I need you here...Darien and

317

I need you to stay here. You can't go down on foot. You'll never make it."

"I can't just sit here, Sam."

"I know. Generate some heat. Move around. Walk, jump, run circles...just keep moving."

"I don't see her breathing," I gasp, covering my mouth with my hands once I dare to look.

"She is, I promise. Help us by helping make it warmer. It's the wind that's the worst."

I remove my jacket and use it and Sam's coat to block the arctic gusts shooting through the two small windows. "I'll be right back." Outside, I look around for anything poking out of the snow. I manage to find broken slats of rotting wood crates and other decaying brush, limbs, and debris to close off as much as the doorway as possible. It's feeble coverage at best, but it's better. At the very least, we can no longer feel the harsh slaps of wind, only hear it's screams.

"S-sssmm," we hear. *Oh my God!* It's Darien.

"I'm here, I've got you," Sam whispers. "Ryan, keep moving."

"I'm going back out there. The horses…they have to be close."

"They wouldn't just leave. Stay. We're safer together. Dean knows this mountain. He knows it better than anyone. He's smart."

"He is," I agree. "I can feel him. He's coming."

#

The horse paths were easier to trail, although some markings indicated trouble, like a fall or several. They took turns taking the lead and circled around. It was a safety measure, two together, one apart. If anything went wrong, one of them would discharge and go for help. However, Reece was looping longer than warranted, longer than Dean was comfortable with.

Once Reece pulled around from the southeast, Dean breathed a sigh of relief, then nodded to Garrett to fall behind. A minute later, Reece was gone again as Dean waved Garrett to stop, quickly cutting the engines. Dean lifted his goggles, pointing to the cabin hidden well within trees. He glanced around. The wind was loud and forcefully carrying the snow sideways. There weren't any signs of horses, not that he could see. But there was something, something barely visible in the windows. It looked like clothing.

"Watch my back," Dean said, starting to push through the deep snow on foot.

Bursting through the makeshift barricade, Dean dove inside, spinning to his side with a gun in his hand. He turned quickly to check the parameters. Garrett was quick to follow with one hand on Dean's back, pressing him down, shielding his friend. When Dean was greeted by two wide-eyed women, he dropped his forehead with a thump against the wet floor, relieved.

With the engine idling, Reece runs inside, heavy-footed. With one hand against the doorjamb, he bends over, winded and trying to catch his breath. "Horses," he gasps. "Two of them about three hundred yards from here. He lifts his eyes, meeting mine. "She's alive?"

"She's alive," I answer, rushing to Dean.

#

The excursion down the mountain was strenuous. The inclement weather conditions, the terrain, the fatigued horses, and Samantha's resolve to not release Darien proved to be challenging. Trained for these circumstances, Dean was patient with his instructions. "Be gentle, keep her covered, keep an eye on her breathing." The list went on.

Two demanding hours later, we arrived like a caravan to the main house, ambushed on sight by local authorities and Jenna Sterling. We were exhausted and leery of everyone around.

In rapid succession, Brittany Saben the doctor, not the friend, shouted a mouthful of clear commands to those standing by. Brittany reached for Darien, attempting to pry her from Samantha with little luck. "It's okay, Sam. I'll take care of her," Brittany promised, before giving orders to two deputies to help carefully carry Darien inside to administer emergency care.

"If I let go, she'll crash," Sam said.

"She won't."

She did.

320

CHAPTER TWENTY-EIGHT

A week ago, I was at a carnival looking at the rides. By looking, I mean just that. Instead of riding any, I wandered from ride-to-ride watching people much braver than I am being tossed into the air. At one point, I waited by a smaller version of the Sky Roller for children who are yet to learn that death is permanent. When I glanced up to the Ferris Wheel, I saw Darien free falling to her death.

I jolted awake from that dream just as I had from all the others. For the past seven days, life has been exactly that—a carnival ride.

I should have foreseen that Darien would require more than passive rewarming. Of course, she would. Her philosophy for everything: go big or go home. Her clinical presentation had included a spectrum of symptoms. I could have predicted which of the three categories—mild, moderate, or severe—she'd go with.

Treatments vary depending on the degree of hypothermia, ranging from noninvasive, passive external warming techniques to active external rewarming to active core rewarming. Sam and I learned that and more, refusing to leave Darien's side. No surprise that the management for severe hypothermia would be much more complex and her outcome depended heavily on clinical resources. Hence our gratitude for being close to town and mostly for Brittany's competence to recognize Darien's atypical demonstrations. Dr. Brittany Saben had acted swiftly, and little did we know, we had front row seats to experience Darien's mortality.

At the Heart of the Rockies Regional Medical Center, Brittany, alongside an adept medical team, struggled to resuscitate Darien with ongoing CPR. At the words "cardiac arrest," I clung to Sam as we were stopped by staff. We were no longer granted access to the behind-the-scenes of the show. Before the door completely closed, Brittany looked up, and I saw the conviction in her eyes. She was working on the mantra that '*you aren't dead until you're warm and dead.*'

Alas, here we are, a week later. Darien is sleeping in the guest room downstairs, while I lie restless and awake in the room above her. It's well past the witching hour, the time of night my imagination runs wild.

Sam is also here and occupying Colby's room. There are times she's reluctant to leave Darien's side. I wonder if it's because she was denied the opportunity to be on this side of Jordan's recovery. I don't intervene, and neither does Dean. We say nothing. This is Sam's journey to either embrace or depart. Whether she likes it or not, and regardless of her readiness, something is evolving between them, albeit slowly.

Waiting for the sun to rise is like watching paint dry, that's true. There's no chance I'll fall back asleep. An idea sparks, and for a nanosecond, I think I should wake Dean. Ice fishing. I'd really like to finally conquer the mountain the only way I know how, which means catching the long-awaited rainbow trout. If I can pull that off, I can make mackerel for breakfast. *Gross, but clever!*

After all, it's during breakfast when I plan to break the news. There has to be a suitable way to tell them I need to leave, but I haven't found that way quite yet. It's not as if I'm leaving for long, a few days at most. Get there and get back—that's the plan. If things go well, I prefer not staying overnight. The tortured soul from Silver Valley is no more. I have one final thing to do, and then I'm closing the book of my past.

Dean stirs, smothering me more. He doesn't cuddle, he conquers. He takes up most of the bed, three-fourths of the pillows, half the blankets, and all of me. Sometimes I think I'll need a prying bar to separate us in the morning.

It takes almost five actual minutes to escape the extraordinary lover in my bed. Not to mention the mad Jedi skills it takes to acquire the appropriate clothing to go downstairs to start a fire and make coffee without waking him. Mid-step and halfway down the staircase, I stop. There's already a warm blaze glowing in the hearth. Samantha is awake.

With our backs against the sofa and our feet reaching toward the warmth of the fire, I sit beside her on the floor.

She scribbles one final word in her journal and closes the leather case. "Hey."

I smile and rest my head on her shoulder. Aside from Dean and Colby, there isn't a person I love more. "Hi."

"I'm sorry I yelled at you the other day."

"I deserved it."

"I can't lose anyone else."

"You won't."

"Then why are you planning to leave?"

I look at her. *Hmm*. "What do you mean?"

"Ryan?"

Ugh! "Okay, must you always be so intuitive. Besides, I should tell Dean first, not you."

"Tell us both." I look up. I should have known it wouldn't be long before Dean realized I'd fled our cozy bed. He's making his way down the staircase then sits on the leather recliner facing both Sam and me.

"I have to go to Silver Valley. It's a quick trip I can't avoid. In and out, and then I'll be back."

"No—"

"I'll go with you," Sam says, interrupting Dean. I look at her.

"Sam, we both know you can't leave right now." Sam breaks eye contact and instead focuses on the edge of the area rug we are sitting on.

"Okay," Sam agrees, far too easily. "You're right, I can't."

I turn to Dean. "Blue, I have to go. I will be in a vehicle during daylight in the last place any psychopath would want to be. You have to trust that I'm not taking any more chances."

"Why now? Why can't it wait?"

"I have to go now and have to help put an end to all of this."

"Don't you see? Both of you" he points at me and then Sam "with the same mindset. You say one thing and do another. "You're still taking chances."

"What does any of this have to do with Silver Valley? Is it Jim?" Sam asks. I nod.

"This is about your uncle?" Dean asks.

"He's not my uncle, honey. It's fine to say it. Jim is my dad. It's nothing more and nothing less than a fact." Ironically, the biological detail is bothering each of them more than me. I am so done caring about things I cannot change, things I finally understand were not my fault.

"I spoke to Ray." I look at Dean. Any mention of his father is a sore spot. Then, it hits me. He's Sam's father, too. *This is all so crazy!* I shake my head. "I had a hunch, more like a nagging voice in my head since we met with Jim in Leadville. It felt like...I don't know. Like I was missing something."

"So, you decided to call my dad?"

"Ray was able to point me in the right direction, to the right points of contact. Before I came back, when I was packing up my condo in Austin, I didn't feel the need to forward my mail. I also don't answer calls from numbers I don't know. In short, I haven't been easy to reach."

"Who is trying to reach you?" Dean asks. I want to laugh. Nothing about it is funny, except in moments like these that's exactly what it is.

"Silver Valley."

"Ryan—"

325

"I'm getting there," I tell him, and stand. "I need some coffee first." I leave the room and am grateful to discover Sam already started that process too. All I have to do is pour the dark bliss into three mugs. My mug has a bear on it with the words *Buena Vista* below it. Sam's cup has Colby's handprints splayed across the front in primary colors from a school art project. And shockingly, Dean's mug is cobalt blue.

When I return, they're whispering. Not so much to keep me from hearing, per se, but none of us are ready for the rest of the house to be up. "Are you all right?" Sam asks.

"I am." I hand them each a mug and brush my hand through Dean's messy hair before sitting in the same spot as before. "As you know, I'm the proud owner of a single-wide." It's difficult to say it and not feel ill. "It turns out there's more to it than just the trailer and the repulsive belongings inside of it."

"The land it's parked on?"

"At first, I didn't want it. Any of it. Then, after getting rid of the chip on my shoulder, I listened. I didn't understand the majority of it and had to seek council for that." I raise my eyes to first Sam's then Dean's. "Ray helped me."

"You do realize," Samantha begins, sidebar'ing the way we often do. "Ray is yet to speak to me. Is he afraid?"

"Probably. I mean…you are super scary," I joke, attempting to ease the mood. "Anyhow, with the trailer and keepsakes aside, there's a royalty account my aunt left to me, not Jim. Two, in fact. Her portion and my mother's.

"Your mom's music?" Dean asks, confused. He's adorable, and both Sam and I laugh.

"Not quite. An account built from gas and oil royalty interest. Inheritance by death and default and power of attorney. Mineral rights."

"Come again?" Dean stands, walks to the window, and by habit, surveys our surroundings.

"The wells aren't major producers, but they produce, nonetheless. The rights are firm at shallow drilling to forty-five hundred feet below. Anything below that belongs solely to DDA Oil and Gas."

"You own land that produces oil? In Texas?" Sam asks, her brow arching to new heights.

"An average of one hundred and thirty-six thousand barrels per year."

"Whoa!"

"Right?"

"I thought they were broke? Your aunt and unc...*him*?"

"They were, honey. I have no explanation for any of it. She must have hidden it from him all those years. Believe me, I've wracked my brain trying to connect the dots."

"Why do you have to go?"

"Because I've failed to respond to any and all notifications, though Ray is doubtful much was offered. We've had to act quickly, which meant naming Ray as my attorney. Apparently, I'm the sole claimant of a class action case. DDA Oil and Gas was informed the afternoon before Darien's incident."

"A lawsuit? Why? It's yours."

"Well, thanks to the investigator Ray put on it, DDA has been skimming the top of barrels per well for the past ten years. Yesterday, they called with a settlement to avoid the lawsuit. Under the conditions, Ray and I both think it's in my best interest to accept."

"What sort of settlement? What conditions? I don't want you cheated out of anything else in your life. You deserve this, Ryan. Every bit of it."

"Ry, I have an excellent attorney, maybe we can have a second set of eyes look at this for you." Sam looks down, almost ashamed. "It's not that I don't trust Ray, but—"

"You shouldn't trust him," Dean agrees.

"What I need is for *both* of you to trust me. I know what I'm doing. The offer is two dollars and fifty cents per barrel of sweet crude per year. As I said before, one hundred and thirty-six thousand are produced yearly on my small parcel of land. Of that, seventy-six thousand is sweet crude, which is pure, uncontaminated oil. The remaining sixty thousand are sour crude barrels. They're offering one dollar and seventy-five cents for sour crude."

"Way over my head."

"That's exactly how I felt, Sam." I run my hand through my hair. "Which is why I needed Ray. What I'm getting at, is if you do the math, and believe me I have, I'll get close to two point nine million."

"You don't have to accept," Dean advises, not even flinching at the amount. That, and he's suspicious of Ray. "This type of thing in oil…it's gotta be common. Fight them. You may get less, but who knows, you might get more. In everything, I always want you to have more."

"I've already settled." I reach for his hand. "I did have a condition, though. I requested to have a check in hand no later than Friday."

"Why?"

"For you. I'm taking this money, and I'm going to use it to save your mountain."

CHAPTER TWENTY-NINE

I'm back from Texas, leaving Silver Valley behind for the last time. Until that final farewell, my heart was never really able to let go of the old familiar ache. But now—*adiós para siempre!*

The door had finally opened. All I had to do was pass through it to collect a very clean slate. And this time around, I didn't have to escape. Believe me, there's a difference.

It's almost bittersweet. Almost. The abuse I survived, and all that it entailed, has shaped the woman I've become, even if it took more than two decades to recognize and recover. It's encouraging, no longer a hardship, to look into the mirror and appreciate the person staring back at me.

I signed, sealed, and delivered. There was nothing left to do but go. That was until I remembered Mrs. Ames and how she always kept me in shoes. Because of her small tokens of help, I was able to rise up as a young girl and stand my ground after every swipe life took at me. I owed her a proper goodbye.

I left Mrs. Ames with my own version of a small token— a donation. Before separating and going our own ways, we had a nice conversation. Mrs. Ames explained that because of me, when I was younger and my living situation, she had started a foundation for abused children. A foundation to help battered, mistreated and molested children rise, and always in a pair of new shoes. One hundred percent of the funds she raises goes toward the cause.

Leaving her small trinket shop, one she's owned for as long as I can remember, I ran into more women. Faces I recognized and a few I didn't. I'd realized then just how much of my life I'd filed away, memories and people I'd unintentionally shut out. There was no better time to shake up my filing system. No better time to reorganize a handful of memories that weren't all that bad and people of who had been kind. And that is precisely what I did. I stopped long enough to willingly partake in conversations with the friendly people of the valley.

"This reminiscing is slower than a country bus, taking just as many detours," Mrs. Ames had said, stepping out of her shop. This was her way of sparing me more of their amplified tales of what they perceived to be the good ol' days. "Leave this child be, let her go already."

Snapping from the reverie, I smile at Sam who has caught me daydreaming once again. She makes her way into the kitchen but not before teasing Garrett that she's going to lower her offer. She's persistent that he includes the riding lawn mower and all gardening tools. Turning, I get a glimpse of a new class portrait of Colby on the mantle. It's her birthday. I cannot wait to give her my present—a t-shirt of the Capulin Volcano National Monument. I picked it up in a truck stop near Des Moines, New Mexico on my way home.

Inclusion is a well-used term in these parts. Everyone is always invited. And *everyone* is here for Colby's big day, even Ray. It's fascinating because both Jey and Jules Jenson are here as well. Sprinkle Dean and Samantha to the mix, and it's an awkward and extremely dysfunctional family reunion. One I wouldn't have any other way.

Aside from Drew, someone is missing, and that is Reece. Despite his best efforts, he's crept back into the dark abyss. His recurring despair is complicated and cruel. His depression is like a hungry predator, gripping and clawing, and not letting go.

He'd come for dinner not long ago, and when the food was gone, and the dishes were done, he'd said something I'll never forget. "I see the dark around lights instead of the other way around because the color in my world has been distinguished."

Darien, on the other hand, she's in fiery form. Whether or not it's an act, she's determined to "brush herself off and get back in the saddle." I had a good laugh at that because the Darien Shay I've always known would never speak in clichés prior to meeting Sam. With Sam, she's more candid now. They're something to watch, something to admire. I'm fortunate that I'm able to see that in them. Not everyone can.

Speaking of Sam, I halt when entering the kitchen. "Oops, sorry." I withdraw quickly. Ray, Sam and Jules Jenson are sitting at the table talking with Colby's birthday cake—a chocolate cake in the shape of a rock—sitting between them on the Lazy Susan. Sam winks. She's fine, and I hope getting the explanations and answers she deserves. I move on.

And that is when it happens.

#

Hello, Interested, it's your penpal, Killer.

Let me start by saying I've got her. I have taken Colby Sterling. Go ahead, look around. She's gone. And before you panic and run to see, please read on.

You were right to be suspicious. Senator Prescott did hire me. I was retained to carry out several unpleasant scare tactics, none of which I've bothered too much with. Evacuation strategies aren't my thing. However, manipulating Jonathan and his foolish children has been quite fun. It's easy to pin everything I know and all I've done on them and then disappear. But then again, why should Prescott get all the glory?

I've left you a packet along with this letter. Consider it a parting gift. There's enough here to indict both Senator and son. Give me props for misleading both with a fabricated military and blasting background to get in and get the goods. You'll soon agree that this packet on Prescott smells like twenty-five to life.

In case your friend is unconvinced or hasn't said, I didn't sexually assault her more than necessary. I prefer Killer over Rapist. And poor Jenna. Do give her my regards. It's unfortunate her mother's death wasn't from natural causes after all. But forget all that, it's Colby who is important now.

Regrettably, we must come to an end. I have enjoyed our exchanges and your company, so I admit to lying. It was me who followed you all those times. I'd also like to apologize for Sarah Prescott. I really did hope to help you out there. Unfortunately, there's nothing more to that woman other than she's a daddy's girl who also happens to be a sharp-minded slut.

I'll leave you with this riddle. Who knows, if you solve it, you may find Colby Sterling. Ready? What runs but never walks, has a mouth but cannot talk, has a head but doesn't think, and has a bed but refuses to sleep?

You must understand, I only aim to take from those who stole from me.

Killer

#

"What runs but never walks—"

"The river," Dean cries, desperate, trapped in psychosis, and living a nightmare. I blink, and he's running, running toward the door, running toward the creek.

Garrett is seconds behind and quick to join Dean entering the water, breaking clumps of ice, snow, and debris with their bare hands, searching below the current. It's forty degrees, and both men are knee-high in icy water, combing the banks to the middle and back.

Garrett slips and catches himself before going under. He's unfazed and crosses the creek to the other side to look for prints. There's nothing, no evidence anyone's been here. Watching, I feel helpless, we all do.

"Let's go," Sam says, yanking my sleeve. My mind is too frozen, too frightened to do anything other than follow her lead. "We need to search the woods around the house. There wasn't enough time, she can't be far." Darien steps in front of us, shaking her head "no" to both of us. Sam and I aren't sneaking away so easily this time.

It was Ava who handed me the envelope with my name scribbled across the top. Ava who had gone looking for Colby after Colby had run off looking for her new puppy, Rox. "Rox sometimes hides under Colby's bed," Ava had told us, her eyes shining with tears.

Five minutes. Five minutes was all it took. Five minutes to lose Colby.

Ava is with Jey and Luke in their car, driving to town. They're meeting Nana Sterling, Jules Jenson, and Mama at the police station, all of which are in the second car. Ray is behind them. The police station is the safest place any of us can think of. From the window of Jenna's apartment, TC is

335

the watchman. We need his eyes. Jenna continues to rummage the riverbank alongside Dean.

"What did you say?"

My head jerks up, surprised by the pitch of Darien's tone. She's gone from Sam to me to Garrett to Jenna and back again several times, managing the area. Her demeanor is so severe that even Dean looks up. Samantha moves toward her, but I reach for Sam's arm, stopping her.

Darien steps forward, planting one foot in the water. Sam takes another step toward Darien, and this time it takes both my hands to hold her back. Inches from his face, Darien is jabbing a finger into Garrett's chest. Garrett shoves her hand aside, sidesteps her, and continues searching. "What," Darien steps a foot forward "did" and then another "you" one more "say?"

There's nothing more I can do. Samantha breaks free, and with stealth speed, she jumps between them. I close my eyes. This isn't helping. Our girl is missing, and we're all feeling the weight of it, beginning to take it out on each other.

"Relax, Red! What the fuck?" Garrett finally shouts back, and then turns to Dean. "We should separate. They can't be far. If we break up, we can cover more area and find her."

"Sam," Jenna warns, as Samantha steps toward Garrett. "Stop it, all of you! This isn't helping Colby!" Jenna raises her hands in a plea. "This is my niece we're talking about here! Our baby girl! She needs our help, so stop it!" Jenna repeats, sinking to the ground, covering her face with her hands.

"She's my niece, too," Sam argues, remorsefully. Samantha glares at Garrett, hating to go against Jenna then shoves Garrett backward. "What did you say to Darien?"

"Are you kidding me? Have you both lost your minds? We're losing time!"

"What did you say to her?" Sam repeats.

"Jesus! Fine! I told her we have to be smart. That we need to turn over every stone, look everywhere."

"What else?"

"I don't fucking know. I told her I didn't want to miss anything because we're rushing. We need to look better, take our time."

"You're lying!" Darien lunges at Garrett before I catch her around the waist and haul her back. "You lying sonofabitch! You said *we've* got time!" Darien fought to free herself from my hold, but she's still weak, not at her best, and fails. "I heard you. You tried so hard to disguise your voice, but I heard you. You were about to rape me when you said, "we've got time," before leaving me there in a hurry to freeze to death."

From the corner of my eye, there is a blur of motion as Dean grabs a fistful of flannel. Jenna and I are both quick to pull Dean off Garrett, but not before he's already cracked his fist into Garrett's jaw. "Where's my little girl?!"

"Dean, *please*...please stop!" That's Garrett, Dean! Garrett!" Jenna cries, begging. She's right, I have to help her stop this. Every minute we waste on this insanity is another minute we're closer to losing Colby forever.

I glance down. *Wait!* Garrett's jeans are wet and snug around his right calf. There's something beneath the saturated denim making them tighter than his other leg. A

337

bandage. I blink and raise my eyes to meet Garrett's. He's wiping the blood from the corner of his mouth and smirks. *Oh, my God!* Darien shot him, and that is why he took her and not me.

I shove Darien aside, leaving them behind, racing back to the house. The air in my lungs evaporates as I stumble into the parking area of Cottonwood Expeditions. The doors to Garrett's truck are locked. I don't hesitate to punch through the passenger window. A sharp sliver of pain slices through my arm, and then I feel nothing, oblivious to the splattered blood and shattered glass around me. I climb into the cab then climb over the console and into the backseat to reach for the wrapped bundle on the floorboard.

"I've got you, baby. I've got you!" I breathe into Colby's head, yanking at the blanket bound too tightly around her then claw at the tape around her tiny wrists. "It's okay, baby, you're okay. Be brave." It's the last thing I'm able to say before I close my eyes and rip the silver duct tape from her mouth. She screams and then pounds her head once and then once more into my chest, crying, gasping for air. "I'm not letting you go. I'm right here, baby, and I've got you," I repeat, again and again. "You're okay."

With Colby in my arms, I have no choice but to go back. I have to tell Dean. He has to see for himself. *Breathe, it's over!* He can't hurt us anymore.

With Colby's head tucked into my neck, I round the bend to see Dean strike Garrett over and over again, screaming for answers. Garrett's arms dangle at his sides. He's not even trying to defend himself, but instead, laughs with every blow. I feel Colby lurch and look down as she leans to the side and vomits.

338

"Dean!" I scream. His bloodied fist is shoulder high when he freezes. He turns his head to look at me, sees his daughter alive in my arms. He closes his eyes, tilting his head to the sky. I don't know if he's praying or praising and then he snaps, dragging Garrett into the creek. I turn away. Colby cannot see her father drown his lifelong friend. Darien and Sam move quickly toward me, both of them blocking us from the fight in the creek.

It's changed and is equally aggressive now. Garrett is fighting back. They're grappling and tangled, wrestling in the current when Jenna splashes in. "Stop, Dean! Stop!" The quaking fear in Jenna's voice, halts Dean. She steps closer to Garrett, his body bobbing in the rapids as Dean tightens his grip with a white-knuckled fist.

"That morning...after you showed Sam your house," Jenna says, shakenly. "You rushed to town. You knew Reece was there...you saw Ryan take the girls to school. You knew you would run into them. It...it was you!" Jenna covered her mouth. "You tried to...to kill him. You pushed TC. You pushed him, and then you went to town to call it in. You put yourself in the middle of it all with Ryan and Reece as an alibi!"

From the back of her jeans, tucked into the waistband, Jenna reaches for then aims the lightweight firearm at Garrett. "Jenna, easy," Dean says, backing away, leaving his cousin to it.

"What about that woman you beat up and strangled? Or Bruce Caldwell, you pushed him too? And...and Darien. Oh, God, Garrett, why?"

"Because I could," Garrett answers, shivering, his body half submerged in icy water. "Because I was in charge. I got to say who and when."

"Those aren't reasons. Tell *me* why? Why TC?"

Slowly Garrett rose, coming to his feet, with his arms up and palms out. "Jen, you don't want to shoot me."

"Answer me!"

"I think you know the answer to that."

"And Drew? You...you killed your own brother?"

Laughing, Garrett lowers his hands. "That kid? My brother?" He laughs more. My dad marries some lady who I despised when I'm thirteen and that makes him my brother? I couldn't stand that sniveling little shit. I can tolerate Reece, but all that stuff Drew used to say...I got tired of him."

Jenna closes her eyes, preparing. When she opens them, her finger trembles against the trigger of the small handgun she swore she would never touch. A gun that Garrett had given her to protect herself. A Glock 43-9mm they'd quarreled about repeatedly that she wanted no part of. The same one she ran to unlock from the safe inside her closet after discovering her niece had been taken. "And Colby? What were you planning to do with her?"

"What else? Make sure she suffered."

Dean lunges, but he's too late. Jenna fires once and then twice into the center of Garrett Dillon's chest, as faint sounds of sirens make their way up Cottonwood Pass.

The upper half of Garrett's body is lying limping on the bank while the rest of him is at the mercy of the water. He's dying. Jenna sinks to his side, crying inconsolably. She reaches for his hand, hating him, yet remembering the years of devotion. Dean kneels beside her with his hand on her

340

shoulder as blood spills from Garrett's lips. Lips that are turning blue.

"D-don't y-yyou see?" Garret stutters, as red bubbles gather at the corners of his mouth. "Th-the bear and her c-cubs?" Slowly, with the last of his strength, Garrett lifts his arm. "I-I let-t-t the c-cubs l-live."

Garrett brushes the backside of his fingers against Jenna's cheek. Her falling tears leave BB-sized holes in the snow. "All of th-this…it was all y-yyour f-fault."

Dean stands, booting Garrett aside to help his cousin to her feet. Garrett coughs, shooting blood like projectile vomit. "You k-killed my baby, Jenna." Garrett shifts his eyes, focusing on Dean. "You were supposed t-to be my best friend. You d-ddrove her to get an abortion. You b-both killed my baby. Dd-didn't tell me. Wa-as only r-r-right I k-kill yours."

Garrett takes one gargled, deep breath and dies.

Samantha reaches for Colby, wrapping Colby safely inside her arms. Jenna weeps, pounding her fists into Garrett's unmoving chest as Dean looms above them, swaying and on the verge of passing out. Reaching for me, Dean blinks, tears blurring his vision.

"It's not her fault," Dean confesses. "I found her and promised her. I promised I'd never tell Garrett. It wasn't an abortion. She had a miscarriage."

CHAPTER THIRTY

Some people call them lifehacks, I call it learning the hard way.

With time, we learned from Colby that Garrett had lured her right out the back door to look for Rox, her puppy. It had been fast and easy. She'd been taken in plain sight. Just like Sam.

There were seven of us there, and one is dead. By the grace of God, Colby will not endure a lifetime of graphic recollections of her aunt killing a man. She didn't see it. It leaves five of us, five who know with detailed precision what went down that afternoon. Five who will never share the whole truth. It is our secret to bear, even if every secret comes with a price.

Jenna killed Garrett. As the sirens grew nearer, we had a split second to deliberate and were unanimous with our unspoken decision to protect her. I knew Garrett carried a fixed blade. I didn't hesitate, nor did any of them question my haste move, to remove the Bowie-style hunting knife from the sheath strapped to his belt. I laid it beside his open palm on the riverbank, not bothering with the small Beretta inside his left boot. It was enough.

As days passed, decisions continued to be difficult, but in the end, it was also Jenna who asked for Dean to destroy Garrett's house. Samantha did buy the parcel of land, after all, and immediately filed for a property transfer, gifting it entirely to Jenna to do with it as she wished.

On the fifth of February, Dean had Garrett's home demolished, just as I had done with the single-wide trailer in Silver Valley. Lawrence Dillion, Garrett's father, had Garrett cremated. He's taken Garrett's ashes with him to Alamosa, Colorado. He is gone for good.

TC remains in recovery, though stronger by the day. He's living with Jenna, and together, they're rebuilding their lives one day at a time. Reece and Brittany went away only to return home just in time for the summer season. Equipped with answers, Reece is better now, and they are engaged. There's a backstory, false family dynamics and rocky relationships of Reece's family dating back to early childhood. Things no one knew. Things we'll never know and will never ask.

Under Article 1, Section 5, clause 2, of the Constitution, Senator Jonathan Prescott was removed from office. His expulsion from the Senate occurred five weeks before the trial, which resulted in life without the possibility of parole. The penalty of being charged with and found guilty to conspiracy to commit murder, murder, human trafficking, extortion and embezzlement.

Henry Prescott's case is ongoing and will pale in comparison to his father's. Sarah Prescott walked free from the scandal with no worse than a smeared name and frozen assets. She was a no show to the custody hearing for Colby and did not interfere with the process of adoption. Colby Sterling is legally mine.

Dean and I were married on Valentine's Day. I have no clue why. Quite possibly because Ava and Colby thought it would be funny. To Ava's credit, we avoided the use of Cupid in all ways. It was a small ceremony with both little people standing by my side at the altar.

My gallery is set to open on the second of June to kick off the summer season. Darien has arranged a grand opening to rival the Macy's Day Parade. Luckily, there's also a Farmer's Market on South Main that same day.

As for the little people…where one yings, the other yangs. They're miniature versions of Sam and me. A friendship so profound, they already understand that only one lifetime together is worth more than an eternity of nothing. They are the future. The story that will live on.

Finally, that leaves me with Samantha. My dearest, most precious Sam. It's only right I let her show the rest.

I got out of bed to get a glass of water. It felt a lot like déjà vu, but this time, I didn't look for you. I know you're gone.

I always believed we'd last the test of time, and in ways, I still do. But things are different now, and I'm no longer devastated by how I feel.

Through music, Ryan's mom attempts to explain that "when God takes you back, we'll say Hallelujah, you're home." Although I do appreciate the sentiment, as well as her love for Ed Sheeran, I'm not quite there yet. But I do believe you now, I believe that my story will continue even after you're gone because you will always be a part of my story.

I need to say something I have found to be true. My anger and resentment were paralyzing. As was my grief. I can finally make you that promise to no longer be woeful of losing you. It's wasted energy and the quickest way to circle the drain. I've figured out how to get up, to stand tall, and to fight. I have figured out that it's time to let go of what I thought my life was supposed to look like.

I'm open to new experiences and people. Maybe it means someday I'll meet someone new. Maybe I already have. Who knows where it will go, or if it will at all? The point is, I am good. I'm really, really good.

You were also right about what we leave behind. It is true, I have never seen a hearse pulling a U-Haul. And why? Because we can't take anything with us, so I'm letting go.

Thank you for leading me home, and for showing me that life is a mystery to be lived, not a problem to be solved.

Until then...
Samantha Xx

THE END

Made in the USA
Coppell, TX
30 December 2020